By the same author

TOUCHING THE VOID

The
Water
People

—

JOE SIMPSON

An *Abacus* Book

First published in Great Britain in 1992 by Jonathan Cape
This edition published by Abacus 1993

A CIP catalogue record for this book
is available from the British Library.

ISBN 0 349 10349 6

Printed in England by Clays Ltd, St Ives plc

Abacus
A Division of
Little, Brown and Company (UK) Limited
165 Great Dover Street
London SE1 4YA

I will go with you then,
if you must play this game of ghosts . . .

Siegfried Sassoon

The Hollow-men live in solid rock and move about in it in the
form of mobile caves or recesses. In ice they appear as bubbles
in the shape of men. But they never venture out into the air, for
the wind would blow them away.

They have houses in the rock whose walls are made of
emptiness, and tents in the ice whose fabric is of bubbles.
During the day they stay in the stone, and at night they wander
through the ice and dance during the full moon. But they never
see the sun, or else they would burst.

They eat only the void, such as the form of corpses; they
get drunk on empty words and all the meaningless expressions
we utter.

Some people say they have always existed and will exist
for ever. Others say they are dead. And others say that as a
sword has its scabbard or a foot its imprint, every living man
has in the mountain his hollow-Man, and in death they are
reunited.

René Daumal, 'The Tale of the Hollow—men and the Bitter Rose'

The Wilderwurm Gletcher by H. G. Willink

Contents

I

The Earth Collapses

When I peered into the grave I saw Jimmy crouched over the cover board of the coffin, bailing the last scoops of muddy water into a red plastic bucket.

'How's it going?'

'Okay,' he said, and stood up blinking at the bright sunshine flooding into the grave opening. 'Here, grab this.' He handed me the half full bucket.

I reached down and grasped the slippery muddy handle. When I had emptied the contents on the downhill side of the grave I handed it back. As I did so I noticed something odd.

'What have you done?'

'What do you mean?' Jimmy said, as he bent to refill the bucket.

'You've done something to the grave. What . . .' I spotted the two scaffolding planks lying by the spoil heap and the four jacks that had braced them across the walls of the grave.

'Oh, my God!'

'What's bugging you now?'

'You've removed the bloody props, haven't you?'

'So?'

'I told you not to touch them,' I shouted. 'What the hell are you playing at?'

9

'They were in the way,' Jimmy said, handing me the bucket. I looked at the uphill wall of the grave. It was noticeably bowed out. It had been raining non-stop for three days and when we had arrived the grave held three feet of musty smelling water. I looked at the wall again. Water exuded from the crumbling mud and trickled down, washing more earth on to the coffin. A fist-size lump suddenly broke away and dropped with a splash into the water by Jimmy's feet.

'Of course they were in the way. That's why I put them there. It was the only thing holding the walls up.'

I grabbed a plank and lowered it into the grave.

'Put them back and be quick about it,' I said, throwing two props into the grave. They thumped into the coffin lid with a hollow knocking sound.

'It doesn't half pong down here,' Jimmy said, ignoring the props.

'For God's sake, put those bloody props up. It's going to collapse.' As I said it several bucketfuls of earth avalanched into the water and Jimmy jumped back with a startled expression on his face. It was soon replaced with a mischievous grin.

'Keep your knickers on, Chris. It will hold long enough to bail this lot out. Give me the bucket.'

'Stop winding me up, Jimmy,' I shouted, and threw another plank into the grave. 'If that wall goes you won't stand a chance . . .'

Another heap of mud dropped from the bulging wall, and Jimmy's grin vanished.

'Maybe you're right,' he muttered, and lifted the heavy plank until it was pressed lengthways across the wall. He leant his shoulder against it to hold it in place and picked up one of the props.

'Can you give us a hand?' He struggled to brace the prop between the plank and the opposite earth wall.

'There isn't enough room.' I was relieved that I didn't have to get into the grave. 'Here, I'll lower this plank behind the prop so you can jack it into position.' I slid the heavy wooden plank down the wall of the grave and watched Jimmy struggling to place it between the plank at his shoulder and the one I had lowered into place.

'It doesn't fit!' He sounded worried. 'I can't get it between them.'

'That's because the bloody wall has bulged.' I looked nervously at the wall that Jimmy was pressing with his shoulder. I was convinced it had bowed out further. 'You'll have to retract the prop.'

'How? I haven't got the handle.'

'Shit . . .' I dropped my plank and searched for the short iron handle that we used to wind the extendable prop in and out. 'Hang on, hang on, it's here somewhere,' I shouted. My stomach felt tight and knotted. The handle was nowhere to be seen.

'You must have it,' I said to Jimmy. 'What did you do with it when you undid them?'

'Oh, bugger.' Jimmy looked wildly round his feet. 'It must be under here somewhere.'

He tried holding the plank up with his shoulder and bracing himself against the opposite wall with his arm. Kicking distractedly at the muddy water, he peered down hoping for a glimpse of the handle. I heard him swearing to himself between what sounded like frightened gasps for breath.

'Get out of there, Jimmy. It's going to go at any minute.'

I could see the wall had pushed out further and Jimmy was really holding it back rather than keeping the plank in place.

'Quick, drop the plank and grab my arm,' I yelled at him, suddenly consumed with the awful knowledge that it was going to bury him. He continued searching for the handle, slashing at the water with increasing urgency.

'I see it,' he cried out. He bent towards where he had briefly glimpsed the iron handle.

'No!' I screamed, as I saw the wall of the grave tumble past his back. As he released his pressure on the plank to grab the handle the wall collapsed. I saw him forced on to his knees by the weight of wet earth and the plank across his back was pushing him under. There was a grunt, a splash, and a sickening slumping noise, and Jimmy disappeared from view.

As he reached for the handle he felt the sudden heavy shift of earth across his back. For a moment his legs held him up, and then with shocking abruptness his knees collapsed under him and he pitched, face first, into the water. He dimly heard a scream from Chris and, glancing sideways, registered the sunlight being cut off into blackness like a light bulb bursting.

He sucked a gritty mouthful of water into his lungs and at once began coughing and retching. There was an immense weight on his back. He felt the sharp edge of the plank cutting into the back of his skull and the length of it pressing his torso into the mud. He lay with his left hand trapped against his cheek. His right arm was pinned behind him, and his legs seemed paralysed so heavy was the load on top of them. He strained against the weight tensing his back and thighs, desperately trying to push upwards, but it did no good. As cramps and burning acid pains in his muscles began he slowly relaxed and was pushed further down. He could feel the hard coverboard over the coffin against his chin and he clawed at it with his left hand.

In the black silence of smothering earth it seemed as if he had been there for hours though he knew it was only minutes. Despite his straining muscles he was forced inexorably down and the plank pressed his head deeper into the water until he was forced to twist it sideways. His face was half submerged. His mouth and left nostril were under the water. Abruptly the downward pressure ceased. He tried to breathe through his one clear nostril but sucked water into the submerged one. Frantically trying to retch the water out only made the situation worse, and he sucked in another mouthful.

Pressure pains built in his chest. Hard hot pains from lungs in critical need of oxygen. He felt himself slowly go. There was a distant thrumming sound in his head and his thoughts calmed into despairing resignation. He thought of his left hand at the last moment of consciousness and his fingers seemed to grope towards his nose without any command from him. He managed to plug his submerged nostril with his thumb and breathed a water-free lungful of musty putrid-smelling air through his clear nostril.

Suddenly a flash of light sparked near his head and then darkness returned. He was vaguely aware of movement on his back. Then another spark of light and a voice.

'Jimmy?' Chris shouted in a high-pitched voice. 'Jimmy? Hang on, we're getting you out. Can you hear me? *Jimmy!*'

He gurgled helplessly into the water and choked as he tried to reply. *Christ!* he thought, *I'm bloody drowning in a grave! They're going to get me.*

Out of the corner of his eye he saw a muddy hand groping towards his face. Unable to move he watched it fixedly as it clutched around in the mud and then brushed his cheek. In a moment Chris had poked a finger painfully into his eye and hooked his thumb into his clear nostril.

'Mmmpphh . . .' Jimmy said, trying to pull away from the suffocating hand. 'Mmmmmpph . . .' he said with greater force as Chris tried to pull his head up by his nostril. He was unsure whether the pain from lack of air was worse than the pain of having his nostril ripped off, but at last the thumb slipped free and he sucked in another desperate lungful.

The blade of a shovel smacked into the coverboard inches from his horrified eyes and was then lifted from view. He tried to pull his head back, but nothing happened, and the shovel smashed back into the board.

'Mmmmpph mmph mmmph,' he squawked, which translated as 'You're going to cut my goddamn head off!' Again the shovel crunched into the splintering board, and suddenly he could breath through his mouth. The water level had dropped. The air abruptly changed and he smelt the foul odour of the not so long departed. The shovel had punctured the coffin lid

13

and the water had drained into it, forcing out the stench of a decomposing resident.

'You're a daft bugger,' Harry said cheerfully as he watched Jimmy retching a thin bile on to the spoil heap. 'Serves you right for taking them props down.' With that he turned on his heel and strode away.

'Who's he?' Jimmy muttered.

'My gaffer, that's who,' I snapped, 'and I nearly lost my job, thanks to you.'

'Well, I nearly lost a sight more than that.'

'Yeah,' I said, 'you'd be bloody dead if it hadn't been for Harry breaking the coffin open. I told you not to move those props, but, oh no, you always know best . . .'

'Look, I'm sorry, okay. Now give me a break.' Jimmy lit a cigarette and inhaled deeply.

'God, they nearly got me that time, you know,' he said weakly.

'Who did?'

'The Water People . . .'

'You're not still on about them, are you?'

'Don't mock what you don't know,' Jimmy said smugly. 'I'll show you what I've written so far when we get home. Talking of which, I'm going. I'm soaked and I smell like a dead dog.'

'More like a dead Mrs Brownlow,' I laughed, pointing to the last name on the stone above the grave.

'Oh God!' Jimmy said with an expression of disgust, and I laughed the louder.

2

The Universe to a Drowned Rat

The Water People have no homes or fixed abodes. They travel freely within the waters of the world. They are unaffected when water changes to snow or ice. They move as easily in the vapour of superheated steam as they do within the turgid creeping pressures of a glacier. They can never be seen. For if you saw them you would know everything and you would die.

They were here when the world came into being. Before that time they swirled through the chaos of the universe. There are some who believe that they existed before time existed, before the universe. Science tells us that the universe began 10,000 million years ago in a massive explosion of galactic material; that all matter was once concentrated into a super-dense body before being blasted apart. It will not tell you that the Water People were there. It can never reveal their journey through space as they raced endlessly away from the centre with the scattered material of the core to form the galaxies and the stars. They, like us, are for ever escaping at unimaginable speed from our creation. Unlike us they were there before; this creation of ours, this universe, may have been their doing.

We think this world of ours is big. Yet it is nothing, a mere speck within a cloud of dust blown violently above the most desolate desert in the world. Radio telescopes have detected galaxies nine million light years away. Put into perspective, a light year is the distance which light travels in one year. Light travels almost six million million miles in a year, and yet we talk of nine million light years. It is beyond comprehension. To understand such a scale is where madness waits darkly.

Our galaxy is a cluster of 100,000 million stars of which our sun is but one, and it spirals within a universe of thousands of millions of other galaxies.

We began as a cloud. An immense, swirling cloud of gas that held within it all the matter sufficient to form the sun and the planets. They also swirled within that cloud. As it collapsed under its own gravity the sun formed in its centre, the planets reaching out from it. The newly formed planets, incandescent with the heat of their creation, expanded as debris from the gas disc bombarded their surfaces.

The sun, an average sized star, was then fifty times its present size and burned with a brightness 500 times greater than today. Those planets nearest the sun had their atmospheres blown away as the star began to shine. Those further out survived intact with thick atmospheres and their assorted collections of moons and satellites. Eventually the Sun will expand once again, but when it does there will be no respite for the outer planets. Four hundred times bigger and burning 10,000 times more brightly, it will consume Mercury, Venus, Earth and Mars before once more collapsing to about the size of the earth, glowing in the sky as a white dwarf, spent of fuel and cooling down to blackness.

Around the earth a thick atmosphere formed and across its surface water poured in torrents from the sky. Volcanoes blasted their gases into the atmosphere, producing vast quantities of steam sufficient to account for all the waters of the oceans today. We call them the Water People because they have chosen to inhabit earth's most abundant and creative surface element: 70 per cent of the planet now consists of water. We do not know what they were before the water formed; particles within a gas cloud perhaps, or shadows across a solar wind. It matters only to know that they move within the water. For thousands of years clouds hid the planet, inundating it with water. Drowning it, cooling it, and shaping it. Running water, rain, ice, seas and the wind carved through the continents. These are the most creative and destructive of all nature's forces.

The Water People have always been there in the gas cloud of the creation and move now through the atmosphere of a new world. They are not made of water but exist within it. Their world is governed by temperature only in as much as it changes the nature of water from ice through to vapour, but it leaves them unhindered. They move freely, choosing where to do their work. In those early millennia they covered the world in a maelstrom of violence and chaos. It took almost seven hundred million years for the earth to cool sufficiently for rocks to solidify from its molten surface and the slow sculpting of the land to begin. Immense volanoes erupted gas and steam into the atmosphere, the steam condensing to fall back to earth as rain and snow.

Over a thousand million years passed before life forms appeared in a world still in the cataclysmic violence of its birth. Time stretched on almost beyond comprehension as mountains formed at the colliding edges of the drifting continental plates. Three thousand million years of mountain building. Seas rose, formed oceans and disappeared; water streamed across the land, eating down through its crust, sustaining life. Without water there could be no life.

Today we look upon our planet as a pattern of fixed continents, and seen from space it shines with unimaginable beauty against the dark back-drop of the universe. A blue globe, wisped with white cloud shapes, and marked by the distinct outlines of the landmasses. We think it has been like this for ever. We cannot see the infinitesimal movements of the continents, the slow rise of nascent mountain ranges and the inexorable grinding down of others.

Yet, if we could film the world's formation as we film, freeze-frame, a rose growing, blooming, closing and dying, we would be struck by the liquidity of it all. As the continents drifted apart from grouped masses into separate bodies and back together, it would look like torn pieces of card swirling over the cloud-streaked blue of the water. The pieces, if jig-sawed together, would roughly match up, and as they drifted we would watch the ripples on their soft soaked surfaces as they collided, see the mountains rising, see continents sub-merge beneath others, see the water take its destructive toll on their edges until we began to recognise the familiar shapes of present time. Above all we would see water.

Early life forms have been present for only one fifth of the planet's existence. As a species we have been here for only one millionth of that time. We are nothing. Soon we will be gone, hastened no doubt by our own success, but we will be gone. Other forms might take our place, or perhaps all life will sink back into the chaos from which it came and the earth will spin on, lifeless again, towards its unavoidable nemesis with the sun.

We are a freakish transience but we cannot see ourselves in such a way. What we can do, and as a species have always strived to do, is change everything that we encounter. Our evolution is a history of change. We have adapted as no other living things have ever done, evolving faster than any others, dominating all life, not by brute force but by intellect, imagin-ation and creativity. We have the ability to imagine the future and see our place in that future. We have not accidentally found a home for ourselves on this earth – we consciously made one. We are tool makers and users, sculptors of our-selves and our landscapes. We are creative. No animal, insect or bird begins to compete with us, locked as they are into the limited worlds of their own shortcomings. Dinosaurs may have left their petrified footprints in the shores of ancient lakes, and the countless fossils of life in the past are proof simply that they existed, but we alone leave evidence of our creativity.

It is more than mere curiosity that drives us to confront the planet head on. We must do it. It is the only way we know to survive. We accept nothing passively without trying to change it first, to mould what we encounter into our sense of how things should be. The harder the task the more determined we are to force a change as if it were a threat to our very existence.

We are the sum of everything that we do. When we are gone the evidence of our existence on the planet, the transformations we have wrought, will stand proof to our passing. Perhaps not for ever, probably not for long at all, but it will be more than any other life form has achieved.

In this way even space has felt the touch of our questing eyes, and the relics of our explorations will no doubt last longest on the distant moons and planets. Footsteps in moon dust left undisturbed for millennia, a moon buggy abandoned where an atmosphere can never destroy it. A vainglorious flag standing motionless in the dust near a place aptly named *Descartes* on the eastern edge of the *Mare Tranquillitatis*, the Sea of Tranquillity. Man's first steps on the moon. Apollo 11. 20 July 1969. *'Cogito ergo sum'*.

And if this is what we are, and what we are likely to become, what of the Water People? Will they also be consumed by the sun? Or will they evaporate back into space, into the endless race outwards from the initial explosion of the universe? What are they doing here, or are they present throughout the universe?

Most would say that it doesn't matter, and many say that it is a nonsense to believe such things. There are those like myself who say they exist and will do so for ever. Others say that now they are dead.

There are many tales of the Water People. In each one they have different names. Each different in form and character, interpreted distinctly by each separate language and culture.

They are not commonplace. Yet there are traces of them to be sensed in every place – in the twitching of the water diviner's forked twig of hazel, in the life forces, the 'dragon lines', that the Chinese believe run through the earth.

This is the Chinese practice of geomancy, or *feng-shui*. For thousands of years they have believed that the earth is a living being and, like the Heavens of which it is a reflection, there is an intricate pattern of energy currents both good and bad, running through the land. The good positive currents, the 'dragon lines', carry good *chih*, or life force. The chih is believed to follow the flow of water beneath the surface of the earth and the magnetic fields of the planet. Every building, business, marriage or funeral is started in places where the dragon lines are auspicious. It is no accident that a traveller will notice an uncanny sense of natural alignment in the placing of a house, or village in China. So deep rooted is this sense of the dragon lines that it is reflected in the language, the architecture, and the very nature of the people. The lines are always curved, never straight, as are all the traditional buildings with their arched walls and roofs.

The spirit world of the Amazonian Indians is drenched in a mythology of rain gods. What of the Aboriginal 'Songlines', the tracks of their ancestors followed by some across the most inhospitable land in the world? There is a feeling of something else running through the earth that the Aborigines intuitively follow.

The great rivers of the Himalayas, the Indus, the Brahmaputra and the Ganges, have nourished and created both the spiritual and material culture of India. These monumental rivers, flowing with the urgent power of the greatest range of mountains, from which they were born, have shaped the whole nature of the Asian continent. Mother Ganges, the Ganga, more than any has become the myth, the dreams, the hopes, and the fuel of this ancient civilisation, so that even today it is impossible to unravel the twisting coils of the river's length from the identity of this huge population. She is a symbol of all they have become and hope to be. She created the vast fertile alluvial plains which are the heart of Indian civilisation. She feeds both the people and the culture, and remains the spiritual artery of India. As Jawaharpal Nehru said of her: '. . . she is the river of India, beloved of her people, round which are intertwined her racial memories, her hopes and fears, her songs of triumph, her victories and defeats. She has been a symbol of India's age-long culture and civilisation, ever-changing, ever-flowing . . .' Washing on the banks of the Ganges in Varanasi, India's holiest city, assures the pilgrim that the sins of a lifetime will be washed away, and dying there breaks the believer free from the cycle of re-birth.

In every Christian church can be found a font of Holy Water and every baby enters the world of God drenched by the mark of water. It is here that water is turned to wine, and wine becomes the blood of Jesus, and Noah rode the flood in his ark to escape the sins of a world turned sour.

They are there. They are there to be found, if never seen.

I once followed the sense of them in a hidden frozen forest where red flowers lay scattered on the path, and five fingered leaves blackened with frost pointed me down through a tangle of pine woods.

I talked to a blind man who felt them move across his eyes. I thought perhaps he more than any of us could have stood the seeing of them. He hadn't seen them. He left me at the station, his stick tapping him home through the puddles left by the rain.

There is an individual Water person for every one of us, and every being that has ever lived. It is said that we always meet that single one, but only once. They fit too completely.

I follow their traces.

'What do you think then?' Jimmy asked. He sat at his paper-strewn desk, nervously pulling on a badly rolled cigarette.

'Interesting.' I handed back the loose sheaf of papers he

had passed me to read with my coffee. 'I liked the bit about space. The insignificance of life and all that.'

'Yeah, but what did you think about the Water People? I mean that's what it's about. The 'space bit' is just the setting.'

'As I said, it's interesting, they're interesting, I mean.' I began to feel I was on dangerous ground. 'Are they part of the story? Is it a sort of fantasy thing then?'

'No!' He almost shouted as he flung the papers on to his desk. 'No, it's not fantasy. It's real. I've followed them . . . so have you.'

'What? When did I follow them?'

'You might not have known it but you have. On every trip we've been on we've heard the stories, seen how they work . . .'

'Hang on, Jimmy, *you* might have, I haven't. It's you who listens to those interminable bloody stories, not me. I some-times wonder how we've ever climbed anything when you're always sitting in some rat-hole village listening to those old gits rambling on.'

'They don't ramble. They tell the stories of their villages. It's what they believe. They all connect as well. I heard things in Africa last month that were the same stories, same feelings, only in different clothes.'

'All right, all right, forget it. Anyway, what is this? Are you writing a book about it?'

'Well, not exactly. I wanted to put my ideas down. You know, get them into some sort of shape. This is the introduc-tion. I'm going to put in all the stories as I record them. We'll get loads in India.'

'You might. Don't include me in it. Come on, let's go climbing.' I stood up, drained my coffee and glanced out of the window. 'It won't rain.'

'Sure, I've heard that before.' He picked his car keys off the desk and headed for the door. As he stepped outside he knocked over a jumble of empty milk bottles and kicked one against the kitchen wall angrily. It shattered. He swore testily and I laughed. It happened every day until he finally cracked and brought them round to the corner shop in his rucksack.

'Are we going to see Alice after?' he asked as he locked the back door.

'Yes,' I said, and stopped laughing.

He walked ahead of me in his usual manner, head down and slightly forward, shoulders hunched, and with a fast bow-legged stride. It always surprised me, the speed with which he walked. It was powerful, intent, and at odds with his small stature. He never strolled. I cannot recall ever seeing him lope naturally and relaxed to any destination. It was as if walking were solely a means of getting somewhere and therefore had to be done with the utmost efficiency.

I was glad to let him steam ahead. My steps dragged. I didn't want to reach our destination as much as Jimmy wanted the walking to be over. When we reached the car the afternoon's brief respite would be over and I would have to face up to Alice.

April had arrived and yet winter still clung to the land. The moors were bleak. Dirty patches of snow showed amid the rolling heather, and clouds scudded heavily across the sky. Rain was coming. The wind pulled insistently at my back. Our attempt at climbing had been unimpressive. The rock, though dry, had seemed to close up in front of us while fingers solid and unfeeling with cold groped blindly in shuttered cracks and over rounded edges, gripping without us knowing what they held. I had crouched, hands between my thighs, a full twenty minutes; knife blades slid under my nails while hot blood returned with agony.

Then, with icy horizontal rain in the air and the western sky threatening worse, I'd thought of giving up. I was sure that I could have persuaded Jimmy to come down and forget this idiocy but I remembered Alice, and our coming visit, and I turned my shoulder to the wind and hunched there in misery.

For sure, Jimmy would not come down first. He would wait for me to beg.

It was growing dark by the time we coiled the ropes and set off along the muddy path, rucksacks stuffed hastily with our gear and the straps stropping in the wind. There was much swearing as I tripped over heather roots and stumbled into holes set for the unwary. It was all the more irritating to notice that Jimmy was never caught out. At the top of a short gully leading to the top of Froggat edge we turned left on a wide smooth path heading for the road. The gritstone lay like whale backs bedded in the moor, smoothed down, weather worn, and marked with the grooves of wind-driven water. A bend in the path running through a rounded outcrop led us away from the edge of the cliff and Jimmy increased his stride. It was now quite dark, a cold late April afternoon, no moon to show for hours yet and even that would be lost above the driving clouds.

It would have been done to her by now. The thought had repeatedly popped into my mind during the day, and each time I would quickly work out how long ago it would have been done. She had said that it would be very quick. Some sort of chemical taken, a general anaesthetic, and then awake and it over with. She had seemed cheerful. I knew she was sad – and scared. She wasn't scared of the operation but of me. Fearful that I would leave her, reject her. I was scared too, of Jimmy, and his mother. I had felt furtive all day. In fact, now that I thought about it, I had been furtive from the beginning. From the moment we decided to keep our love secret I had felt ashamed, and now we had dirtied even that. Now it had to be even more secret. We were bound to it.

I suppose we should never have started it. More to the point, I should never have let it begin. Alice was ten years younger than me, the darling of her mother's eye, doted on by her father, an unexpected gift to them so long after Jimmy was born. Unexpected, unplanned, and loved all the more for it. And Jimmy had loved her with that ferocious power of a brother who had never expected a sister to come along. Suddenly, in that half-way world between childhood and adulthood, she had released him from the asphyxiating embraces of doting parents and left him free to develop.

When Jimmy and I had plundered the countryside on one of his questing adventures, the day had always started with tearful scenes as Alice was persuaded that she was too young to come with us. 'Next year. You can come with us next year when you're bigger,' Jimmy would say, and her beautifully wide eyes would darken and glisten before she turned abruptly on her heel and marched back to the house with all the dignity a six-year-old could muster.

It was on that day that the killing stopped. We too had grown bigger and beating water rats to death in the stream had lost its fascination. At sixteen we had delighted in trying to hit them with stones as they swam furiously across the pools in the stream. Jimmy always knew where to find them. Armed with sticks, we would roam the banks until he gave the signal. Crouching at the edge, we would reach round the mud overhang and thrash wildly into the shelved hollows where we hoped some old male would be sheltering. Often nothing happened, and I would hold Jim's ankles while he leant right out over the water to see if there was anything lurking furtively below. I never could bear to lean out like that. I feared a leaping dark shape and a vicious bite in the face. It didn't seem to bother Jimmy. When least expected there would be a splash and an excited yell from him and the male would be paddling furiously across the pool – a sleek dark shape cutting a vee across the surface with stones splashing violently all around it. Once, in an excess of zeal, having run out of stones, I saw Jim hurl himself off the bank, arms outstretched as if to catch a beach ball, and land full square on the poor rat. Both disappeared in a welter of spray and two thrashing arms. I expected him to come up with the rat's teeth sunk deeply in his cheek, lashing itself from side to side. He stood instead sheepishly on one leg, massaging his shin, the rat swimming off downstream unhurt. The water was two feet deep, the stream bed strewn with rounded boulders. Blood trickled from his shin and his nose began to bleed.

After Alice walked morosely away in rejection Jimmy set off to the stream carrying his recently acquired air rifle. He had spent the previous week killing anything he could hit, starlings, blackbirds, robins and wrens. We had gone ratting in the abandoned sheds of the old pig farm next door. I had kicked the door open and shone the flashlight in on nests of startled rats. Jimmy had fired and missed every time. They were too quick for him.

'We need a shotgun. I don't have time to load a second shot with this thing,' he muttered, disgusted at his lack of trophies. 'Water rats!' he exclaimed excitedly. 'We'll get them at the stream like before. They're not fast.'

And so we went to the stream. I didn't like it. Somehow it seemed unfair. After all, we had only ever got one rat in all the previous years of sticks and stones and catapults. In any case, we were too old to be out killing rats. A rifle was cheating.

'Hey, are you serious about this?' I asked as we reached the bank.

'Of course,' Jimmy replied. 'Why do you think I bought this?'

'I don't care why you bought it. I care what you're doing with it.'

'You never complained before?'

'We never bloody killed anything before,' I retorted angrily. 'The last few weeks has been a slaughter. This isn't the Sands of Iwo Jima you know.'

'Come on, stop being wet, Chris.'

'Wet! What's wet about not wanting to kill things? We're a bit beyond the sissy stage now.'

'Well go on home then,' he replied with a familiar determined look on his face.

'Oh sod it!' I was seething, as much because I could never properly remonstrate with him. Either he ignored me or launched into an irrefutable argument about how we must do it. Whatever plan or scheme he came up with, we did it. I stayed. Somehow I felt that I might win the argument if I saw him kill one. Silently I hoped he would miss.

As we had walked down to the stream I had wondered what arguments he would produce this time to justify killing a water rat with an air rifle. The rats in the piggery had seemed fair sport. At least they were a health menace and the farmer wanted to be rid of them. Water rats harm no-one. I liked them, and was glad we had been so inept in the past. To me they conjured up images of *Toad of Toad Hall*. To Jimmy they were merely targets. It was stupid to be doing this at sixteen. We could have gone climbing. I followed him nevertheless.

He held the rifle in front of him and marched purposefully behind it, as if it were leading the way. When we reached the stream, he stopped to let me catch up. He searched the opposite bank, swinging the barrel left and right, leaning out over the stream. I hoped he would fall in and ruin the gun.

'They're here,' he whispered conspiratorially, and I burst out laughing.

'It's not man-eating lions we're after.'

He ignored me and crept stealthily off to the right, hunching down over his knees and bringing the butt of the rifle up to his shoulders. I slouched up behind him.

'Come on, Jim, forget it. Why not just have some target practice?' I said.

'I want to get a rat.'

'What for? It's done nothing wrong.'

He didn't answer me and, thinking of the birds he'd shot off his mother's bird table in the last few days, I saw that it was pointless. Such ideas didn't come to him. I could have walked back home and just left him to it. I didn't. I suppose I wanted to see what would happen. Perhaps I also wanted to see a rat die.

It was late afternoon, September time. The stream seemed smaller than I remembered. We hadn't been there in years.

The water seemed darker and reluctant to flow. There were some half-rusted cans jammed against rocks out in midstream. A white plastic bag caught on a branch near the far bank swayed to the rhythm of the weeds among which it lay. There was an oily infected look to the water. It had changed.

There was a spitting muffled report and metallic clack. One of the cans jumped from its trap in the rocks and rolled slowly beneath the surface as the stream took it. Jimmy cracked open the rifle, pulling the barrel back towards him with the stock braced against his thigh. He fiddled a little lead pellet into the breech and snapped the barrel shut again.

'There's nothing here. It's all dead.'

Almost as I said it there was a soft plopping sound and we turned to look upstream. A large rat was swimming languidly across, letting the flow take it down towards us as it headed for the opposite bank. Jimmy raised the rifle to his shoulder. I wanted to put my arm out and stop him; reach out and push the barrel aside. I did nothing but watched the rat gliding towards us serenely unaware of the danger. It was a difficult shot given the poor light. The rat's nose and forehead were clear of the water and I saw the slight hump of its back slicked with water, oily on its pelt, cutting a silvery wake across the stream. It slid forward effortlessly on invisible pumping legs. Jimmy kept re-adjusting his aim, unsure of a moving target. Motionless blackbirds were much easier.

The first shot splashed with a thwacking meaty sound into the water where the rat's hindquarters were submerged. It jerked sideways threshing the water.

'I got it. I got it. Did you see?' Jimmy yelled as he frantically cracked the gun open to reload. I stared at the rat, fascinated. It had calmed its struggles and resumed its progress across the stream. I fancied I could see its black un-lidded eyes squinting sideways for the source of its pain. It swam differently. The hindquarters twisting awkwardly and the head further out of the water as it pressed forward with its front legs. It had been hurt. I wondered whether it was frightened.

The second shot cracked into its exposed back just behind the neck and for a moment it disappeared. The impact rolled it over and it sank beneath the darkening water. I heard the rifle click open as Jimmy again reloaded. He fumbled in his pocket for a pellet, swearing excitedly. Then I heard him click the barrel shut. The rat had not surfaced.

Jimmy leant forward, tense and expectant, staring at the point where the rat had last been. I wanted to break the silence and pull him back from what he was doing. I was ashamed of being part of it. I could have stopped it. Even if Jimmy had refused me I could have disturbed the rat, frightened it off. It was unfair to have killed it like that. I didn't understand why we had decided to do it in the first place.

Suddenly a high keening scream came from the stream. I jumped. It was an awful high scream, kept at the same pitch and volume, a continuous unnerving wail of pain and fear and confusion.

'Where is it? Where the fuck is it?' Jimmy muttered as he stared at the stream through gathering gloom. He swung the rifle from side to side, aiming it down at the water.

It didn't stop. There was a maniacal edge to the sound. Fury and agony and upset. I shuddered at the sound of it, wanting to block it out from my head but it went on and on.

'Oh God! It's hurting.'

'Course it's fucking hurting. So would you if I shot you twice,' Jimmy snarled. The thin high sound was eating at him as well.

'Look, you've got to find it and finish it off,' I said. 'We can't leave the poor thing like that.'

'I know. *I know*. Don't tell me. I'm looking.'

He stepped cautiously into the stream. The water swirled below his knees as he waded into the centre. He was feeling for footholds on the rocky stream bed and nearly lunged backwards into the water as his foot slipped on a tangle of weeds. The screaming hadn't abated. I didn't understand how something could scream for so long. It seemed to have been going on for hours. How could it breathe? It wasn't a scream so much as an unbroken searingly high whine – something that perhaps didn't require breath. It pierced into the head like fingernails scraping on a blackboard.

'There! It's over there,' Jimmy yelled, pointing to the now barely visible group of exposed rocks in mid-stream where he had shot at the tin cans. I saw a darker mass move spasmodically among the rocky shapes. Jimmy edged towards it.

'I can't see a thing to shoot by,' he said. 'I'll never hit it with this.'

'You should never have done it in the first place,' I retorted. He said nothing and sneaked forward. I saw him raise the rifle. His figure was darkened to a shadow but I could make out his elbow right-angled from the stock on his trigger arm and his head bent forward along the barrel. He lifted his head, then lowered it and again took aim. All the time the keen piercing noise continued. I heard a splash as he dropped the rifle and sudden watery thrashing sounds as he lunged forward towards the rocks, arms outstretched as if to catch a beach ball. A loud splashing came from the darkness and the screaming stopped abruptly. I heard a yelp of pain and vaguely saw his arm rising and falling from the rocks on which he lay.

He was quiet on the way back. Sucking the bite on the ball of his thumb and spitting out the blood. He couldn't find where he'd dropped the rifle and after a stumbling search he had given up saying he would come back for it tomorrow. I knew he wouldn't. His passion for the air rifle had gone. The screaming had scared him off as it had sickened me. I asked why he had shot it but he wouldn't say.

When we reached the house Alice asked if Jimmy had got one. He ignored her and brushed past to go to his room and change. She looked questioningly at me, her eyes unnervingly wide. When I told her, she smiled and lights seemed to glint in the dark of her eyes. She was proud of Jimmy. Indeed she approved of anything her brother did with an innocent faith in his infallibility. I couldn't explain to her the pity of it. The sordid way the rat had died. The screaming and the smashing to death against the rocks. She would not understand the shame I felt nor Jimmy's obvious embarrassment with me. To her Jimmy was the great white hunter, the mighty slayer of rats, even if they were only independent little fellows harming no-one, just out for a swim to catch some food for their young.

That had been fifteen years before. A lifetime ago. Jimmy had never killed again, and as far as I know the rifle still lies rusting in that choking weedy stream, and maybe rats still swim it. Five expeditions have gone by, two failed attempts at bettering ourselves; mine in academic mutiny at the Poly and Jimmy's in an abortive year as an apprentice draughtsman. I'd wanted to be a journalist. No, a photo journalist, heroically covering stories from the hottest spots in the world. The media and communications course had finished that idea off. Jimmy simply couldn't stand the inactivity and the sterility of his chosen work. He could now boast an ability to draw perfect circles freehand – it had taken him a year to learn. I had recently got a job digging graves. I liked it. The money was good; good enough to save some for India anyway. I liked Harry. Harry dug the graves with me. He was sixty-three and had dug graves for the whole of his working life. He said he would teach me the tricks. So I dug the graves and he stood above me, smoking and drinking tea from his flask and telling me the best way to dig. At least I was getting fit.

3

Facing Up

Alice had blossomed. She had wide eyes, dark and silky, and a mane of auburn hair. In the mornings she twisted it into a long single plait which reached to the middle of her back. Sometimes she braided two thin plaits from the sides of her forehead and drew them back around her head and fixed them together with a coloured band so that the mane of her hair spread down her back below these thin restrainers. However much she combed and braided, it always rebelled against her and wisps of autumn gold popped free and in sunshine her hair seemed to glow with an aura of saffron and amber. I see her often in my mind's eye, back-lit by a low winter sun.

Her face should have been pale and freckled, her eyes a watery blue. She should have burnt easily in the sun. Instead her skin was smooth and evenly tanned a creamy brown, her eyes dark and liquid where flecks of light seemed to glimmer when she smiled.

I remember her through half-closed eyes. I could never bear to look directly for fear she wouldn't be what I thought she was. So, glancing sideways through my lashes, I'd examine her as she slept, white teeth glimpsed through parted lips, and auburn hair luxuriant against the white pillow case. When her eyes opened her face changed. They dominated me, those huge dark eyes where shadows seemed to shift and wetly dissolve and flecks of light glinted.

I had come back to Sheffield from the last adventure with Jimmy and there she was, fully grown and glowing. She had left her parents' lonely home on the Durham coast and come to Sheffield to study Literature and Fine Art at the Poly. She told me that the stream had finally dried up. It had become smaller and dirtier each year, taking on a dark fetid look of stagnation. The water rats had long since left, driven out, she said, by the rubbish and the petrol-slicked water and a lack of food. The rats in the piggery had also gone. The farmer had brought in the council rat catcher. There was a battery chicken unit there now and a huge pit of slurry.

Her eyes drew me to her. I could not stop from staring, and every time she caught my eye she smiled and shadows flickered and I would look quickly away, wondering what on earth I was doing. If Jimmy was near I had to force myself to look down. I couldn't let him know what I felt.

Maybe we could have avoided it. I tried but she didn't. She said she had always wanted me. She said she loved me. She kept looking and smiling and I stopped trying. I thought I loved her.

For a year we had played the part of lovers. Meeting secretly we would walk long handheld rambles through the peak district, over Kinder and Bleaklow, following the barren gritstone edges in September. The heather bloomed purple and Hathersage sat snug in its tree-surrounded valley and strengthening winds of coming winter boomed in from the north. We avoided Jimmy as best we could, and the sense of secrecy, the illicit assignments, added strength to a love we had not bothered to question.

This last year I had not gone on any climbing expeditions while Jimmy had fallen in with a company of dubious worth playing to the current trend for adventure holidays. May and June had seen him leading trekking groups in Peru, and in August he was in Africa acting as a guide on Mount Kenya after an illegal foray into Tanzania to make a solo ascent of Kilimanjaro. When the treks had finished he had moved on alone to Zaire and paddled into the rain forest. His two-week adventure to follow the river to the sea and find the nearest road had turned into a four-week epic journey that had seen him half-starved on a diet of roots, grubs and bugs. The stories, he said on his return, had made it all worthwhile, and he showed me the crumpled and stained notebooks packed with his disorganised scrawl.

He returned to Sheffield in early October yellow with hepatitis and shaking feverishly from malaria. He regretted that he had decided that it was best not to take the pills because they never worked and he thought the side effects would be far worse than a dose of malaria. Despite admitting this he still wouldn't accept that he had made a mistake. So for most of October he lay quarantined in the infectious disease unit of Lodge Moor Hospital complaining bitterly that there was nothing wrong with him. They wouldn't let him go until they had completed all their tests, and when he tried to leave of his own accord, he was forcibly reminded that he was a potential danger to society and couldn't discharge himself from an infectious diseases unit.

We already knew this and laughed at his inability to get his own way with the doctors. It also meant that our time together could last a bit longer. It was natural for us to visit him together. It felt as though Jimmy and Alice were my brother and sister, and our relationship seemed more insidiously incestuous as the days drew on. The fact that he never once suspected us made me feel worse. It seemed I was deceiving him, betraying his trust. I often hoped he would ask vaguely if anything was happening between Alice and me. I could have answered him then, straight-faced and honest. We both could, but he didn't ask, and the longer we kept the secret the harder it became to reveal it. We had become too adept at secrecy. Silently we sensed that everything would change if it all came out in the open; not once did it occur to us that it might change for the good, convinced as we were that it would destroy the sense of family for ever.

I was relieved that Alice didn't want Jimmy to know about us. She said he wouldn't understand. She was his little sister. He called her Sis or Ali Pali or other childlike names, as if entirely unaware that she was an adult now. I kept wondering if she would blurt it out someday. It was uncomfortable even to consider broaching the subject myself with him and I shied away.

When she told me that she was pregnant, for a moment everything seemed to collapse. We had reached the top of Grindsbrook, a rocky gully leading down from the Kinder plateau to the tiny village of Edale. It was an icy, cold and clear day, windless and silent. The heather and wild grasses stood petrified in a fine white gauze of hoar frost, and water lying between the tussocks of heather had frozen hard enough to walk on. Kinder downfall had glistened with a thin sheen of ice but the main stream still flowed unhindered. Alice had been silent since we left the downfall and headed back to Grindsbrook and the path to Edale. At the edge of the moor, I had already started down when she called me back quietly. Her eyes were troubled, dark and tearful from the cold I had supposed. She held my hand as she told me, then let go.

'Are you angry?'

'No. No, of course I'm not angry,' I said, looking over the moor edge into Edale. 'I'm confused.'

'I don't want it.'

Her voice had a deadened flat sound. I looked at her and she raised her eyes to mine, pushing forward her chin. Hoar frost had crisped the spray of auburn hair escaping from beneath her woollen hat.

'I don't want a baby.' She repeated it firmly, as if I would protest.

I was too shocked. A baby. We're pregnant, or rather she is by me. There had been no time to think. And we had been so careful.

35

The Water People

'How . . .' I muttered to myself.

She shrugged, looking away over Edale. A white plume of smoke rose directly into the windless sky from the cement works in Hope. Loose Hill and Mam Tor humped solidly in the way so that the smoke seemed to rise from a volcanic caldera near the top of Mam Tor. I heard sheep calling from the slopes below Lord's Seat and the shrill whistle of the Manchester train as it emerged from the Edale tunnel and shuffled busily down the line for Sheffield.

'I made a mistake,' she said.

'Well we both did, then.'

She shook her head. 'No, it was me. I couldn't be bothered fitting it that night after Sally's party. I thought it was safe.'

'Oh! . . . that night.' I vaguely recalled. A greater part of my memory seemed to have stopped functioning.

'I can't go through with it. I don't want it.'

I couldn't think straight. I took her hand, saying nothing, and we walked carefully down the heather bank leading into Grindsbrook.

It seemed very quick. The learning of it, the planning and the abortion. Less than two weeks had gone by and now it would be over. There had been no doubt in her mind. She had asked me once more what I thought. I said very little. It was her decision. She said she would tell her mother, but not about me. Her mother didn't know about me. She would tell Jimmy she needed an operation, call it 'women's things', and that would shut him up. Alice and her mother would sort him out.

Jimmy had reached the car well before me. The boot was open and the interior light was on. He had taken off his boots and thrown them in with his rucksack.

'That was bloody horrible,' he said, getting into the driver's seat of the Mini. He slammed the door against the cold and a piece of rusted bodywork clattered to the ground from the sill below. He opened the window to check nothing important had fallen off. Bits of rust rattled inside the door. I threw my boots into the boot and hefted in my rucksack. It didn't quite fit so I shuffled the sacks around and after some heavy shoving managed to close the boot. As I moved round to the passenger side the boot sprung open and I heard Jimmy laugh.

'You have to twist the coat hanger round the bumper,' he shouted as he started the engine with a throaty shuddering roar. I struggled with the wire, keeping the boot shut with my knee, and tried to ignore the deafening roar from the cracked exhaust pipe as Jimmy gunned the engine enthusiastically.

'No time to drop the gear off. We'll go straight to the hospital, shall we?' He shouted above the engine and the cassette player at full volume delivering 'Bat out of Hell' to the sheep. I nodded as he reversed out from the layby, craning over his shoulder to look between two huge Goodman tannoy speakers stolen from Vinners when the factory had been pulled down. There was a constricted view between the fourteen-inch square boxes bolted to the rear window tray. 'Is she coming out tonight?' Jimmy yelled, gunning the Mini up Froggat Hill through a twisting road overhung with the darkened shapes of wet trees. They were barely visible as a tangle of black leafless branches against the night sky.

'Maybe,' I said.

She stayed in that night. Too much blood lost, we were told. Her mother was there, sitting close by the bed with one frail and wrinkled hand laid possessively on Alice's forearm. Alice looked drawn – a mixture of drugs and pain. She lay very still, not moving when we came into the ward. She smiled weakly at Jimmy and looked quickly at me and away again. For a moment her eyes held mine, pleading. I could say nothing. I wanted to go to her and hold her, hug her close and bury my face in her hair. It spread around her head on the antiseptic white pillow like flames against the snow.

Jimmy asked how she was, and she said 'Okay' in a dull dispirited voice, and her mother glared at him sharply in rebuke.

'She's lost a lot of blood,' she stated and turned to Alice, patting her arm. 'But you'll be fine love, don't you worry.'

Jimmy wandered over to the large plate glass windows of the ward. Alice's bed was closest to the windows and she could look out over Sheffield. She could see my house, she told me later. Hospitals unnerved Jimmy. After asking Alice how she was with exaggerated brightness he could think of nothing more to say. He looked out at the city bejewelled in its night-time finery of street lights and considered how best to leave the ward without indecent haste. The car would be a good excuse, parked as it was on double yellow lines. If he had brought Sis a present it would have been easier to leave quickly, conscience salved. But he had forgotten and resigned himself to wait out the minutes dutifully.

I asked if she was coming out that night and earned a frosty glare from her mother, which reminded me of the blood loss. Alice smiled, a bit more cheerfully, amused at our discomfort. I felt on the brink of discovery and that any word uttered would incriminate me. I imagined the two of them turning to stare at me. Mother, with the white toothmarks of anxiety on her lower lip and a cascade of prunish wrinkles on her upper lip, would wither me. Jimmy, well Jimmy probably wouldn't connect for a long time and perhaps he would forgive me in the end. He would with Alice supporting me, but Mother never would.

I shuffled uneasily, unsure if it would be improper to move closer to the bed. If Mother was angry with Alice she didn't show it, but the strain was clear to see. She had her daughter's wide dark eyes, but crow's feet of age spreading from the corners of her eyes seemed to close them down. Her hair had thinned since I saw her last and she wore it tied up in a severe salt and pepper bob.

I had expected tears but instead the scene was silently unemotional, except for the occasional searching looks that Alice directed at me when her mother looked away. Jimmy had stopped staring at the city and was fidgeting with the oxygen control system above Alice's bed. A staff nurse stripping the nearby empty bed with starchy efficiency told him to stop which he did with a sudden guilty shrug and a sheepish grin at me.

'I think we had better get off now, Sis,' Jimmy said, with a mischievous grin at me. 'The car's on a double yellow.' Mother glared crossly at him.

'Go on, Jimmy. You're no good here,' Alice said.

'Right you are,' he said, brightening immediately. 'We'll be off then. Take care of yourself now. Come on, Chris.' With Jimmy tugging at my elbow I reluctantly turned to leave.

'Bye Alice. Ring me when you get out if you need anything,' I said, conscious of her mother's stare.

As Jimmy bundled me towards the lifts outside the ward his mother came after us.

'James!' she said in a sharp flat voice. I saw his shoulders sag as his chances of escape were cut off.

'James, I want you to look after Toby for me. Just for tomorrow mind. I can't leave him in the car and Mrs Foster wouldn't like him in the house.'

'But, Ma, I'm working tomorrow. I can't take him to the factory.' Jimmy's employment as a welder in a local light fittings firm was two days old and I doubted it would last much longer.

'It's all right, Mrs Banks, I can look after Toby for you. I've only got one job tomorrow and he can come along. He'll enjoy it.'

'Thank you, Chris,' she said. 'What is it you are doing now, exactly?'

'Ah, yes, outdoor work mostly. You know in the park, digging and so on.'

'Gardening?'

'Well, yes – landscaping, that sort of thing,' I replied, and she accepted the lie.

'Good. Well, he's in the car, James. The door is open and his food, bowl and basket are in the boot. I'll pick him up from your house when I leave for home tomorrow evening,' she said as she picked lint off Jimmy's sweater. 'Is that all right with you Chris?'

'Yup. Fine by me.'

'Right then, we had better be off. Bye, Mother.' Jimmy hopped into the opening doors of the lift and pulled me in. As we sank quietly to the ground floor Jimmy sighed.

'God! I hate hospitals,' he muttered, and then smiled. 'Fancy a pint?'

I was quiet on the way back from the hospital. The visit had seemed strangely normal, as if nothing had happened. I suppose I was relieved. I didn't know if I could have dealt with tears and wailing. Then again, Alice would never have behaved like that, I thought, although I wasn't entirely certain. I had braced myself for it. Perhaps I didn't know her as well as I thought. The idea unsettled me.

Some people would believe that we had committed murder; abused the sanctity of human life. I'd heard the arguments and in the past had felt swayed towards them, especially after seeing photographs of nine-week-old foetuses with fingers, toes, bones and a brain all formed. It was difficult to refute the evidence, until it happened to us, and then it seemed so remarkably easy. Convenient to be able to drop one's moral notions so painlessly, though I couldn't stop it impinging on other convictions and beliefs I held. There had been no attempt to discuss the decision, to find any other solution. Alice had been so determined. I had no say. I had no right to persuade her otherwise. So I said nothing and was relieved to have had the problem removed from my mind. There was the shock of being told and almost immediately the announcement of what would be done about it. I felt belittled by my silence, and ashamed that, now it was over, I should choose to roll these breast-beating ideas through my mind.

The wind had built up to a strong gale since our return from the crag. Wet leaves tumbled along the pavement flags and the petrol price sign at the Mobil station span crazily with a staccato clacking sound. A few broken branches were scattered across the forecourt. A man refilling his car had to lean forward and grip the rear window pillar against a sudden swirling gust. I glimpsed a few stars through the rush of low broken clouds. It was warmer than the afternoon. A front was passing over.

A grimy yellow double decker pulled in with a hiss of air as the door opened and we moved sideways to avoid the group waiting at the unprotected bus stop sign. Mostly young girls between fifteen and eighteen dressed to dance in tight-fitting skirts and bomber jackets, hung with chains and bangles and over-done with make-up. They giggled and shrieked as the wind ignored their finery, buffeting them into each other. A few surly boys in stone-washed jeans and garish patterned nylon bomber jackets stood to one side trying to be cool. One was in the throes of an acne attack so severe his face was a pock-marked scar, livid purple in the street light.

Jimmy, head down, shoulders hunched and with his hands dug deeply into his front jeans pockets, made no effort to side-step the spotty youth and expertly shouldered him aside. There was a muffled protest.

'Townies!' Jimmy muttered.

We passed the local working men's club half-hidden up a lane crowded with chestnut trees. The driveway was strewn with twigs and branches and crisp packets swirling in eddies of wind. A large poster-board swayed in the wind, some of the posters flapping and ripping from the plywood. Those more firmly glued announced female mud wrestling at seven-thirty.

As we passed the sign we saw a man swaying behind it, one outstretched hand grasping the sign as he leaned forward, head-down, in a tangle of nettles. He retched and a dribble of bile strung from his mouth. He tried to spit it away but it remained firmly glued to the stubble of his chin. Unsteadily he wiped it off on the sleeve of his free arm, at the same time retching and vomiting a gush of beer and chips on to his hand.

'He's a bit early to be in that state,' I said as we passed by. Jimmy laughed.

Music came like a shock wave as Jimmy pulled the pub door open. The heavy bass of the juke box at full volume vibrated through the floor.

'The snooker table's free,' he shouted above the roar of a Stones track. 'I'll set the balls up. Mine's a pint of Castle.'

I headed for the bar. The pub filled rapidly, as it always did on a Friday night. We were fortunate to have got the snooker table so easily and, after the first game, decided to play doubles with the next two people on the blackboard. Jimmy was playing well and as usual I was playing erratically. Before I re-racked the balls for the game I noticed Jimmy involved in a heated discussion with Lono. I kept a sly eye on them as I moved around the table retrieving the balls from the pockets.

Lono was a regular. He was also dangerous. He towered over Jimmy, who seemed unconcerned by the difference in size. Lono was powerfully built, with an aggressive close-cropped hair-style, razored at the back to produce a cross-hatch effect. Bullet-headed and with a deceptive smile, he had a habit of trying to bully his way on to the table. I had never seen him get violent, but that was probably because most people backed down from his aggression. The thin scar running from his left eyebrow into his hairline was warning enough to most. I had often wondered whether he had deliberately cut himself for effect, but had never attempted to find out. Lono dealt quarters of dope on a regular basis by the football table in the smoky recesses of the back bar, and I had no doubt he could look after himself.

He leaned over Jimmy's shoulder and wiped several names off the board, ignoring what Jimmy was saying. I knew his temperament; Jimmy hadn't met him before. A few people standing near the table were looking at them and laughing. They looked an odd pair – Lono, wearing a grey tank top with LONSDALE printed across his clenched chest. Strong shoulders above bunching biceps, the smooth ridges of muscle, veins standing proud of the skin, shone a silky ebony in the deflected glow from the snooker lights. Jimmy's head barely reaching Lono's shoulder so that he seemed to be speaking directly at the LONSDALE sign. He stood characteristically hunch-shouldered, head forward and meeting Lono's stare without flinching. A slight smile had formed at the corner of Jimmy's mouth, giving him a patient tolerant appearance, an easy touch for Lono, except that I knew what it heralded. What Jimmy lacked in stature he made up for with shockingly fast reactions and an almost demented ferocity.

I had seen him smile that half-sneer droop of the lip only twice before and had been unable to intervene in time. As I moved quickly round the table towards them I heard Jimmy talking in that coldly controlled and polite manner of his.

'I'm sorry, mate, but I reckon you're mistaken there. What's your name? Lono, yeah Lono, well, you see that name wasn't on the board when we started this game. In fact, it still ain't there. Put it down and you are on after us, okay.'

'No way, man!' Lono said in a surprisingly high voice for such a big man. 'No way. It's been rubbed off, right, don't give me that shit, man.' He turned to the table where the colours and red were now in position and leant across to cue up the white ball. Jimmy stepped sideways and slapped his hand across the cue before Lono could strike.

'Come on, Lono, stop hassling us,' I said, hoping he would back off when he recognised me. He straightened up. Jimmy's hand remained on the table, firmly pressing the cue against the green baize. He hadn't taken his eyes from Lono's face. Everything happens first in the face, he had told me once; look at the face and you'll know what's coming. Lono tried to snatch the cue up from the table and showed momentary surprise that he hadn't succeeded in moving Jimmy's hand. Jimmy smiled again, still looking Lono in the eye.

'Fuck it, man, who cares.' Lono loosened his hold on the cue, and suddenly his whole face changed. He smiled a broad open smile. I smiled back, recognising that the flash point had passed. He had backed off. Jimmy released the cue and Lono threw it heavily across the table, scattering the reds. I felt a rush of relief come over me. Lono swung on his heel, grinning his infectious smile to the onlookers, most of whom smiled back as he loped past them with a cocky swagger.

Jimmy leaned across the table and re-set the red balls in the wooden triangle. As he lifted it away and re-placed the pink he glanced over at me and said quietly, 'He's all front, that guy.'

'Yeah, well, you didn't know that when you started,' I said in annoyance. Jimmy seemed unaffected by the encounter, but I was suffering the nervous after effects, feeling angry at what had nearly happened.

'I didn't start it. He did. I don't like being pushed around.' He collected the white and began cueing up to start the game.

The cue ball snicked off the red at the back right of the triangle and bounced smoothly off three cushions to finish snug against the baulk cushion in a near-perfect break. I shook my head, exasperated by his lack of concern, 'For God's sake, he would have slaughtered you.'

'Possibly,' Jimmy said, handing his cue to one of our doubles opponents, 'but I doubt it. He was just trying to front me out and it didn't work,' he added as a matter of fact. 'My round, I believe.'

We lost the doubles. I was too distracted to play well and Jimmy didn't seem to care. He had won before we started and I envied his confidence.

We found a seat near the table and talked about India. The plan was to spend June there before going on to Pakistan. Jimmy talked of staying on after the climbing and cruising round India. He wanted to visit the seven sacred cities, then travel down to the southern tip with a view to crossing the Gulf of Mannar and visiting Sri Lanka. It seemed typical that he was quite uninterested in the fact that Sri Lanka was embroiled in violent civil war.

He spoke quickly and urgently, a faraway gleam in his eyes.

He talked as if he had already been there, as if what he went seeking he had long since found. There was an arrogance in his words. He had asked in passing if I wanted to join him and then had continued before I could answer, accepting my silence as acquiescence. I couldn't be bothered to correct him. Alice had come back to mind, and the idea of leaving for India depressed me. I felt we were on the watershed of our relationship and sensed in the hospital that already we had begun to slip down separate slopes. I would go, but only to the mountains. I stood up.

'Come on, let's get out of here.'

Despite my protests Jimmy insisted on driving the Mini back to his flat. I watched him gun it along my street, seven pints down, a broken rear brake light, fractured exhaust pipe roaring competitively with the heavy beat of reggae music blasting from the speakers. His flat was ten minutes' walk from my place but he wouldn't listen.

'I'm too pissed to walk,' he shouted from the driver's window. 'I'd better drive!' And flicking the cassette and graphic equaliser into a dance of coloured lights in the glove compartment he accelerated away in a burst of blue exhaust and crashing sound. Sometimes I wondered how people ever got done for drink-drive.

4

In Memoriam

Toby jumped enthusiastically on to my chest when the radio alarm burst into life at seven the next morning. His tail thrashed excitedly, his rear legs kept slipping on the duvet and he breathed a foul stench into my face with a cheeky toothy grin.

'Phew! God! What have you been licking?'

I shoved him off the bed. He immediately jumped back and barked one sharp excited command at me. I got out of bed and gingerly padded down to the kitchen. Toby darted out the back door and cocked his leg against the next door neighbour's neatly washed and ordered group of milk bottles. He grinned at me over his shoulder, as if to include me in his mischief.

When I called him back he darted into the kitchen and on up the stairs. The previous evening Jimmy had left the kitchen as he left everything – in a mess. Empty cans of lager were stacked in the sink. A sideplate floated in the washing-up bowl. Hand-made cigarette butts floating on the greasy surface. I lit the ring and filled the kettle, regretting that I had given in to Jimmy's idea that we take a few cans back. Three black coffees and several cigarettes later, things had not improved. I whistled Toby down from whatever he was destroying in the bedroom, stuffed his lead in my pocket, and

46

stepped out into the cold windless day. A cold grey cloud layer hinted that winter hadn't fled entirely; snow was on the way. Toby followed at my heels, pausing occasionally to sniff lampposts and cock his leg for a territorial squirt. The bus driver tried to charge me for Toby but I ignored him and he let the bus into gear and pulled away sharply, checking in the mirror that I hadn't sat down. I pitched down the aisle of the almost empty bus, grabbing for a seat as the driver stabbed the brakes to make me lurch backwards. Two men laughed, and I heard the driver chuckle as he set off again at a more leisurely speed.

Toby yapped excitedly and jumped on to one of the red vinyl seats. I sat beside him and studied the graffiti scrawled in unintelligible Arabic on the seat back in front of me. I wondered what the words meant. 'God is great', or 'Down with the Zionist oppressors', or more probably 'I wuz 'ere'. I decided that the curly Arabic script seemed preferable to the scrawled 'Sheffield Wednesday Rules' that crossed a slashed cut in the vinyl. 'Fucking Pakis' in thick black felt-tip partly obscured a familiar Arabic symbol of Allah.

Toby put his front paws on the metal window sill and scanned the passing streets, mouth open and tongue lolling between pristine white young teeth. Occasionally he glanced at me over his shoulder to check I was still with him, then returned to his view.

The bus ground noisily up Woodseats Road and swung right, out of town on Chesterfield Road. The shops hadn't yet opened. A newsagent's advertising Benson and Hedges in lurid gold gave a cheery early morning glow from its windows. A man bent over the red headline board of the *Sheffield Star* and removed yesterday's news from behind the wire. The air brakes squealed as the bus drew in at deserted shelters for no-one to get on or off. Air hissed as the doors opened and let in the cold, then hissed again as we shuddered on up the hill past Meersbrook Bank. The wooded hills above Graves Park were shrouded in lingering fog, though I could see it lifting from the trees of Coneygree Wood as I turned to look across the city awakening slowly below us. Street lights competed with the flicker of car headlights. It was a fine view of houses spread in patchwork squares, red brick and glistening black tiled roofs, a city seated within hills, dipping down from the moors to the north and south.

The imposing block of the Hallamshire Hospital jutted up from the sprawl of houses, with Walkley Bank rising behind in stepped streets of terraced houses. Black smoke rose pencil thin and straight from the roof of the hospital, where incinerators converted sheets and dressings, organs, limbs and foetuses, the diseased and unwanted detritus of sick people into an oily black line of smoke above the windless city.

They would have woken Alice by now, I thought, remembering the numbing routine of hospital treatment. I looked away and stared out of the wide front windows of the bus at the moorland edges to the west. A brownish shade of wintered heather marched away over Hallam and Burbage moors, dipping into tree-filled valleys and up again in a sweep of trees, giving out to heather and the top of Derwent moors where Alice had walked with me and we had hidden so well from Jimmy and his mother. We had followed the Derwent edges with the swooping drop of heathered hillside to our left and a low hum on the wind of traffic toiling up the valley below towards the Snake Pass and the lights of Manchester. It seemed as if, by looking at the vague promise of rolling brown lurking through the dirty glass in the west, I could see for ever across the moors and remember those cold rain-swept days we had stolen. We had watched the rain swaying towards us in serried ranks of shadow, falling as columns of needle-grey light across the moors. Ladybower reservoir had darkened as they passed over and the waters rippled under the spraying rain. Then it would sweep over us with a flurry of cold wind and heavy-bellied clouds rolled above shadowed blue-black and darkening the sky until they passed and the waters glimmered below in damp sunshine. We kissed each other's hands and blew on them for warmth. Alice took off her hat and shook the rain in a fine spray from her hair. I looked through the frizz of autumn gold beside her cheek at a low winter sun, and we waited for the next rains to come scudding over.

The bus swung left up the hill of Derbyshire Lane. My stop next. I listened to two men on the back seat complaining about beer prices, the Poll Tax, the Tories, Sheffield Wednesday losing away, Poll Tax rioters, fucking students, and Pakis in a monotonous dialogue delivered in gruff South Yorkshire accents, non-committal statements of fact as they saw them, never speaking to each other or with each other, simply stating views alternately without judgment or discussion. There was so little difference between each aggressively worded wisdom that I had to turn round to check they were both talking. They looked up as I did so and fell silent for a moment as they concentrated their early morning bile on me, staring down hard and cold so that I turned my eyes quickly away. 'Fucking students . . .' I heard one begin his diatribe again and smiled at how they thought of me. If I had opened my mouth it would have invited only further scorn as they heard my bland private school accent. The very sound of my voice would have condemned me to a few well favoured prejudices. Student, poofter, wouldn't know the meaning of hard graft, thinks he knows it all . . . I listened instead to their stream of racist, sexist invective and wondered at how wrong they had it down south. I reckoned they had no idea in London of the depth of reactionary working class vitriol, so alive and corrosive in the heart of the country. I laughed at the idea of Camden council providing for the minorities of race and sexual leanings and answering to the acid scorn of these two men. If I loved the north it wasn't for the likes of these mean men, or what they thought, but for the plain speaking that came with it. At least they spoke straight. I didn't have to look beyond their smiles and guess their postures to understand what they meant. They disliked me. They didn't know me and didn't care. I disliked them, heartily, and knew clearly the reasons why. At least I knew.

Despite the chill, Spring was struggling through. The budding fresh green foliage of the trees slapped against the roof of the bus as it passed down a street lined with horse chestnuts. Daffodils had already made their appearance and in the park yellow clumps bloomed by oak trees isolated at the sides of playing fields rolling down the hill towards the city. A couple walked by the oaks. I saw the man throw a stick for his dog, a squat brown bull terrier, legs braced widely from powerfully muscled shoulders hunched against a thick steel-studded collar. The dog ignored the stick and pissed against a tree. The woman laughed, unheard by me, with head thrown back and white teeth flashing and dark oiled hair hung across her shoulder, swinging forward and covering her face as she leant over and covered her mouth with her hand. The bus pulled away from the park.

I stood up, conscious of the two men's sudden silence, and pressed the bell. The driver braked hard at the stop and I nearly fell. There was laughter from the back as I straightened up. Toby sprang off the seat with innocent enthusiasm and headed down the aisle. The doors hissed open and Toby jumped down to the pavement and turned expectantly, tail wagging and wet eyes reflecting the orange flashes of the indicators. As I took the first step down I turned and leant into the aisle, looking back at the two silent men who were scrutinising my every move. They stared coldly back, one jutting his chin and bracing his mean mouth in a sneer. I smiled at them as I clenched my fist, index finger pointed up, and jerked my wrist back.

The doors shut, but not before I heard the angry shout. As the bus pulled past me I grinned at their outraged faces and circled my forefinger to thumb and wagged a slow lewd gesture. I saw mean mouth pulling himself up angrily, but the driver held no grudges and accelerated sharply, forcing him to tumble back into his seat. I turned and walked down the hill to the cemetery.

Harry was waiting for me at the entrance to the cemetery. As always he wore a heavy black donkey jacket with leather shoulder and elbow patches. 'Can't get them with leather now,' he said repeatedly. 'It's all plastic now . . . never lasts.'

His boots were army issue, steel capped and stained a reddish brown from mud and water and a dearth of polish. He wore ill-fitting jeans that hung in rumpled folds around his knees and exposed flabby spotty buttocks from above the waistline whenever he bent to dig. I was glad he rarely did so, preferring instead to initiate me into the finer traditions of digging holes. He was a short fat man with a cheerful face, blue eyes, and a mischievous schoolboy humour. A muddied woollen hat was pulled over his ears and wiry bushes of white hair sprouted rebelliously from its sides. His beard was full and wild, and nicotine-stained yellow at the corners of his mouth. He was sixty-three and though he was fat, a huge beer belly swelling over his belt buckle in a pregnant roll, he appeared younger. He laughed a lot, mainly at me, but not in the derisive vicious manner of the men on the bus. Life was amusing to him, endlessly so.

'All right then lad,' he said and bent to chuck Toby under the chin and ruffle his ears. 'And who are you then laddie, eh lad, what you playing at, eh?' Toby played delighted at the attention, rolling his head from side to side as Harry cuffed him gently, and eventually getting a grip on the tattered leather-lined cuff of the donkey jacket. He shook his head vigorously, tugging at the cuff and growling in the back of his throat. Harry laughed and straightened up, lifting Toby clear of the ground until he hung by his teeth, growling and shaking his head so that his hindquarters swung from side to side.

'Gerrof, you cheeky bugger!' Harry shook Toby free and, hooking his boot under his stomach, lofted him gently away.

'Right, Chris, let's get on,' he said and headed through the wrought iron gates.

'What have we got today, then?' I followed him into an imposing gatehouse building of gritstone blocks and leaded glass windows. Inside was a messy sprawl of scaffolding planks, pieces of chock wood and adjustable props. A wheelbarrow lay upside down on the flagged floor. A pick and two shovels leant against it. Harry moved the shovels and kicked the pick aside.

'An opening, down at the bottom end,' he answered.

'When was it last opened?'

'Dunno. A while back I reckon. Can't remember working the bottom end.'

He turned the barrow on to its wheel. The tyre was flat and the left rear foot rest broken so that it leaned drunkenly. Harry piled the props, pick and shovel into the barrow balancing them on the right side so as not to upset it. I fetched the planks. Four for round the grave and two for support inside.

'Put another in,' Harry said, throwing two more props in, 'it's wet, and there's no burial till tomorrow.' I balanced another plank in the overladen barrow. Two large panelled boards the size of doors tottered precariously atop the pile.

'Come on then, lad,' Harry said as he walked into the cemetery carrying a couple of sticks in his right hand and clicking his fingers at Toby, who bounded after him. I muttered a curse under my breath and bent to lift the overloaded barrow. Since it had been loaded to compensate for its rickety standing position it had to be pushed in the same way. I staggered after Harry crouched over with my left hand dropped lower than my right to keep everything balanced. He was throwing a stick down the gravel path for Toby as I wobbled after him, hunchbacked by the awkward load and forced to walk in a strange bent-kneed hobble down the narrow path.

The grave stones rose dark and weathered on either side, aged by the years of city smog and bitter westerly winds, blackened with soot and green lichens. These old burial sites told a silent history of the city in generations gone by. Some were simple upright flags of stone with scrolled carvings round

the edge and words carved in an arch at the peak of the stone.
'In loving Memory' or 'Rest in blessed Peace' seemed the
most common inscriptions. I liked the view and the sense of
being high over the city, able to look at the promise of
moorland in the distance.

I located Harry by the sound of excited barks and ground
the heavy barrow round the corner on its punctured tyre, the
flabby rubber rolling sideways off the rim so that the boards
slithered across the planks. When I tried to ride the wheel up
on to the grass, it stopped obstinately at the kerb and the
barrow tipped sideways, spilling boards, planks and tools in a
jumble against a headstone.

'Have some respect, lad,' Harry said, laughing at my curses
and bending to lift the boards, one in each calloused hand. I
brought the tools over to the grave site. A small white stone
jutted from the turf, and behind it a large headstone threw a
shadow towards us. There was hardly room for more names. I
counted five and the associated words explaining the relation
of each to the other. 'Much loved wife of . . . beloved son of
. . . dearly beloved husband to . . .' The first name was dated
1889 and the lettering had worn down. The stone faced the
moors and a century of wind-driven rain had eaten at its sharp
edged lines and smoothed out the chiselled letters. The last
name had been added in August 1959.

'Thirty-two years,' Harry said as he returned with the
planks stacked sideways across his arms. 'I hope it wasn't a
cheap 'un.'

He was referring to the coffin buried beneath our feet.
What little I had learnt in the past four months had come from
Harry's often gruffly clipped statements. The rules had
changed in recent years. No more than four internments were
allowed in any one grave, and now even that was prevented by
demands for deeper earth above the coffins. Owners of some
plots discovered too late that it was no longer possible to use
the last grave space they had purchased years before.

Harry would let me dig most of the hole until he judged I

was near the top of the coffin. He probed down with the bar, a long thin loop-handled iron rod which he pressed steadily down through the stone-sharded clay. When he could press no further he withdrew the bar and slid it up and down a few feet before plunging it down hard. A thunking, dampened wooden sound confirmed his guess, and he measured off the depth left to dig. He had a knack of guessing correctly every time. He guessed as right on graves he'd never worked as those he remembered digging in years past.

'Go on lad, put your back into it,' he'd said during my first grave dig. 'You've a long way to go before you hit wood.'

'What?' I said incredulously, staring at the steel toecaps of his boots protruding over the edge of the grave at chest level.

'Yup. Should be a couple of feet yet, I reckon.' He sucked deeply on a battered old pipe. 'See there. Nineteen twenty-three. It will have settled a lot by now.'

I glanced at the headstone. Suddenly I felt unsafe in the hole I had dug almost single-handedly. I imagined a sucking, crunching sensation as I crashed through into the previous occupant, and shuddered. I flung the shovel out on to the planks at the edge of the grave and began to lift myself out.

'Gerron with it, now. It won't bite.' Harry kicked my hand off the edge and I slipped heavily in a crouch on to damp earth at the bottom of the grave. Something crawled up my spine and made the muscles in my back spasm. 'There's three more beneath him. Man and wife and a bairn.' He leant closer to the headstone and squinted at it. 'Seven months. Poor mite,' he muttered to himself.

Twenty minutes later Harry lowered himself ponderously into the new opening. I passed him the spade and he scraped it gingerly over the lumpy clay floor. I peered into the shadowed grave while he skimmed a few spadefuls from a point near his foot, then straightened and looked triumphantly up at me.

'There you go. Solid,' he said thumping the tip of the spade down between his feet. A wooden knock echoed clearly from the shadows. He bent forward again and scraped more soil clear.

'Told you. They don't make them like that now,' he said with obvious pleasure. 'That's the coffin lid. There ain't even a cover board.'

I turned away apprehensively, feeling that grave-digging wasn't for me.

'It's all in the wood you see,' Harry explained as he dug the soil clear. 'Heaths. Now that's a good box. Solid elm, mostly, sometimes oak. They last years, them. I helped clear the churchyard in Derwent village before they flooded the reservoir and every Heath was solid. We slipped straps beneath 'em and hauled them out whole. It's all chipboard now. Cheap and cheerful.'

'How do you mean?' I asked.

'They don't last a year in a wet grave. Bye, you can tell before you're halfway down. Yer can whiff it. Phew!' He wrinkled his nose contemptuously. 'Can't get much elm now what with Dutch elm disease and all. Mahogany or oak. They're best 'uns. Good hard woods.'

'Elm isn't a hardwood,' I said.

'So some say,' Harry agreed, 'but it's best wood for water. All them lockgates in the canals, they're all elm, those are. Hundred and fifty years in water and still like iron. Aye, elm's the best.'

'What do we do with this?' I asked, pointing at a small white marker stone hanging perilously on the edge of the hole.

'Oh, I'll move that, lad.'

I knew that there was no body laid beneath it. The small stone was dwarfed by the dark looming grave stones around it. There was a striking simplicity about it. The clean sharp white lines of the stone, the etched figure of the Royal Air Force emblem. A bird of prey, wings outstretched and its tail fanned beneath it, and laurel leaves circled round with the words 'Per Ardua Ad Astra' following the upper half of the circle. Beneath the symbol the words 'Buried Elsewhere' were a chilling reminder of the lonely deaths of past battlefields. A name followed by rank, Aircraftsman 1st class, and the date, 1943, evoking a sense of sadness in me that the other stones had failed to do.

Harry was careful with all the graves, respectful in an honest smiling way. With these war graves he was quiet and would not let me help him. 'I'll do it son,' he'd say firmly. I had never asked him about his family or his past and suspected he may have lost more in the war than he ever mentioned.

We were finished by noon. A solid cover board hid me from the coffin and Harry had finished off boarding the sides with support planks and props braced between them, pressing back the leaning wet clay walls. A musty damp smell emanated from the grave. The spoil was piled neatly between the two boards propped up by sticks and covered over with heavy canvas. The grave edges trimmed and laid with planks.

Toby followed me as I pushed the barrow to the entrance gate, empty now and easy to manage. I studied the inscriptions on the stones, noting the ages and the abundance of infants at the turn of the century. The name of a soldier caught my eye, a young officer, 'Killed in France 23rd October 1918'. Nineteen days before the war ended. Some were plain unlucky. The more wealthy families had life-size statues of angels with wings drooped and arms embracing a tall cross. Folds of stone garments flowed down to the tiered plinths where a generation of names was etched. I looked for the small circle on some angels' shoulders – the symbol of a fallen halo, usually for an unmarried mother. There was none to be seen; either an upright community or less than honest. The arm of one angel had snapped at the wrist and the hand lay abandoned in a tangle of frost-dried grass.

In the midst of the cemetery a spray of colour flickered between the stones as I passed by. Fresh earth in a high mound covered with bouquets of cellophane-wrapped flowers marked a recent burial. An orange tape flapped in the wind and the cellophane creased against the flowers. I stopped at an ancient grave. The last burial had been ninety-three years past and subsidence had tilted the stone precariously. A small ornate wrought-iron fence six inches high and set into a limestone flag covering the grave was twisted and misshapen. The flag had sunk deeply at the lower left corner and the whole grave and headstone seemed to be sliding sedately beneath the soil like a sinking ship, the superstructure of the headstone defiant against the clouds. I wondered whether the family line had petered out and there was no-one to look after the site. A rose bush rattled drily in the wind, dried grass snagged in its thorn branches. One yellow rose stunted by cold and fading brown at the edges clung to life at the foot of the slab.

'Right, lad,' Harry said, extending a calloused hand for me to shake. 'Be careful in India on those fool mountains you're after.' He slapped his thigh and Toby jumped up and rested his forepaws against his leg, closing his eyes with pleasure as Harry ruffled his ear. 'Nice dog, this 'un.' He pushed Toby away and clapped me on the shoulder. 'I don't suppose we'll meet again. You're not for digging graves, are you, lad?'

'No.' I smiled at him. 'Well, take care Harry. I've enjoyed working with you even if I did do all the work.'

'Get away with you.' He laughed and pushed me roughly away. He turned and walked down the hill. I saw the bus pulling in to my stop and, shouting farewell, ran up the hill waving my arm at the driver for him to stop. He waved back and grinned as he gunned past me with a throaty diesel roar. 'Bastard!' I yelled after it, recognising him from the morning. I set off after Harry.

I found Jimmy had let himself in when I returned with Toby. He sat at the kitchen table rolling a cigarette. The paper was folded out under his arms. I noticed he'd completed the crossword. A flash of irritation rose up. I had looked forward to relaxing with it after work.

'So how was the last day then?' Jimmy said.

'Okay. We were finished by twelve,' I said, pouring tea from the pot. The tea was cold. 'Fancy a walk up Kinder?'

'You're kidding! It's going to snow.'

'No. Rain, I reckon. Come on.'

I was subdued when we came out of the gully on to the heathered moortop. The wind boomed in from the Edale valley, a clean power of air driving in from the east. I sat facing into it, perched atop a small gritstone pedestal. Toby sat beside me, leaning forward into this wind the like of which he had never encountered in his short cosseted life. Clouds rolled in with the wind, sweeping over in an unbroken mass and past me across the bleak Kinder plateau on their way to Manchester. There would be rain soon.

I struggled to fix the little wicker basket securely against the wind. The posy of dried flowers was barely visible among the gritstone blocks. I stood, head bowed into the wind, my jacket buckling in the gusts, face hidden, lost in my own world. I doubted Alice would ever see this memorial to what we had lost. Thoughts of what could have been came and went unasked for, now superfluous. What would it have been like, the thing which had died unborn, unseen, unsexed even, of so little importance to everyone except Alice and myself? Even we hadn't wanted it.

I had lost the certainty of knowing myself, perhaps I had never known. The future scared me. So many things in the last year had gone out of my control.

I glanced over and saw Jimmy approaching. He knew nothing of the flowers I had hidden in my daysack on the way up. I moved away from the pedestal so that he wouldn't notice them shivering crisply in the wind. He walked across and smiled wistfully when he saw me looking at him. Toby pricked his ears, leaning round me to see Jimmy, before jumping up, tail wagging so hard his hindquarters swayed. A patch of blue sky appeared briefly above the wind-rent clouds, then closed up and was whipped away across the moor.

'I'm glad I came.' Jimmy sat down beside me and scanned the valley below. 'I feel different already. It was worth it.'

'Good,' I said. 'Come on. We'd better make a move. It'll rain soon.'

We half-walked, half-ran down the open slopes leading into the gully, and Toby sprinted in bounding hops through the heather, letting out yelps of excitement as he criss-crossed back and forth between us. As we walked into Edale village the threat of rain lifted. The Nag's Head was closed for renovations, so we drove down to the Traveller's Rest and hurried in for the last hour before closing time.

We talked quietly. Jimmy spoke of India, and I spoke of the fears I felt at what was happening to me. I wanted to explain the reasoning behind the small memorial act I had performed. Then I remembered, as I began to speak, that he knew nothing of it and I could never explain. I would never know what it might have been, a boy or a girl, but decided irrationally that she would have been a girl. It seemed easier on my mind. The flowers would soon be gone. Perhaps the basket would be there next year, but it didn't matter. I decided to return each year, a penance for my guilt. Jimmy returned from the bar with two more pints of Pedigree.

5

Days Lost in Delhi

I watched a figure standing motionless on a knife-edged ridge of snow. Blue shadows lurked on either side. The snow glared white heat shimmers around his legs as if they were wreathed in tendrils of smoke. Light sparkled from a myriad scattering of diamanté ice crystals strewn across the snow. He wore a red wind suit. He shielded his eyes with white woollen-mittened hands, examining the ridge rising steeply ahead of him to a rocky summit flecked with ice smears. I seemed to float above him as if in flight, though I knew I couldn't fly.

When I looked at the summit I wanted to be closer and I was there as soon as the thought had occurred. I looked down the sliver of ridge to a distant speck of red looking up at me. Far below the man I saw a dark shape moving. I passed over the red man to see the shape but it disappeared and the red man turned to smile at me. I recognised myself. I was the red man and no longer floated. I saw through his eyes and turned to seek the shape.

A very old man moved slowly up the ridge towards me. He was bare-footed. The sharp crusty snow broke over his leathery brown feet with each careful step and slithered in icy crumbles into the blue shadows. Four birds circled on a thermal in the shadowed valley to his left. Ravens rising to feed – a sign of good weather. Clouds twisted in thin streamers high in a lapiz lazuli sky. Signs of bad weather coming. The valleys were hidden below a carpet of unbroken cloud. A temperature inversion so perfect that only the peaks were visible bursting through a flat white cloudscape. I was tempted to descend to the cloud level and step off the ridge on to the softly undulating whiteness. I could be God, I thought, and then I saw the man appear from beneath the cloud, climbing smoothly up the ridge and breaking through the layer into dazzling sunshine. For a moment, as he emerged, a diaphanous train of misty white trailed from his back and shoulders and swirled below him in the vortex of his passing. A cape of smoky white was drawn up from the sea of cloud that slowly dissipated in the beat of the sun.

I recognised his face but I didn't know him. He seemed untroubled by the cold and never once hesitated in his stride. His feet didn't slip in the snow and I noticed red dust on his legs. The snow had not washed them clean. He wore a rough brown blanket wrapped twice around his shoulders. It draped to the level of his knees, and as he lifted each leg, I glimpsed bare skin and thin sinewy legs powdered red with the valley dust.

He stopped ten feet from where I stood and looked up the ridge. He looked through me or past me. He did not know I was there. I noticed then that it was silent. There were no sounds. Just windless calm. When the snow rolled from his feet into shadows there were no scratchy slithering sounds. I saw the clouds of his breath in the freezing air but couldn't hear him breathe. I moved sideways on the ridge to let him pass and heard nothing.

On his head he wore a magnificent turban. A bright splash of colour contrasting with his dull blanket and brown dusty skin. It was saffron orange, twisted in whorls around his head. One blood-red twist of cotton curled up from above his right ear in a distinctive crescent and folded back into the layers of saffron above the centre of his forehead. A vermilion caste mark on his forehead was banded on each side with triple layered patterns of white rice-paste. Below the caste mark, on the bridge of his nose, was a smaller white paste dot. A leaf-shape in white reached the tip of his nose, and split into two arms drawn out to each eyebrow and up, passing the caste mark on each side in straight lines into the folds of his turban. It seemed as if someone had painted a white tuning fork laid handle-down along the ridge of his nose.

His eyebrows were finely marked in thin plucked lines that curled above his eyes giving an air of inquisitive surprise. The pupils were black, the whites yellowed. There was no emotion in his eyes.

'Who are you?' I said, and heard nothing. He looked at me then, as if noticing me for the first time, yet his eyes did not register seeing me. His face was riven deeply with lines. From his forehead to his nose parallel grooves swept down to the corners of his mouth. From his eyes crow's feet spread out and curved down across his cheekbones. I fancied they were lines worn by tears, the way they flowed through the leather of his face. He smiled. His black moustache curled at one corner and I glimpsed a set of even white teeth. He raised his arm, lifting the blanket that had hidden it from view. I saw a thin red cord tied tight around his neck. It dug deeply into the tendons, and faint cicatrices of grey ridged scar tissue formed a groove through which it ran like a scalpel wound across his throat. I wondered how he could breathe.

His hand was bone, skeletal. The nails arched from bony pad-less tips. He reached towards my face and I tried to move but my head refused. The nails scratched down across my eyes and I seemed to be looking through an opaque gel. There was no pain though I could feel my skin cutting open in five clean gouges and felt cold air on my cheek bones.

I heard him laugh, and blinking through the gel in my eyes I saw water cascading from under his turban. It splashed in sun-danced droplets from the ridge of his brow and streamed down the lines in his face. The water seem to flow out from his skin. It exuded, as if under great pressure, from widening pores in the leathery face so that fine needles of water lanced out through the curtain dropping from the edge of his turban.

As he withdrew his hand the flow of water stopped and I felt my face itching where the cold air touched my cheek bones and bared teeth. A cold wind blew through the ragged slits in my face with a hollow sound. His eyes were unchanged. They were black, a dry deep black that swallowed the sunlight and the reflected glare of the snow and gave nothing back. He turned and stepped slowly down the ridge. At the edge of the cloud he twisted slightly and, looking across his shoulder, he smiled. The cloud sucked him in smoothly. I watched the saffron turban float momentarily disembodied above the cloud. A swirl of white as of a galaxy seen on a clear night swung slowly round the point where the saffron colour had sunk from sight.

My face itched with the tickle of rough hairs and I opened my eyes, slowly raising my hand to my face. A horn blared from the street and the ceiling fan span erratically above my head with an electric whine and the protest of poorly maintained bearings. A strong stench of the blocked toilet dispelled the last images of dream.

I touched my face and felt something hard and scratchy fall past my cheek. I closed my hand over my mouth and felt something move inside. As I bolted upright I saw a small shower of cockroaches fall on to the sheet. I shook my head and spat and thrashed around me with my hands, cursing in panic and revulsion. The one in my hand had been investigating my upper lip and as I sprang from the bed I saw a sinuous single file of roaches crossing the floor from the toilet door. They moved towards the nearest bed leg still undisturbed by my antics above them.

When I had calmed myself after the slaughter with my flip-flop, and stopped shuddering at the feel of them on my face, I lay back on the sweat-stained sheet and lit a cigarette. It was my second day in Delhi. I had yet to find Jimmy. He had flown out a day earlier, saying on the phone from Heathrow that he would meet me at the Barnaj Hotel off Connaught Circus. He spoke with his usual urgency and I could barely make out what he had said. In the background the echoing sounds of a departure gate announcement drowned out his voice.

'Where?' I yelled querulously into the mouthpiece.

'. . . Connaught Circus . . . Flight BA176 is now boarding . . .'

'What?'

'. . . dead easy to find. Section D, I think.'

'No! The hotel! What's it called?' There was a series of rapid pips from the phone and a muffled curse as it went dead. He didn't phone back. I swallowed my irritation at his assumption that I should know Delhi like the back of my hand. I'd never been there before.

It was seven in the morning and suffocatingly humid. Sweat pooled in the hollow below my sternum and I dipped my finger into my belly button and flicked droplets sideways on to the damp sheets. There was a wheezy feel to my breathing. Too many cigarettes, I hoped, though I suspected a chest infection was developing. Two days' tramping through the exuberant dusty chaos of Delhi had probably caused it. I stubbed out the cigarette and swung my legs off the bed. A clatter of falling bottles scattered from my feet. Four empty bottles of Black Pagoda Lager span like tops on the floor amid a massacre of cockroaches. Some span crazily away on their toffee crisp backs. I saw the antennae of one twitching tentatively and leant forward to crush it slowly with one of the bottles.

The toilet was a bare concrete room muggy with heat and the stench of sewage. A cracked plastic bucket sat beneath a tap which twisted at an angle from the wall. A shower head above dripped rusty coloured drops with metronomic ticking into the bucket. I kicked the half-full bucket on to its side and the water splashed warmly over my feet, splashing against the base of the lavatory bowl. Two cockroaches were washed from their hiding-place beneath the stained piping and I expertly stomped them.

I struggled to push open the shuttered window. A cracked pane of glass let in a meagre yellow light through a film of street dirt. Hot air flooded in as the frame reluctantly parted company with the window and dust puffed out over the street four storeys below. I returned to the bedroom and increased the speed of the fan so that it whirred in an unsteady blur above the bed, shaking and groaning in protest. The wind blew cigarette ash from the ashtray and an unfinished airmail letter to Alice fluttered into the bathroom and settled absorbently on to the wet floor before I could catch it. The words merged in a smudged blur of expanding ink. Gingerly I pressed a button by the light switch. A tangle of ancient corroded wiring climbed the wall by the door frame and exited through a crude hole near the ceiling. My hands were wet.

The boy knocked softly a few minutes later and I let him in – a timid lad dressed in a maroon bellboy suit far too large for him. The suit was faded and ragged. A pathetic string of gold braid hung from one cuff. He was no more than twelve years old and peered shyly round the room, obviously nervous but unable to contain his curiosity. A jumble of climbing equipment, ice axes, crampons, ice screws and plastic boots were piled at the foot of the bed. My Walkman and several tapes lay on the rumpled yellowed sheet beside my passport which bulged with four thousand rupees held together by an elastic band.

I showed him the blocked toilet and he nodded solemnly.

'Yes sir, I will make it good.' He smiled a bright white smile at me, and his dark serious eyes lit up as he self-consciously touched his hair back into place. Like many young lads he groomed himself fastidiously, trying to emulate the looks of the latest Indian film star. What dreams he saw in those films of macho heroism and sickening romanticism I could not guess except to know that they were beyond anything that would ever come his way.

'Okay, good, and bring coffee. Big pot,' I said demonstrating with my hands.

'Yes sir.' He backed towards the door, smiling at me. The coffee arrived hot and acrid. It was mostly chicory, but it cleared the hangover taste in my mouth. I scanned the map of Old and New Delhi, finding Connaught Square and Connaught Circus. I had looked for the Barnaj Hotel in that area and found nothing. A note left at the Indian Mountaineering Federation would have to do, I decided, gathering together my money, pen, writing paper and the map into a plastic bag. I finished the coffee and left.

The street had awakened to another furious day. A few people still slept in the doorways of their shops, laid out on crude wood and rope beds. A large and malevolent-looking cow leaned against a black and yellow scooter taxi. It rocked unsteadily on its three wheels as the cow scratched its flank on the wing mirror. Its ribs protruded in a bony rack and an open sore oozed a smear of pus along the side of the scooter. Flies flicked expertly around the wound. A large hump above its shoulders flopped over to one side and its dewlaps swung heavily as it scratched.

The classic holy cow of India. To feed and care for it was accepted as an act of worship, a devotion to the pantheon of Hindu Gods believed to reside within the cow. From a useful and productive domestic animal providing for the owner butter, milk, ghee, curd, cow-dung and urine for curing diseases, it had become an adored symbol of sanctity and wealth. The products from a cow are all used extensively in temple worship, in the sacrifice of offerings to the gods. It stands as a common centre to all Indian life, ensuring the well-being of the people and bestowing blessing if treated accordingly.

That said, this particular cow had been given the rough end of the stick as the residence of the Gods. Its pelvic bones arched out from its rear and the flaky white hide seemed on the point of breaking open where they jutted to the sky. One horn had been twisted in a grotesque curl down and into its flank. The tip had sheared off. It fixed me with a baleful one-eyed stare. The right socket was empty and scarred. A strip of plastic swung from the corner of its mouth as it ruminated on it with little sign of relish.

There was a shout from inside the scooter and a bare foot kicked out from the driver's doorway, thudding into the cow's shoulder. It moved a few steps towards me and then swung its heavy head back across its shoulder. A thick rough-surfaced tongue snaked out to lick at the open sore.

'You want taxi?'

The Sikh driver leant out from the scooter and peered at me between the arched pelvic bones of the cow. I recognised him from the day before. A short bandy-legged man with a poorly wound red turban on his head. He wore loose fitting trousers that hung in folds around his shins like a skirt pulled up between his legs. A long-tailed white shirt, crumpled and stained with dust and sweat, opened at the chest to reveal an emaciated torso. He grinned a broken set of yellowed teeth and his face was wreathed in sun-weathered wrinkles. His beard spread riotously from his face in an unkempt growth of grey stained dark red at the corners of his mouth from years chewing and spitting betel juice. He was the leading purveyor of opium, hashish, cocaine, heroin, LSD and women in the district, he had conspiratorially whispered to me on our first meeting. I had declined his offer.

'You want to change dollars. I give good rate,' he said this morning hopefully.

'No,' I said. 'No taxi, no change.' I smiled at him and waved my hand in salute. Sidestepping the cow, I headed into the bustle of Pahar Ganj, looking for a breakfast restaurant on the way into the heart of the old city.

It was early and the streets didn't yet have the frantic chaos of midday. Puddles of filthy water, the remnants of last night's storm, edged the side of the road. Here and there piles of garbage and rotting vegetables lay in festering heaps. Cows and emacitated calves nuzzled through them, occasionally selecting something to chew on in a lazy resigned manner. The majority seemed to prefer plastic and cardboard, though I noticed one cow less gaunt than the others rooting out cabbage leaves and clumps of damp straw. A woman bent over the pavement, holding her sari clear of the wet flags with one hand and sweeping the stones clean with a small straw hand-brush. Her young daughter stood beside her sprinkling water from a plastic jug in front of her brushing.

I turned down smaller streets, leaving the roaring traffic sounds of the main road behind. Glancing back once I saw a pall of blue smoke rising with the dust from the six-lane stream of vehicles. On next turning to look back the view had been swallowed by a curtain of fabric banners stretched high across the street. Sun flashed through gaps in the canopy of billboards and shop signs jutting from the sides of the buildings. I soon lost count of how many sideroads I wandered down and looked up only to fix the sun and know roughly that I was moving in the right direction. Although my senses still reeled at the assault of sounds and colour and smells, the claustrophobia I felt on first arrival had waned and I no longer felt an urgent desire to escape from the squalor and mayhem. Suffocation seemed to be a part of life here. Sweat ran into my eyes, and the air felt heavy and hard to breathe, and humanity crushed me with demands too insistent to block from my mind.

A constant throng of people moved up and down the road amid a bustle of scooters, rickshaws, ox-drawn carts, bicycles and black and yellow Morris Minor taxis. Bells, hooters and horns blared a cacophony of warning sounds which competed with the thrum of voices selling and buying on the pavements. The buildings overhung the road festooned with signs, col-oured billboards advertising products, shop names; bolts of cloth were racked one upon the other above sari shops, walls lined with flip-flops or aluminium pans of every possible size and shape. Fronds of tinsel and great vibrant coloured bunches of flower necklaces swayed in a hot breeze above the head of an ancient man whose long white beard tickled the keyboard of his typewriter. He sat cross-legged on a rush mat typing right to left in Arabic script for a patient queue of young men clutching paper.

Snug doorways led into crude tea houses and pungent steam drifted from stalls set on the pavements cooking vats of basmati rice on single-burner paraffin stoves. A man ladled hot ghee over onion bhargis and neatly tucked pastry envelopes. They sizzled and spat droplets of oil from the wide shallow pan. A fragrant steam of spices crossed the street.

I walked cautiously, constantly glancing behind and to the side to avoid being run over. Dodging foul pools of slurry clogging blocked drainage channels, turning to a shouted question from a shop doorway asking for me to enter, to buy, to change money, sidestepping the bustle of life on the pavement. On the road I was conscious of my unprotected sandalled feet and the brush of vehicles from behind.

I ducked into a darkened doorway past a boy squatting on his haunches on a trestle table as he tended two steaming pans, a neat stack of sweetmeats, parathas and samosas, fresh fried and still hot by his side. The pans held curry of some sort bubbling a sheen of ghee from its surface in one, and lumpy spicy dahl in the other. He reached into a sack on the table and withdrew a large chappati and gave it to a man who stood eating dahl and rice from an aluminium plate. Two Europeans sat at a lino-covered table near the door. They were in their twenties, dressed in the uniform of the cheap travellers in Asia – multicoloured cotton shirts and small wallet bags strung on long leather strings around their necks. The man wore jeans and trainers and an unkempt half-grown beard of blond hair. He looked gaunt and hollow. His hair straggled in tangled blond dreadlocks across his forehead. His eyes were pale blue, washed out, an indifferent lazy stare as he looked up at my passing. The woman rose and came past the table I had chosen at the back near a rusty noisy fan. She wore Jesus sandals, and a long flowing dress of fine sari material stained damply at the hem. The sun coming from the street shone through from behind, and I watched the outline of her thighs moving in shadowy lines against the sunshine.

Over ginger tea in an aluminium mug and a plate of egg and fried potatoes I again composed my letter to Alice. The sense of her was lost to me and the words I wrote seemed no clearer than those now smudged on the toilet floor. The girl in Jesus sandals returned from the lavatory I could smell behind me, swinging bony hips against my table to avoid the waiter who stood staring at her breasts jiggling loosely beneath a thin cotton T-shirt. The table wobbled unsteadily and the pen drew a line across my words. She did not notice. The waiter's eyes followed her towards the sun, naked in his mind and bent over ready for him.

We had said farewell four days before – Alice and I. It was an awkward embrace, as if we both knew we had lost each other and words were mechanically said because they had to be said. I looked at the girl now seated with her bearded companion. The sun touched her hair and motes of dust moved in a haze against the backdrop of the street. Her hair was long and blonde in a plaited rope down her back. She curled a thin twist around a finger as she leant forward and spoke to the man. He nodded in agreement and looked back into the shadows at the waiter who returned his stare. I imagined Alice's hair glowing against that sun and wet dark troubled eyes turning away from the glare to search me out in the shadows. A shiver tingled my spine as I realised what I might have lost.

I left to resume the search for Jimmy, or so I thought, though I wandered aimlessly through crowded streets and looked at signs and shops and vehicles and never once at Europeans. Jimmy's enthusiasm for this trip angered me. Why wasn't he here? Why did I put up with him, and follow him, and do whatever he decided we should do and never follow my own desires? Why did he have to be Alice's brother and I so dishonest that he knew nothing of us? The less he knew the more acid my resentment became.

I walked through Sadar Bazaar parallel to the rail tracks and looked for a crossing point. I passed a milk stand where a middle-aged moustached Indian ladled curd into plastic bags and eggs were piled high in a perfect pyramid. At his feet a man crouched setting out his wares in intricate patterns of stacked colour. White muslin cloth squares mounded in cones of glowing yellow turmeric, red chili powder, and hessian sacks with the tops peeled open to reveal rice, lentils, beans, dried powdered tomatoes and countless colours of foods and spices I had never seen. A shout from behind warned me to step aside as a wide-horned ox dragged a creaking wooden cart past me. Its chest bore a froth of sweat, the dewlap swinging wetly and its neck arched, eyes rolling with the pain of the load. The cart was piled high with sacks of flour, and the driver sat cross-legged atop them, flicking a long thin handled whip at the ox's flapping ears. Crude wooden wheels ground past higher than my head, the iron hoops round the rims screeching on the cobbled street.

Across the street a row of clothing and tailor shops hustled for trade under a variety of multicoloured signs. 'Mohinda Saree Printers & Artists' written in bold red letters above a wall of material fluttering in the dusty air almost obscured a much smaller sign reading 'DOCTOR quick no waiting.'

I turned down an alleyway between 'Vijay Pressure cookers & quality footwear' and 'Jagan Nath & sons, Bra and Panties'. Soon the shops petered out into a dusty abandoned broken alley. Steam from a locomotive rose ahead of me above a tangle of wire fencing and weeds. At the wire I looked across a hundred yards of tracks and saw the red sandstone of the Jami Masjid mosque, the largest mosque in India, standing majestically above a sprawl of covered streets, the perfect proportions of its domes and minarets towering serenely above the chaos below. Pigeons swung in circles above the domes before settling precariously once more upon the curved slopes. Each dome pointed an ornate golden spire into the sky.

An old bridge led across the tracks. A wall now lay between me and the street from which I had come, and damp clumps of shrubs grew from red mud where people stared from a collapsing huddle of lean-to huts of corrugated iron and cardboard. As I picked a delicate path through puddles of foul water and heaps of rubbish, I felt panic rising. I should not be here. This was the world of the poor. I felt hostility breathing from darkened alleys between the dismal dwellings and the heat suffocated me with the stench of disease and despair. I heard taunts from blank-eyed men standing in the squalor though they said nothing and watched my passing in silence. Babies played in excrement, a man washed in sewage water, a woman breast-fed her child and looked up at me. I smiled uncertainly and she looked away.

Sweat stung my eyes. My skin seeped in the muggy grip of dead air, feeling as if I had poured sugar on it. I flapped my shirt at the neck and warm air pushed rivulets of sweat into my waistband. I abandoned all ideas of the bridge and made a run for it over the wire fence and across the converging lines not looking for oncoming trains nor looking back. I burrowed into the bustle of street life on the other side. Shameful of my complacency and wealth, I fled from the crushing weight of these abandoned people into the bustle of the street life on the other side of the tracks.

I had not the patience nor the time to absorb these myriad lives held together by bonds of desperation. I had come for the high mountains, for the silence of empty vistas, and cold throat-burning breath steaming in the early morning air. I had not come to learn these lessons.

'Hello! How are you? Change dollars, want hash . . .'

I drifted past the hawkers and shop keepers, each turning expectant eyes on the sudden appearance of a day's bonus in dollars. Laughter pealed above the din of voices and scooter horns. In a tight crowded passage two young men burst fighting from a doorway. One shouldered me aside, stepping on my sandal and almost tripping me. They tumbled wrestling to the ground and older men separated them roughly. Onlookers grinned conspiratorially at me as I retrieved my sandal. It was no different from the pub on a long Friday night. I bought fruit at a stall to quench my thirst, slices of pineapple cut with a rusty knife and tasting sugarless, as if poverty had starved the soil as well. A mass of pineapple heads were heaped by the stall on wheels and a calf chewed quietly on the spiky morsels. In an open doorway two women squatted among heaps of rags sorting each according to colour and fabric.

There was a shout from behind and I gave way to four toiling porters in dhotis pushing an overladen barrow of rusty iron rods and linked chains. Sweat cut dark clean lines through the red dust on their backs as they struggled with the load. As they passed one man turned his head and looked at me with curiosity, and I was unnerved by his unsmiling eyes, the most beautiful eyes I had ever seen. Then he looked back to his companions' trudging feet and bent his neck into his task. They were indistinguishable in colour from the stacked piles of iron that they pushed. A young couple followed the barrow on a scooter, the driver pressing hard on the high-pitched horn, a woman sidesaddle behind him with folds of silk-embroidered sari flapping in the wind and a baby held one-handed on her hip. A dog lay crushed on the roadside with three sore-covered puppies whining nearby. I saw a line of women carrying wet clay mud on hessian sacks balanced upon their heads. They were all one hue, even their clothes, and I thought of a procession of mud wrestlers who fought in saris rather than leotards. They dumped the mud in a mound by a man who patted out bricks between two platters of wood and laid them in the sun to dry.

A Sadhu passed me, a holy man, one of the millions travelling the roads of India in search of enlightenment, with their begging bowls and matted hair, ash-streaked faces and hash chillums smoking, a glazed stare in their eyes that could be confused with the tranquillity of true enlightenment. There must be some who find that state of perfect realisation and detached tranquil consciousness, but not many. He looked at me once and knew I would not reach into my pocket.

6

The Major

A scrum of Morris Oxford taxis and scooters blocked the view of the entrance to the mosque. One scooter was tipped on its side and wires trailed from its innards as an oily driver delivered hammer blows at the clutch-plate assembly and colleagues clustered round with advice. Suddenly I was tired of walking, tired of the tension of new sights and sudden alarms. At the back of the mosque I found the bazaar laid out in the pattern of a Mogul garden with pathways lined in sandstone, and fountains by terraces and every imaginable type of stall staffed by dark-bearded Pathans – soothsayers and snake charmers, hawkers and beggars. I bought sweet milked tea in a thick chipped glass and sat resting on sun-browned grass watching the Hakims sell their wares. The midday sun hung in a cloudless sky directly above the domes of the mosque. It was refreshingly cool in the open esplanade of the park, free from the stifling claustrophobia of the covered street of Chandni Chowk. I had learnt that in the past caged cheetahs, greyhounds, hooded hunting leopards and Persian cats had been sold in those darkened lanes. They were gone now, replaced with the plastic squalor of consumer goods but the fervent desperation of the sellers was no doubt the same. I had walked through the spice market, Khari Baoli, steeped in a heady aroma of scents, and the jewellery displays in Dariba, the street of silver.

As I drained the last of the tea a man approached and sat cross-legged beside me. He shouted to the young boy at the tea stall who at once came over. There was a rapid exchange in Hindi to which the boy nodded frequently and smiled. The man turned to me, smiling.

'From what country do you come, sir?' He spoke in a melodic modulated accent, pronouncing each word with studied care.

'England.'

'Ah! England. Yes, a fine country,' he said with satisfaction. 'Yes I have always admired the English.'

I listened to him talk wistfully about English gentlemen and cricket and facets of the country that had long since disappeared. The boy returned with two glasses of tea and offered one to me. I put my hands up, palms outward, to indicate that I hadn't asked for tea.

'You will take tea with me, sir,' the man said. 'You look tired and hot. The tea will revive you. It has ginger in it, most refreshing.'

I took the tea and handed the boy my empty glass and a five rupee note. The man spoke to the boy who returned the money to me with a smile.

'I would be honoured to buy you the tea.'

We sat there for half an hour talking of India and England. When I mentioned that I had come to climb a mountain in the Garhwal Himalayas he became animated.

'How fine,' he said. 'Yes, very fine indeed. I have seen the great mountains once in my life. I will always remember them. I am no mountain climber, sir, but I have walked among them.'

'Where were these mountains?'

'It was an important thing for me. You see I went to the very source of the river, of Mother Ganges. I saw her birth from the ice of the mountains. I prayed for my ancestors and washed in the waters.'

76

'You went to the Gangotri then?'

'Yes! Yes!' he exclaimed in an excited voice. 'Have you been there also?'

'No, but it is where we are going.'

'Oh that is fine, very fine.' He smiled.

His whole demeanour had changed with the mention of the mountains and he sat quiet for a moment lost in memories of the pilgrimage he had made. He had a friendly open face, shaped to smile. Behind small wire-framed glasses his eyes twinkled in amusement and laugh-lines crinkled out across his cheek bones. It seemed as if the lines in his face had formed from laughter and merriment; I could not imagine him scowling. My usual suspicion at the approach of a stranger had fled the moment he sat down and smiled at me. I felt I knew him well and yet had shared only a glass of ginger tea with him.

He wore a white cotton shirt with a peculiarly old-fashioned wing collar and soft grey flannel trousers with turn-ups. A white-spotted bow tie added an eccentric charm to his appearance and I noticed his brown leather brogues intricately decorated with a pattern of punched holes, polished and gleaming in the sun. He had placed a leather case, similar to an old schoolboy's satchel, carefully by his side when he sat down. A black umbrella lay beside it. The handle was of dark sandal wood and carved in the shape of what appeared to be a dragon's head.

'My name is Major D. N. Cheema, originally from Rajastan.'

He held his hand out to me and I shook it. 'Christopher Banks,' I replied.

'A good name for a traveller.' The major smiled and nodded and, seeing my bemused expression, added, 'You know of Saint Christopher, of course.'

'Ah, yes. Well, I am not a religious person myself.'

'But that is a sad affair. All religions are vital. They are the spirits of life in all its forms. We Hindus would be as nothing if there were no Gods. There are thousands of them, you know.'

'Yes, I have heard that.' I didn't wish to be drawn into a religious discussion. It was far too hot.

'And why are you here at the bazaar and not travelling north to the mountains?' the major asked.

'I am looking for my friend, my climbing partner. He arrived before me.'

'And he agreed to meet you here? That is a very strange place for a meeting is it not?'

'Oh no, we were to meet at a hotel off Connaught Circus two days ago but I cannot find it. I've given up. He can find me.'

'That is not a good plan. You must be methodical about your search. What is the name of this hotel?'

'I don't know,' I admitted sheepishly.

'I see.' He looked thoughtful for a moment before standing and holding his hand out to help me up. 'Perhaps someone here could help you find your friend,' he said. There was an amused look in his eyes.

'Here?' I said. 'Why on earth would anyone here know where Jimmy is?'

I looked at the crowded stalls and pavement displays. Across the path from where we stood a makeshift canopy of coloured blankets supported by canes and guy lines shaded a woman who sat cross-legged before a small audience of attentive men. Her long dark hair was partially covered with a white shawl and tassels of coloured cloth were tied to braids hanging across her ample bosom. Layers of bulging brown flesh wobbled from beneath her breasts, barely restrained by the sheer purple top she wore. A necklace of copper hoops and beads jiggled on her cleavage as she berated her audience in rapid fire Hindustani. The overall effect was of an outlandish gypsy in voluminous cotton pantaloons and forearms encircled to each elbow with silver bangles.

The major noticed my stare and laughed.

'This is a very special bazaar, sir. Here you will find many things stranger than the appearance of your friend, Jimmy.'

He walked over to the stall. On a beautifully woven carpet with tassels at the edges and carefully brushed clear of dust she had laid out an exotic display of herbs and spices, roots, twigs and powders in stoneware pots. Garishly coloured fluids in Pepsi Cola bottles were lined in ranks behind the dried plants and powders.

'She is from the Gond tribe of Maharashtra. She comes from Nasik, just north of Bombay. It is a very holy city, a place I must go to bathe and pray at the next Kumbh Mela.'

'What is that?' I asked.

'It is a very important day for us Hindus, an auspicious day for prayer. It is a celebration of the winter solstice and happens only once every twelve years. The next Kumbh Mela will be held at Nasik and I will be there to wash in the waters of the Godavari river.' The major talked in his careful precise English but there was a faraway gaze as he spoke.

'Do you go on many pilgrimages then?' I asked and he seemed to come back into focus again.

'Oh yes, I have been to many places. I have travelled far with the army, you know, so I have been lucky. Now I am retired. I work a little at the National Museum keeping records and accounts – that sort of thing – but I have a lot of time to travel at my leisure. You know, sometimes I wish I had been a holy man, a Sadhu. Do you know what a Sadhu is?'

'Yes, I have seen them in Nepal. Naked and covered in mud and ash.'

'Ah, yes, they are Naga Sadhus. The naked ones. There are many different orders. Very holy men, good men. I met many in Haridwar at the last Kumbh Mela. It was after that festival that I went to the mountains above Gangotri.'

'I've heard of Haridwar.'

'Yes, you will travel to Haridwar when you leave for the mountains. I recommend that you visit this sacred city. It is

79

one of the Seven Sacred cities of Hindus, and the Ganges is very beautiful in Haridwar, powerful and strong.'

'Is she a holy person then?' I asked, nodding towards the woman.

'No, no,' the major chuckled. 'No, she is a Hakim, a traditional seller of potions and cures. Her tribe have sold medicines such as these for thousands of years. And they work, well, some of them do.' The major smiled at me and, taking my elbow in his hand, he led me closer.

'You see this?' he said proferring a twiggy root, 'this is Balamkheera, very good for bad stomach, I believe.' It looked to me as if that was exactly what it would cause. 'Semul roots for dysentery and stones in the kidney, and here are flowertops of Hoarhound . . . good for coughs and breathing sickness.'

The woman suddenly noticed me and stopped her tirade at the watching men who now laughed and gazed expectantly at me instead. I smiled awkwardly at them, wondering why they were so amused. The woman addressed me in a flood of incomprehensible gibberish. The men laughed delightedly. Others joined the crowd. She held out a straw mat with various roots and herbs strewn across it.

'What is she saying?' I asked the major.

'Ah, well, she is saying that you have sexual problems.'

'What?'

'She sells many cures and remedies, but mainly she is . . . how can I say? She is what you might call a sexologist.'

'A what?' I looked at the woman, who returned my stare with a babble of sounds and proffered the mat at me again.

'She will cure all your difficulties with love making.'

'I don't have any . . .'

'This is Safed Bahaman,' he said waving aside my protests. 'It is a traditional and very ancient medicine. It is a very fine aphrodisiac.' The major took the mat and stirred the crudely ground mixture with his finger. 'You take it as a tea, I think.'

I sniffed the pungent aroma of the mixture and handed it

back to the woman. She smiled and said something to the major, who laughed.

'She wants to know if you suffer any inconvenience in satisfying your wife?'

'I'm not married,' I replied, and the major spoke again to the woman.

'She says this is because you are lacking in sexual power. She thinks you are too old not to be married and if you take this you will soon find a wife and have many children.'

'What is it?' Dubiously I eyed the small bottle of evil-looking liquid that the woman held out for me.

'It is Sakamber. The most expensive of her formulations.'

'Surprise, surprise!' I muttered cynically.

'Yes, she thinks you are very rich.' The major laughed. 'She also says you are impotent!'

'Charming,' I said, carefully putting the bottle down on the carpet.

We left the woman waving the bottle, beseeching me to buy in her high-pitched staccato. The major strolled ahead of me, his satchel slung across his shoulder and the dragon umbrella swinging imperiously in his right hand. Voices clamoured from all sides above the roar of traffic. A pall of exhaust fumes drifted in clouds of dust above the canopies. I blinked sweat from my eyes and flicked flies away from my face. The air hung hotly around stalls thick with the dense aroma of spices and pungent smoke. Small boys pounded pestles into stone mortars. Paper packages were offered to attendant groups by a tall, thin-faced, dark-bearded Pathan.

Occasionally the major would stop at a stall and point out an item of interest with the metal tip of his brolly.

'Those are the dried male organs of bears,' he said as I peered curiously at some shrivelled brown leathery objects laid on a sheet of newspaper.

'Oh!'

'And these,' he exclaimed, disturbing a small cluster of smooth green pebbles, 'are Bezoar stones from the stomachs of mountain goats. They cure you of poison. They are rare indeed.'

There were dried owl tongues, skins and wings of bats, feathers, bones and claws of all descriptions to be ground down and eaten, used as talismans to bring good fortune or hung in amulets to ward off evil spirits. The dried tongue of a crow would ensure a dumb child could speak. Powdered tiger bone brought from the forests in the foothills of the Garwhal where Corbett had shot his man-eaters would give strength and courage.

The Pathans, proud warrior people with cruel faces, sold oils made from animals and plants. There was much laughter around their stalls as they regaled the crowds with anecdotes of their sexual prowess and lewd jokes usually at the expense of embarrassed listeners. The major was uncomfortable when I asked him to translate the stories and hustled me away.

'Major?' I asked when he stopped at a tea stall. 'Why did you say I might find someone who would know where Jimmy is?'

He handed me a glass of sweet black tea. 'Well, there are some here who claim to see the future. You understand? To read minds, that sort of thing?'

'Surely you don't believe they can?' I said laughing, but the major did not laugh.

'There are many things I believe. Yet I understand very few of them. This is the difference between you and me. You always need proof. You need reasons, evidence, exact answers. This is not so in India.'

'Yes, but predicting the future, I mean that surely is a bit far-fetched.'

'No more than believing in Gods. When I washed in the Ganga at Haridwar I was blessed. I know that to be true. There is more magic in this land than you could ever comprehend. It is easy to mock, sir, but much harder to believe.'

'I am sorry major. I did not mean to insult you.'

'That is quite all right. I am too old to be easily offended, and I think maybe it might have been hard to find your friend through some of these people. They are not all honest, you know.'

With that he laughed, swallowed his tea in one, and reached into his satchel.

'Here, take this.' He handed me a small card. 'Call on me any time. I will be honoured to talk with you again.'

'Thank you.' I read the address on the card. 'Where is Barakhamba Road?'

'It is near Connaught Circus. Any scooter driver will find it. Just show the card.'

'Right, I will, and thanks again for showing me the bazaar. It would have meant very little to me if you hadn't been there to explain it for me.'

'It was my pleasure.' He grasped my hand firmly, gripping my shoulder with his left hand. 'Would you do me a small favour, I wonder?' he said.

'Of course, if I am able to, I'd be delighted.'

'When you go to the mountains, can you bring me back some water from the river?' He rummaged in his satchel and picked out a small brass bottle with an ornate top. A thin chain hung from the top. 'Perhaps you could store it in this. It is water-tight.'

I took the bottle from him and promised to do my best. He shook my hand again vigorously and beamed a happy smile. Then, turning abruptly on his heel, he raised his umbrella in an elegant salute and bade me goodbye and good luck.

He disappeared almost at once into the milling throng and I stood examining the brass bottle in my hand. If I had not been given it I doubted I would have believed what had just happened. I had known him for little more than two hours and yet he had given me, a total stranger, an exquisitely engraved brass bottle to fill with water from the source of the Ganges and return, God knows when and if at all, to his house at 216

Barakhamba Road. Strangely he had not asked how long we would be gone. I was overwhelmed by his trust in me.

After much haggling a Sikh driver took me back to the hotel in a battered scooter cab. He wanted twenty rupees for what would have been a good forty-five-minute walk, and I felt guilty for harrying him down to five. The herbal smoke from the bidi he smoked competed with the rush of smells blowing through the scooter windows. I lit a cigarette and gripped the driver's seat-back to counter his sudden swerves from side to side as he avoided cows and bicycles and made outrageous attempts to overtake.

As the scooter lurched into the Pahar Ganj district with a continuous blaring of its horn I spotted a familiar figure stood hunch-shouldered outside a restaurant.

'Jimmy!' I yelled, leaning out of the door and almost losing my head to a Suzuki jeep. He turned as I ducked back into safety. He hadn't seen me. I shouted at the driver who turned to look at me, the bidi clamped to his lips, and the scooter careering on down the road with no lessening of speed.

'Stop!' I screamed almost in panic as I saw a rickshaw looming on collision course. It flashed by with an angry tinkle of bells as the scooter shuddered to a halt and stalled. I jumped out, stuffed a ten rupee note in through the driver's door, and ran back the way we had come.

I recognised the Punjabi Book Shop & Stationery Co. sign projecting from the wall above the restaurant. It was where I had eaten breakfast. I ducked into the shadowed room past the boy who still sat cross-legged on his table stirring his vats of curry and dahl. I squinted in the darkness, waiting for my sight to adjust from the glare outside. Jimmy was nowhere to be seen. I ran out, nearly knocking the boy off his table, and looked hastily up and down the street standing on tip-toes in an effort to scan over a sea of heads.

Immediately opposite was a shop front gaudily draped with multicoloured cotton trousers, shirts and saris. A confusing sign reading 'Hosiery Ready Made Exhibition and Gum Sale' hung askew above the doorway. A figure that had previously been bending over straightened up inside the shop and at once I recognised Jimmy's shock of curly brown hair. I crossed the road, dodging a rickshaw and two men, one sidesaddle, astride an ancient rickety bicycle.

'Hello Jimmy,' I said to his back and he turned quickly, beaming a huge smile at me.

'Chris! There you are. Where the hell have you been all my life?'

'Where have I been! Bloody looking for you for the last two days, that's where!'

'Well I've been at the hotel,' Jimmy said with an air of innocent confusion.

'Yeah, and I would have been as well if you had given me the name of the bloody place before you got pissed at the airport.'

'How did you know I was pissed?'

'Come on,' I replied, feeling defeated, 'let's have some tea and sort things out.'

'Do you like my strides?' He grinned at me, holding the sides of his cotton trousers out at full stretch. They were three feet wide at the hips and tapered down towards his ankles in columns of variegated tie-dyed colours that would make the average house-cat sick.

'Very fine,' I muttered heading for the door.

7

The Hunter

It was cold and damp in the low early morning mist. The sounds of scree falling into water echoed up from the shrouded glacier somewhere ahead of me. I shivered. I was dressed in socks, a threadbare T-shirt, and a pair of disintegrating underpants. They provided little comfort at five in the morning at over fifteen thousand feet. Behind me, from the direction of the tents, I heard an odd clicking sound. I craned my head round and peered into the mist, twisting my chest and torso but keeping my legs facing forward. I arched my back and tried to expel the urine faster. It spattered noisily amid the boulders. The clicking sound came again, closer.

I tried to think what was making such a sound. A bird calling its mate or defending its territory? At this hour, God no. There isn't a bird that stupid up here! Was it Attar, the cook, moving about the kitchen tent? No, the sounds would be stationary, not coming closer. Perhaps he was coming for a pee as well?

The clicks came again. Delicate and bony, a quick rattle. Four, maybe six, soft clickety sounds, then silence. They suggested caution, and fear. I felt afraid. Standing in the mist, shivering, peering into the shifting banks of white gauze with my hearing trained towards where I had last heard the sounds, my eyes seemed to dance erratically in their sockets as they tried to make shapes out of the greyness. I hunched forward twisted, protectively clutching my penis with both cold hands.

A sound of pebbles trickled down a rock face. I tucked myself away, still peering into the mist, and then stepped gingerly towards the sounds. My stockinged footsteps were silent. The wool gripped the damp boulders well and I felt sharp edges bite painfully into my cold numbed feet. A slight breeze drifted into my face. Whatever I was searching for would not smell me first. I sensed it was lightening already. The sun would be burning bright upon the mountains rearing above this valley-filling mist. Soon it would burn the valleys clear.

It seemed an age ago that I had padded sleepily from the tent for this call of nature. I was fully alert now but considerably colder. It was strange to hunt sounds in the mist, almost naked, over sharp rocks in stockinged feet. Strange in that it had never occurred to me not to search. What if it were a snow leopard, I thought, crouching ready to leap at my soft bellied body? Rubbish. They're too small and I'm too big. Then again, I'm not much heavier than an ibex and they'd eat that, wouldn't they now?

I slowed to listen to the shifting mists that looked as if they should make soft rustling sounds, but they were silent. They blended into each other in distinct shades, like the moving dark shadows seen when looking into deep water; the sort of shadows that pull you in and scare you as you hang floating above an unending depth of them; shadows that lurk and threaten and hide dangers you had never considered until you saw them shifting below. I had always thought of cloud and fog as a uniform blanket of white. Yet moving uncertainly through it, looking for the shape behind a clicking noise, I could see endless varieties of shade and colour and density. These shadow shapes were a different colour from those seen moving in great dark planes below the surface of the sea. White mostly, with hints of grey, and higher, nearer the sun, a glow of marigold tainted with hints of washed out blue.

I shivered. Anyway, I thought, they don't have snow leopards in this area, and even if they did they are so rare that there was very little chance of being attacked. Could a bandit be lurking in the cloudcover? The idea popped into my head as a darker shape revealed itself to be a large angular rock jutting fifteen feet above the boulder field. The mists clung tenaciously to its sides. I reached out and touched the wet grey surface. It was the perfect time to attack a sleepy campsite, the crucial hour of early dawn when the senses are most vulnerable; the taking-time favoured by secret police and vicious cloud-lurking bandits all over the world. Somehow the soft clicking sounds didn't connect with my idea of the creeping stealthy approach of a bandit. Apart from my breathing I had made no sounds at all in my movements, so why should a bandit, especially one about to attack a campsite?

As I peered ahead I noticed a gap between the rocky ground and the underskirt of the mist. I wondered whether it might be lifting. I saw the dull gleam of moisture on the rocks and the slight gap between their surfaces and the mist. I crouched down, placing my hands on the cold rocks, and cocked my head sideways, hoping to see a long distance through the gap as if looking under a car. Perhaps I would see the booted feet of a bandit, or even his face as he crouched to look at me. The gap closed and I saw nothing, but I heard the clicking again.

Rising I rubbed my hands on my thighs and decided that enough was enough. I was too damn cold to creep round the boulders chasing sounds. I began stepping from rock to rock, no longer attempting to conceal my presence. As I approached the tents, which I instinctively knew were in front of me, the breeze increased and the shadows began to tear apart.

It stood, front legs braced high on a boulder so that its hind-quarters were hidden from me, its tiny cloven feet set neatly together. A ruff of brown hair flecked with white sprouted from its chest. It stared directly into my eyes.

I stopped, catching my breath with the shock of seeing him there. We watched each other unmoving – I too scared to frighten him away, and he arching his neck so that his magnificent knobby horns lay against his back and his nostrils flared, questing for me. He sniffed the air inquisitively, searching for the scent that would tell him I was Man and make him wheel round and flee in a panic, death smells reeking in his brain. The wind ruffled my face. He could not smell me. He turned his head aside as if to examine me from a different angle and I did not move, scarcely dared to draw breath. The saddle of his back was a beautiful silvery white and his face seemed to be that of a grizzled bearded old man, peppered white with age and hard winters. I noticed a dribble of mucus coming from one nostril and a dull rheumy look to his eyes and wondered whether he could see at all. An old man of the hills come low into the valleys when he should have been safe up on the high crags. His horns were longer than the reach of my arm, as much as forty inches, and deeply corrugated with notches. He lowered his head and pawed uncertainly at the ground. The heavy horns swung his head low between his forelegs. He was a marvellous sight, standing there silhouetted against the shadowy mists like a Himalayan monarch of the hills.

I barely moved. Perhaps it was only my leg shivering convulsively but he spotted it immediately and swung his head up with sudden force and for a moment held my eyes with his. Then, with a rapid clicking of hooves, he sprang sideways from the rock, turning in the air as he jumped and, with a white flash of rump, he was swallowed by the mist. I heard the clickety rush of his flight fade and imagined each precisely placed step as he ran unerringly away from danger.

Silence returned, broken occasionally by water sounds from the glacier. As I walked into the camp a deep ominous rumble echoed from above the clouds. An ice cliff, breaking away on the peak above the camp, was roaring in destruction down the flanks of rock and ice to be swallowed by the sea of mist. I heard a clatter of metal pans and the throaty sound of the primus heating into life. As the tents became shadowy domes solidifying in the mist I saw Attar crouched by the cook tent, a tarpaulin stretched against the wall of a high boulder, breaking ice in an aluminium pan. He looked up, smiling broadly as I approached, and not for the first time I envied him the perfection of his teeth. There was many a film star that would pay good money to have teeth such as his.

'Hello, sir!' He swung the pan of broken ice on to the primus. 'Chai ready.'

He poured a mug of fragrant steaming tea, flavoured with thin slices of fresh ginger, and handed it to me. I was still trembling with the excitement of seeing the ibex. It had been so close. I felt I had only to lean forward and could have stroked its wet muzzle. I could still smell its strong goaty stench.

'Ibex,' I said to Attar, pointing downhill into the cloud. 'I have just seen a big male.' I pointed at my chest and Attar's smile widened as he shook his head.

'No ibex, sir,' he said, smiling at me. There was a constant confusion of signals coming from Attar, for he smiled at everything. Even in the most vehement argument, usually about money, he fought his case with a broad smile on his face, as if he were enjoying it all hugely, though he was deadly serious about getting his way. And he did so now, like Russians nodding their heads and saying 'Niet' so you had no idea what they meant.

'What do you mean, Attar? I have just seen a huge male. Very old, he was.' I spread my arms to show the span of his horns, but Attar shook his head and smiled.

'No ibex, sir,' he said again as he carried a mug of tea towards the tent where I could hear Jimmy snoring.

I followed him, suddenly aware of how cold I was, and how odd it must seem to Attar to find me wandering near-naked from the clouds at this time of the morning gibbering about ibex. Jimmy grunted and reached his arm through the doorway to take the tea from Attar. I pulled the flap back and reached in for a pair of polar trousers and a fleece jacket. Jimmy glanced blearily at me through the steam from his mug.

'You're up early.'

'I was busting for a pee. It's all I seem to be doing at the moment.'

'Yeah, well, it's a good sign. Shows you are acclimatising properly.'

'I'd have thought we would have been fully acclimatised by now. I mean we've been here over a fortnight.' I crouched down by the door and looked over at Attar rolling the dough for the parathas. 'Oh God, not parathas again.'

Jimmy groaned. Attar washed and groomed his hair constantly and took great pains with his appearance, having already pinched my spare sunglasses for that special filmstar look. He spoke passable English and performed his duties as cook efficiently and without complaint. Unfortunately he was a lousy cook, which was annoying because that was what we had hired him for. True, his parathas were especially unpleasant because the flour had been contaminated by a paraffin leak on the walk-in, but the rest of his culinary endeavours were no better.

'Why the hell did you hire him?' I said bitterly, feeling my stomach roll over at the thought of the parathas.

'Well, he looked the part,' Jimmy replied, and grinned sheepishly at me.

'And what about that bloody thug you've become so tight with?'

I was referring to one of the nastiest specimens of humanity I had ever laid eyes on. He had drifted into camp late one afternoon and Attar had made him tea and given him cold parathas left over from the morning. He had eaten them without complaint, which to my mind had immediately marked him down as someone to be distrusted. There wasn't a great deal to recommend him. He was particularly uncommunicative. He grunted a lot and occasionally barked at Attar for no good reason. Attar was scared of him and almost stopped smiling.

The man was armed with an ancient rifle that he carried everywhere wrapped in a filthy bolt of cloth. He wore heavy steel-capped boots, which in itself was a rarity since most of the porters wore flip-flops, or moth-eaten gym shoes, or else walked heavy-laden in bare feet across the sharp hard ground. This man had a pair of shalwar trousers, baggy hipped and stained a tobacco brown from mud and dust. A red shirt tied at his neck with thin leather laces was covered by a stout black jacket-cum-waistcoat, belted with a wide strip of leather, the elbows so worn his red shirt could be seen. All in all he was indescribably dirty and for the most part smelt like an old yak skin.

But it was his face that was strikingly hideous. He wore a greasy black hat that I was convinced was an old Breton sailor's cap. I didn't ask where he had obtained it. His hair hung in a tangle of dreadlocks, not for any religious reason, simply unwashed and unbrushed.

His deeply lined forehead of dark leathery skin sported a huge wart in its centre, from which two astonishingly long black hairs sprouted. The wart seemed to dictate the few expressions the man ever bore – all variations on a theme of malevolent discontent and imminent violence. The wart seemed to move as he looked at you. It swelled, hairy and carbuncular, from the dead-centre of his forehead, just above a set of beetling eyebrows that grew in a single unbroken tufted bush above his eyes. His brow had a bulging neanderthal look. His eyes were set deep, overhung by the bushy brows and set back above hard-cut cheek bones. They were dark, almost black, and the whites were a jaundiced yellow. There were scars on his left cheek; signs of a vicious attack. A wispy drooping moustache and salt and pepper stubble added to his glum, unwelcoming appearance. I thoroughly disliked him; in fact he scared me. Jimmy seemed to admire him. The man didn't seem to care either way and responded to Jimmy's awkwardly spoken Hindustani in a gruff monotone. I noticed he never asked for food, money, water, anything. He took what he expected was his due and stated a price of hire to Jimmy so emphatically that Jimmy's usual delight in haggling dried at once and he nodded agreement.

'Hassan. Oh he's not that bad. A bit of a tough nut but he's quite interesting when you get to know him,' Jimmy said.

'Yeah, well, that's exactly what I don't want to do. I'm surprised we haven't all been murdered in our pits. What do we need him for anyway?'

'He's strong. Better than Attar any day. We'll need him when we cross the col into Guligad. Attar will never get over that.'

'Okay, but there's stacks of porters we can get, why get him?'

We had had this argument four mornings running. I knew it would make no difference. Jimmy wanted him so we had him.

'I've told you. He's okay. He tells me brilliant stories.'

I had watched Jimmy jotting things down over the past weeks. Anyone who could talk would be probed for tales. I reckoned they made them up. They knew what Jimmy wanted and out it all came, sufficient to ask for baksheesh and then be off for a laugh with their mates.

'I know,' he had said when I mentioned this in the tea house at Gaumukh. 'But there is always some truth mixed in, you see, and I've already got enough accounts that are sufficiently the same for me to know they come from the same source.'

With that he had continued talking with a porter carrying a tourist's load up to Gaumukh. It was the grimy ice cliffs at the snout of the Gangotri glacier they came to see. The source of the Ganges. A small tented village sprang up in summer to supply refreshments for exhausted and dehydrated Indian tourists experiencing altitude for the first time. Blankets were spread under overhanging boulders, and babas sat cross-legged in clouds of ganja smoke, occasionally rising to wash in the freezing grey waters and offer libations to the gods, or rub ash into their naked bodies and knock out the burnt ashes from their chillums. Track-suited Indians, grey faced with the altitude, tottered by with bemused expressions, uncertain whether they had reached the end of their pilgrimage and, I imagined, a little disappointed at the very ordinariness of the place.

It was there that Jimmy had first met Wart Face, and a week later he had turned up at the camp with his rifle and an enormous and ferocious-looking dog. Of the two, neither Attar nor I was sure which was the more frightening; in the end the dog came a close second.

'Where is he anyway?' I said, spitting tea leaves to the side and walking over to the primus where the kettle sat steaming.

'He said yesterday that he was going hunting. I don't know what for.'

'Well, I just hope he has a serious accident,' I muttered – and then thought of the ibex. 'Oh, no . . .'

'What?'

I started telling Jimmy about the encounter with the old ram, until he interrupted me.

'There aren't any ibex in the Garwhal.'

'I've just bloody seen one,' I said, feeling the resentment of the unbelieved beginning to boil up. 'It was a great big ram, horns this big,' I said, spreading my arms.

'No. They don't exist any further west than Zanskar, and certainly not this far south. It must have been something else. A bharal probably, maybe even an urial, but they are pretty rare now.'

'What the bloody hell is this?' I shouted. 'How come you and Attar are suddenly ibex experts? I'm telling you it was an ibex. A sodding great big old male ibex. And I won't be surprised if that warty maniac of yours isn't blowing it to pieces at this very moment with that howitzer of his.'

'It's a Martini Henry actually. Quite old.' He knew he was

irritating me and he compounded it by smiling smugly to himself.

'I know an ibex when I see one. Swept-back knobbly horns, silver saddle, white bum, dark everywhere else. The horns on a bharal sweep out to the side, not up and back – and theirs aren't knobbly.'

'Urial horns go up and back.'

'Yes, but they are not knobbly. These were the knobbliest horns you could ever see, for God's sake. I've seen loads of ibex horns in Pakistan. I do know what they look like, you know.'

'Hey, Attar?' Jimmy called. Attar looked up from his kneading and smiled. 'Have you seen ibex here?'

'No ibex, sir.' He shook his head vigorously.

'Well, what do you expect him to say?' I said acidly. 'He wouldn't know an ibex from a donkey. In fact, I wonder whether he knows anything about these hills at all.'

'He doesn't. He comes from Rajastan. He just happened to be around.'

'What? Well, is he a cook then?'

'Oh no,' Jimmy said calmly, 'I think he said he was studying to be an engineer.'

I looked incredulously at him and then at Attar cheerfully preparing another stomach-churning breakfast. 'Forget I mentioned it.' I filled my mug with tea and ducked under the tarpaulin of the cook tent.

Hassan Ghyias had been blessed with few attractive characteristics, and from the earliest days of his childhood he had set himself apart from the children in his village. He was ugly and paid the price in abuse. His face was heavy browed, rounded in the mongoloid features of a people alien to the area.

The villagers never knew where his father, the Hunter, had come from, with his sickly wife and infant son. The hunter seldom spoke to them except to sell meat he had shot or trapped, or to exchange vegetables for money to buy ammunition. They did not care for the family but it was good to have a hunter in the village; and he was a good hunter.

The friendless couple did not believe in the same gods as their neighbours and took no part in the annual festivals. The woman was occasionally seen praying in her small field but not to anything they knew or understood. Once, when a snake was trapped and killed in the spinach fields the woman became hysterical and screamed high and shrill, wailing a grief that no-one understood. The hunter came and took her to the house. He returned to take the snake, picking it from the tangle of trampled spinach where it had been clubbed with sticks and sharp rocks, and laid it reverently on a small but beautifully woven cloth of gold and red and orange. The villagers thought it strange and laughed and chattered among themselves about the foreign family that had settled among them, but they said nothing to the hunter. They were scared. There was a hard and distant look to his eye and scars on his face that warned them off.

Then in a cold and snow-bound mid-winter the hunter did not return, which at first caused no great surprise. He hunted alone and ranged far from the village. After a week of harsh weather had passed with no sign of the Hunter the boy left the village. Three days later he returned carrying the rifle wrapped in cloth and the hessian sack that the hunter always carried. His face was set hard and his eyes had a distant stare. The village echoed to the wails and ululations of grief coming from the hunter's house, and on the third day both woman and boy went into the fields and worked. No-one asked how or why but they all knew that the hunter was dead.

The children became bold and their abuse increased. The boy said nothing and his eyes seemed to darken and focus more distantly with each passing year. His father had died when Hassan was twelve years old, but not before he had taught the young boy the ways of the hunter. His mother had been left to look after the few goats they possessed and scrape a meagre existence from the barren and stony field in which they grew potatoes, onions, spinach and barley.

He had shunned the crowded gangs of children that shouted taunts and insults. His mother was ostracised by the village. Hassan never understood why. He knew that the children were scared of him. He was a big child used to hard days with his father walking great distances in the hills in search of prey. He could walk in a near sleep, and keep walking when his feet burnt with blisters and his muscles screamed for rest. It was a matter of pride that he did not fail his father who strode ahead with his rifle slung across his back wrapped in greasy cloth to protect it from the rain. And when his father had gone he took the rifle and laid it in buttered rags and buried it in the hard packed soil beneath his bed.

He had worked alongside his mother until he reached sixteen. Then he unearthed the rifle and, taking his father's boots that were too big for him, he had left the village under the cover of night. He said no farewells, not even to his mother. When she awoke to find him gone she knew he would not return. Within the space of a year she had died of pneumonia and her field and dilapidated two-room mud and stone house had been taken by the villagers. There were no relatives. Everyone knew that the tall dark boy would not return; he would not be welcomed if he did.

At first he had travelled south, following the river out from the wet jungled valley. He hunted as he travelled and traded skins, and horns and meat for provisions in villages that he passed. He rarely stayed in houses, preferring instead his cape and the canopy of the forest. If asked, he would say that he would always run in the forests, as his father had, and his ancestors, rather than mix dung into the earth and live in houses. Once out of the Arun valley he headed east, away from Kathmandu, which his father had talked of but never visited. He kept to forest paths, crossing the grain of the land, up each wooded valley and over and down to the deep-cut rivers at the floor of the next. Occasionally he fell in with men of like mind,

97

honey hunters with flintlock guns or sadhus walking in regions of which they knew nothing. These men fascinated Hassan and he talked for many hours with them. He understood their desire for silence and felt a closeness to them because they were so different from the chattering villagers.

For twenty-five years he travelled alone. His memory of his mother and the village that he had left faded with every mile he walked. The memory of his father and the stories that he told and the skills he had taught glowed brighter with every animal he killed. He added to his father's tales from stories he heard on the journey. He hunted in the high forests of Sikkim, and stood one smoky grey morning on a high exposed hillside watching a small herd of urial sheep grazing upwind of him, with the mighty flanks of Kanchenjunga rearing up into a blaze of a rising molten sun and the blue-black night sky flooding westward before the power of the dawn. He crossed into Bhutan, walking a long dark night of forest noises over the border where no-one stood to halt his progress, and followed the young river Amo Chu south into the lower lands.

He crossed into the rolling green hill country of Assam and lived with a family on the banks of the great Brahmaputra, working the fields and letting his rifle rust. He took their young daughter to his bed and talked with her as he had only talked to his father. They consulted her parents about marriage but the father was greedy and saw no dowry of worth from the dark hunter and became angry in refusal.

They left together on a dark monsoon night, crossing the turbulent river in terror and heading through the Garo Hills near northern Bangladesh in search of a place to settle. She died of cholera as the monsoon rains dried and sun brought lush green growth to the hillsides. Hassan recognised the disease as plague and fled her burial, fasting hard for a week, walking north, retracing his steps and passing her village silently in the dark of a moonless night. He left her aprons and silver waist buckle wrapped in the silk of her best sari on the outskirts of the village so that they would know.

He learnt many languages and forgot as many. He killed animals that his father told him of but that he had never seen. He took musk from the canine tusked male musk deer in the Barun valley of Nepal and sold it in the clamour of Kathmandu. The first time he had ever felt ill at ease. The great wealth he accumulated from the musk – more than he had ever imagined possible and far less than he should have received – sent him north-west along the spine of the Himalayas until he crossed into Uttar Pradesh, in the Indian Himalaya, and lived on the banks of the Alaknanda. There he hunted and talked with sadhus and pilgrims.

He met the foreigner at Gaumukh. He had been carrying loads for two fat tourists from Jaipur and resented their arrogance and the sweating corpulent softness of their lives. They laughed at his rifle, saying it was old and useless, so he left them. He was a hunter, not a donkey or a muck spreader. The tourists shouted and waved money and squealed outrage in high-pitched angry voices but he ignored their entreaties. He had spent a lifetime cutting people from his mind, closing his senses to their presence. He found no difficulty in leaving them and they did not shout too much abuse; they were afraid of his dark distant eyes and scarred face.

The foreigner, young and fresh-faced, spoke bad Urdu, a language Hassan also found difficult, and showed no fear of him, nor of his dog, and bought him tea unasked for. Hassan was intrigued by the young blue-eyed foreigner. He had come to accept that others feared him and it was strange to meet a man so young without fear. At first he felt anger; his prowess as a hunter and as a man insulted. Gradually he recognised an innocence in the distant blue of the young man's eyes. He posed no threat to the hunter. So he put away the knife he had unsheathed to frighten the foreigner and accepted the tea.

'Where do you come from?' Jimmy asked.

'I am a Hunter.'

'But where do you go to after hunting?' The man was puzzled by the question and looked darkly at Jimmy.

'I go where I hunt,' he answered after much thought.

'Have you travelled far in your hunting?'

'Yes,' the man replied, and he seemed suddenly distant from Jimmy, distant from everything surrounding him. Jimmy felt he was looking through an invisible aura around the hunter; looking at shadows of times past that clung to the man like an odour. He felt uneasy. For a moment it seemed as if he were being drawn into the shadows. The sounds of others chattering and drinking tea nearby slowly faded to a muted far-off washing sound as of waves lapping a shingle beach, and he felt a cold stab of fear, and at once the moment passed. The Hunter turned to look at the foreigner and a slight smile curled at the corner of his lip. He had noticed the fear in him; he had seen the rush of panic in the young man's eyes swelling his stare and his nostrils flaring as he had gasped with alarm.

Jimmy smiled uncertainly back, unsure of what had happened. The clamour of the tea-sellers and the customers had rushed back like the sudden noise of a door opened on to a noisy pub, and the Hunter had turned slowly to look at him with a sardonic smile. Perhaps he was sickening for something. He had felt dizzy, as if fainting, yet he remembered it clearly. Was it possible to faint consciously?

'What country do you come from?' Jimmy asked.

The Hunter smiled and said, 'You do not need to know this thing. I know the forests and the animals and the ways of hunting. I do not need countries in which to hunt, only forests.'

'Are you hunting here?'

The Hunter looked at the two fat Indians sitting opposite at the tea stall. They glared at him in silence.

'I will look and see if there are good animals here,' Hassan said, standing up from a cross-legged position on the stony ground with fluid ease that suggested great strength. He walked over to the Indians, picked up his cloth-covered rifle and slung it across his back. He bent to untie a long strapped hessian sack from the side of the load he had been carrying, then straightened and looked hard at the two Indians. One reached into his shirt pocket and produced a small wad of rupees. His companion said something sharply and gripped his arm. The Hunter stared unsmiling at them and the money was handed over without further protest.

Jimmy approached the man as he turned to leave.

'I am camped with my friend and a cook further up the valley,' he said pointing vaguely in the direction of the mountains. 'We are mountain climbers.' The Hunter appeared uninterested.

'I would like to talk further with you. You will be welcome in our camp.'

The Hunter nodded, said nothing and turned away. He whistled. A very large rangy dog rose from the shadow of a large rock and padded after the Hunter.

8

Mad Dogs in Guligad Bamak

I saw the dog first. It slunk into the camp with hindquarters low to the ground and nose questing forward for danger. Its lips were curled back, exposing yellowed fangs. It occurred to me that I had never seen such malevolent eyes on any living creature. Then Wart Face arrived and I revised my opinion.

He strode in as if he owned the place but that was no surprise. I had become accustomed to the regal aura that seemed to emanate from the man despite his appearance. It was as if he owned everything, knew it all and needed nothing.

He poured himself a mug of tea and selected a cooling paratha from the pile that Attar had prepared. He flicked it to the dog which flinched back in fear, ears laid back and tail between its legs. Cautiously it edged towards the paratha, sniffing the ghee, flour and paraffin, and drooling a slimy string of saliva from one jowl. With a sudden dart and a clacking of teeth he grabbed the paratha and fled, wolfing it down as he ran.

I examined Wart Face as he chewed steadily through the pile of parathas and wondered what torment he had visited on the poor cur to make it so terrified of him. It was probably the wart, I decided. It had a peculiarly mesmeric effect on me.

Jimmy popped his head out of the cook tent and greeted the

man with his open smile and startlingly direct gaze. Wart Face grunted and spat out some half-chewed paratha. He muttered something, and I looked inquisitively at Jimmy.

'We cross into Guligad tomorrow,' he said with a grin. 'Oh yeah, and Hassan said he's just seen your ibex.'

'Did he . . .'

'No. He said it was too old. No good for meat apparently.'

'Good.'

I couldn't be bothered to say I told you so. Jimmy had conveniently forgotten his denial that any Ibex had existed in these parts. He was deep in discussion with Wart Face planning the crossing of the pass. As far as I was concerned he was Wart Face. Hassan seemed too human a name for him.

Attar struggled manfully to pack the bulky aluminium cooking pots into his dilapidated rucksack. He smiled sheepishly when I glanced at his chaotic efforts, and I bit back an irritated comment. He was an engineering student after all, I reminded myself. *Thanks, Jimmy*. I almost said it aloud as I gazed bitterly at Jimmy's small receding figure on the moraines above the camp.

I re-read the card he had fished from the depths of his rucksack. It was crumpled and stained. Some of the words were so badly smudged it was difficult to read them.

'Here,' he had said with a nasty smirk on his face, 'just found it, sorry.' He flicked it towards where I sat on my rucksack smoking a last contemplative cigarette before the hard walk ahead of us. He had turned on his heel and strode purposefully away before I realised what it was.

'You won't be long, will you?' he said, as he walked away. 'We need to get going.'

As I read the postcard and it slowly dawned on me what Jimmy had done I felt all the anger boiling to the surface. After Wart Face, the dog and Attar, this was the last straw.

I recognised the writing at once. Precise, neat, feminine writing. Alice. It was addressed to me at Jimmy's hotel in

Delhi. Dated a month ago to the day. Judging by the stamp it had reached Delhi the day I had met up with Jimmy.

'Bastard!' I muttered vehemently, and Attar looked at me in alarm. I ignored him and stared at Jimmy's dwindling figure. Why didn't he give it to me in Delhi? Why did he smirk? For a moment I felt like running after him. *And then what?* I couldn't very well start beating him up, and I knew that if I met him now I wouldn't be able to hold back. *Anyway,* I thought ruefully, *he'd probably beat the shit out of me.*

Feeling helpless and impotent fuelled my rage until the whirl of questions running through my mind became confused and unanswerable.

It was a light happy message: 'How are you? Wish I was there. Take care of yourself – and Jimmy. Have a great trip, hope Jimmy doesn't find any Water People.' That surprised me. I didn't know Jimmy had told her about them. And then:

'I thought I'd go to Italy with Andy. Get it out of my system. Be like old times, just good friends.'

'What old times?' I said aloud. 'And who the fuck is Andy?'

Attar smiled hopefully at me. '*Just good friends.*' I'd heard that before, and I felt a hot rush to my head as a volley of jealous thoughts came to mind. *Who the hell was this Andy bloke, and what old times had they had? Christ, for all I know the child might have been his. No, surely not.*

I re-read the short card for the fifth time, desperately looking for some different way of interpreting it. It was signed 'All the best, Alice.' No kisses, no love you. *God! If only I could phone.* As the idea occurred I remembered Jimmy. *Why had he waited so long before giving it to me?* I tucked the battered card into the top pocket of my rucksack and heaved it on to my shoulders.

'Come on,' I said harshly to Attar who wobbled and nearly lost balance trying to swing his clanking rucksack off the ground. I set off along the dusty tracks made by Jimmy and Wart Face wondering what he knew about Alice, but I couldn't think of anything that might explain his action. As I approached the shattered moraines of the Chaturangi glacier my anger had subsided. The dry heat and heavy rucksack had sapped it away. *He must have forgotten*, I thought, *I mean, he is pretty daft*. I tried to convince myself but the memory of his smirk as he flicked the card at me kept alive the idea that there was something malicious afoot. *And if she didn't send me love and kisses, well, obviously she didn't want to give anything away. She knew Jimmy would see it.*

As the questions kept repeating themselves to me and I tried to justify it all I felt something sour had come over the trip. It was tainted now and a cold shiver ran up my back. *Something bad would happen if we went on like this*, I thought. Although there was no logic to the thought it worried me and I looked back anxiously to see Attar struggling along behind.

Jimmy and Wart Face had already crossed the dangerous loose ground hanging above the meltwater that burst in a grey roaring torrent from the snout of the Chaturangi glacier. I could see dust clouds trail behind their footsteps as they toiled painfully up the scree. Small rocks and pebbles trickled down with a rattling sound before plunging over the hard black ice cliffs carved out from the snout. Like some evil eye, it bulged free from a chaotic mound of boulders and rubble hiding the glacier. It formed a cavernous semi-circle of dark ice walls pitted with rock dust. A twenty-foot hole at the centre of the black crescent spewed highly pressurised meltwater from beneath the glacier.

A sinuous yellowish path was visible contouring an erratic and forlorn line above the black cliffs. The two figures were still visible climbing steadily away from the threat of the glacier's snout. I had watched them edge cautiously along the path, each step carefully placed to balance the unwieldy weight of their rucksacks, hands outstretched to the screes for support. The drop of over a hundred feet below the path was made all the more frightening by the steady fall of debris from their steps which dragged my eyes down to the surging torrent below. If they survived such a fall they would be torn to bits by the meltwater.

Looking up the valley, I saw a wilderness of brown rocks, humped in tortured drifts, extending towards the distant white summit of Kalindi Khal. Occasional black streaks showed where the glacier exposed itself. These were the sides of gaping crevasses, fringed with unstable moustaches of broken rocks. The constant cracking sounds of the rocks tumbling into the crevasses broke the early morning silence.

Behind me I heard Attar stumbling over the last awkward boulders blocking the approach to the snout. From where I stood the thin yellow path snaked off to the right. I examined it dubiously. My suggestion to Jimmy that the lower, safer route would be better with our heavy loads had been dismissed. Wart Face had even had the temerity to sneer scornfully at me. He mistook common sense for cowardice and I bristled at the implied slur and said no more. I regretted that stupidly macho reaction.

Attar sat down heavily with a jangle of cooking pots. His load had begun to fall apart again. I bent down to readjust and tighten his straps, pulling unnecessarily hard in exasperation. Attar was a bloody liability, and of course Jimmy was nowhere to be seen. I resented the way Jimmy deferred to Wart Face all the time. He had hardly spoken two words to me since the man had turned up, I thought bitterly, and when he did it was only to translate at my request what he had been planning with Wart Face. Attar sat staring at the precipitous path, and for the first time he had stopped smiling. I patted his shoulder and gave him a stern look.

'Now be very careful here, mate,' I said, 'because if you fall, that will be it. Do you understand?'

He nodded nervously. He understood only too well. I noticed he wore a pair of torn baseball boots with soft rubber soles and no edges. They were almost worse than going barefoot.

'Come on, then, take it nice and slow and do exactly what I

do. Okay?' He didn't take his eyes from the path except once to follow the fall of rocks down the black ice.

A rush of ice-cooled air billowed up from the surface of the torrent far beneath me. It dried the sweat on my face. After the first few fragile steps I became engrossed in the task ahead, stepping warily on to the crumbling steps made by the others. I could sense the drop sucking at me in the cold breath from below. A hint of dark ice, the slithering noise of scree falling away into space, and the numbing roar of the water reminded me of the consequences of a slip. As each step shifted under my feet I felt instinctively when it was time to step again or regain my last step. I progressed in halting fearful movements, absorbed totally in a suddenly contracted world where all my thoughts were fixed on a few miserly feet of loose rocks and yellow gravel, only distantly conscious of the roaring meltwater.

At its end the path became more solid and climbed steeply away from the crescent of dark ice walls in a series of switchbacks. Reaching a group of large rocks firmly embedded in the earth of the slope, I sagged gratefully into a sitting position, removed my rucksack and jammed it securely among the rocks. I turned to encourage Attar over the final few steps.

He was nowhere to be seen. My stomach cramped with the instant thought that he had fallen. Looking back along the line of the path I saw no wide area of scuffed yellow that would mark his last desperate effort to stop the slide. There had been no scream. I wondered whether I'd not heard it above the roar of the water. There was no point in examining the torrent for any sign of him. He would have been whipped away instantly – a tumbling lifeless rag-doll in seconds.

I looked back to where I had last seen him. No sign. My worst fears began building into a panic. I turned and screamed Jimmy's name at the now distant tiny figures high on the scree above me. They stopped and waved. I shouted that Attar had fallen. Jimmy shouted something unintelligible in return and pointed at the far side of the path. I looked and saw nothing. I heard Jimmy shout again but the roaring water drowned out his words. Then a deeper voice echoed down from above. A harsh command.

On the far side Attar crept into view from behind the boulders at the start of the path. He had the apprehensive skulking air of Wart Face's dog, which was bounding effortlessly up the screes above.

'Attar!' I yelled furiously. 'You stupid bastard!'

I could see he recognised the fury in my voice. He ducked his head a few times, as if avoiding a blow, and then flinched as another abrupt command came from above me.

By the time I had retraced my steps across the path and reached Attar my anger had faded. He looked utterly miserable, his eyes filling with tears of fear and failure.

'It's okay, mate.' I smiled at him. 'Look, I'll take your load across and you follow. All right?'

His smile regained a little of its old infectiousness.

'Yes, sahib,' he bobbed his head, 'thank you, sahib, thank you.'

A third of the way across the yellow path I heard Wart Face bellowing something from above and turned to see that Attar had frozen in terror on the crumbling steps. He was at the highest point of the cliffs directly above the spout hole of rushing water. He leant into the slope, forehead pressed into the dusty rubble, eyes squeezed tight and fingers clawed into the earth on widespread arms. I could see his feet creeping down the slope and showers of dusty pebbles falling away into space. At the sound of the voice he jerked his head up and stared fearfully over at me. I smiled encouragingly.

'Come on, Attar, you can do it,' I wheedled, silently cursing Jimmy for hiring an engineering student as a cook. 'Look,' I continued, 'don't just stand there. Those steps are collapsing. It is bad to stay still.'

He looked pleadingly at me and then back across the way he had come, trying to gauge which was the best option. Another stark command came down, and in a rush of fear-induced courage Attar came towards me in a series of rapid crab-like side-steps. His eyes were wide with fright and, having committed himself to the task, he had thrown all caution to the winds. Rocks and scree poured into the abyss from his carelessly placed steps. I watched, horrified, as his baseball boots slithered repeatedly off the disintegrating steps. I turned and set off towards my rucksack as fast as I dared. I didn't want him catching up with me in a panic while still perched above the cliffs.

I reached the safe haven of the rocks just before a wide-eyed Attar, whimpering in terror, clawed his way past me and tried to bury himself between them. His chest was heaving, his breath coming in uneven gasps.

The sound of laughter came from above. Even from so far away I recognised the sneering contemptuous tone of Wart Face's laugh. Attar glanced up from his foetal position among the rocks and tried to smile; he looked hopelessly out of his depth. His meticulously combed hair was straggly with sweat and dust, and tears had cut dark lines down his yellow dust-powdered face.

'Well, you got here, didn't you?' I grinned at him and held my hand out. I meant him to use it to pull himself upright, but to my surprise he reached out, grasped my hand, and shook it with great formality.

'Thank you, sahib,' he said without a trace of a smile. 'Thank you. I am owing to you.'

He smiled eventually, when his uncertainty at my laughter turned at last into pleasure and he beamed at me. His load had nearly fallen apart in the headlong dash across the path, so I repacked it and tied it firmly into place.

When Attar had regained some of his composure I indicated that it was time to leave. Looking up, I saw that the others had disappeared. They had reached the top of the scree slope that formed the left bank of a deeply cut glacier valley and gained the high-level shoulder bounding the left bank of the Swetvarn glacier. This small rubble-strewn glacier cut steeply up towards a snowy headwall that Jimmy had seen from an observation point on a ridge above our camp. Wart Face had said there was a difficult high pass leading across into the next valley, the Guligad Bamak. I could see a jumble of ice cliffs threatening any approach to the pass and sighed, resigned to yet another test of nerve.

I wanted to be rid of the scree slope and the roaring torrent and the shaky fear of Attar's close escape. Forcing the pace, I started up the long zig-zagging trail of footsteps freshly made by the others. No-one else had been this way for a long time.

The heat was oppressive. The sun reflected savagely back from the yellow rocks, and dust rose in occasional gusts of wind from my footsteps, temporarily blinding me. Sweat trickled into my eyes and soaked through my thin cotton T-shirt, mixing with the gritty dust and rubbing the skin from my shoulders. The rucksack began to fight me, a dead weight suddenly come alive and malignant. At every panting rest I stared up the slope and seemed to have made no progress.

Attar struggled far below, his stooped figure outlined by the black shadows of the cliffs below him. The sound of the water had receded to a distant grumbling murmur. Occasionally the clattering of rockfall came sharply on zephyrs of wind from further up the glacier we had crossed. Once, loud thunder made me look up in alarm to find the source of the avalanche, but I could not see it.

When I reached the crest of the slope I saw a level shoulder of land. A thin strip of earth perched between the soaring dark rock buttresses and glistening ice walls of Sudershan Parbat and the chaotic boulder-strewn mess of the Swetvarn glacier. I saw sagebrush growing in isolated tufts, and a dry brown sun-scorched grass, and smelt the pungent fragrant scent of herbs growing hidden among the rocks and boulders. Compared to the desolate lunar landscape I had just struggled up it seemed a paradise. Strange flowers sprouted defiantly from the rocky ground – isolated flashes of colour amid the shattered mountain rocks. White daisies, delicate long-stalked yellow poppies, strange red rubbery-leafed plants, and a few forlorn sprigs of desiccated herb-like shrubs that seemed to have lost the battle for existence.

The air was suffocatingly hot and the earth was baked into dust. A huge granite wall towered above me on my left. It seemed to hang suspended, as if frozen in the moment of collapsing. Crack-lines and corners split the glowing shield of golden red rock. Its topmost edge hung out over space in a broken-toothed cornice of shattered blocks two thousand feet above. I felt small and threatened.

Two black specks wheeled on the thermals of scorched air. Lammergeiers – huge red-eyed bearded vultures banking in graceful circles on seven-foot wingspans. Greedy scavengers of the high mountain, like the bald ugly condors of South America, they carried the stench of carrion and death among their feathers. From a distance they were impossibly beautiful, elegant monarchs of the skies, but seen hunched over their rotting victims, or staggering drunkenly into flight with swollen bellies, they were foul and odious things.

I sagged gratefully into the shadow of a large boulder, leaning back on my rucksack and facing the way I had come. I heard the faint screech of the lammergeier and, looking up, saw the two circling dots like small sparrows riding swiftly up the sun-blistered granite walls. I expected to hear the pistol-shot reports of rocks cracking in the heat. There was a scratching sound close by and the sudden warning cry of a marmot, a quick fire '*crik-crik-crik-crik*', then silence as I turned to look for it among the rocks where it would be standing sentinel for its neighbours. A scraggy plant grew from a crack in the boulder. Its leaves had the look of burnt paper dusted grey and yellow, ready to disintegrate at the slightest touch. It reminded me of wild mint, and when I crushed a leaf, there was a smell of mint and lavender on my fingers. I rubbed it into my forehead.

After half an hour I went to the crest and looked down to find Attar slumped on the path clutching his arm. He shook his head weakly in response to my call and mumbled something unintelligibly. When at last he looked up, I saw the trickle of blood coming from his eyebrow and a violent purplish bruise reaching from the cut across to his temple. His eyes were glazed and unfocused.

I shouted Jimmy's name, hoping that they were waiting for us within earshot, and then descended to Attar. He smiled weakly as again I removed his rucksack and swung it on to my back. He followed me slowly, still clutching his arm.

By the time I had reached the shelter of the boulder I could see two figures approaching us, kicking dust up with their feet as they came across the gently undulating rocky ground.

'What's up?' Jimmy demanded as he dropped his sack by the rocks.

'It's Attar.' I nodded towards Attar who was looking fearfully at Wart Face and the dog standing silently beside Jimmy. 'He's been hit by rockfall. I think he might have broken his arm.' Attar smiled uncertainly and lifted his injured arm towards Jimmy.

'Shit! That's all we need!'

'For Christ's sake, Jimmy, it's not his fault,' I retorted angrily. 'For all I know I was probably the one who knocked the rocks on to him. Anyway, he shouldn't bloody well be here, as you well know.'

'Yeah, well, he was cheap,' Jimmy said defensively.

'Cheap!' I yelled. 'Cheap! Oh sure he was cheap, cheap and cheerful, but bloody useless. It wasn't a Bring and Buy Sale, you know.'

In a fury I had leapt to my feet shouting at Jimmy. The dog let out a horrific menacing growl, baring its yellow fangs, and lunged towards me. It had grabbed my right hand in its jaws before I could jump clear. A harsh command barked out from Wart Face. The dog released my hand but stood close to me, jaws open and teeth bared, snarling from deep in its chest. I could see its body quivering with excitement, anticipating the delightful order to attack. I stepped back and the beast moved forward.

'Tell that guy to call this killer off,' I said quietly to Jimmy, hearing the fear vibrating in my voice. 'And tell him to keep it a long way from us at all times.' Jimmy turned to speak to Wart Face, who clicked his tongue and the dog swung round and padded back to him.

'Away.' I pointed to where they had come from. 'Go away. Now!'

The dog crouched, ready to spring again, at the sight of my lifted arm, but I locked eyes with Wart Face, who scowled ferociously, making his wart appear as if it would burst free from his forehead. He was a fearful sight. Fortunately he turned abruptly away and trudged up the valley from which he had come. The dog followed obediently, but not without a glance over its shoulder and a pointedly nasty snarl. Like master like dog, I thought as I sank into a sitting position on Jimmy's rucksack.

'How on God's earth did you meet up with that guy?' I massaged my hand. The skin was unbroken, which was a relief, but it felt as if I'd slammed it in a car door. 'I wouldn't be surprised if that damn dog was rabid. Did you see how quick it moved?'

Jimmy started laughing. He knelt down slowly, convulsed with sobs.

'Well, I'm glad you find it amusing,' I said. 'I can hardly move my fingers now.'

It only made him worse as he tumbled on to his side, gasping for breath and beating the ground with his fist.

'God, you looked scared,' he managed to say.

'Oh, and you weren't, I suppose.'

'It was just the expression on your face when the dog had your hand in its mouth.' He sat up and wiped tears from his cheeks with the shoulder of his T-shirt.

I was shaking more from shock than anger. I glanced at Attar and saw that he was utterly bewildered. Blood trickled from the gash in his eyebrow. His eye had nearly closed. He squatted on his haunches, rocking gently back and forth, and I noticed the glazed, slightly unfocused look still in his eyes. A smear of blood was visible under the hair by his right ear. I leant towards him anxiously.

'Attar,' I asked calmly, 'how do you feel, mate? How's your head?'

'I am okay, sahib.' He said it painfully slowly, stammering over the words.

'Jimmy, speak Hindi to him.'

'What?'

'Speak Hindi. I'm worried about his head.'

'So? What will speaking Hindi do?'

'Look,' I said patiently while Jimmy sat anxiously searching the horizon for Wart Face. 'Look, this is serious.' I grabbed his arm. 'He's been hit hard. There's blood from his ear, his speech is buggered, and he has a funny look in his eyes. I don't like it. I think he may have fractured his skull.'

'So? Why the Hindi?'

'Because I want to know if his speech is bad in his own language, why do you *think*.'

'Oh, right.' Jimmy turned to Attar and spoke rapid Hindi to him. After a brief exchange he turned to me with a grin.

'He'll be right.' He announced it confidently. 'He was scared of the dog, hence the voice,' Jimmy laughed, remembering my expression. 'His ear is cut. The blood is coming from the outside, not inside. I reckon he's just a wee bit shocked.'

'More than a wee bit, youth.' I told Jimmy how Attar had nearly finished himself on the yellow path above the glacier's snout. 'He's traumatised, out of it, doolally,' I said in exasperation. 'He is even less use than he was before, and that was pretty hopeless. He'll have to go.'

'Go where?' Jimmy looked astonished. 'And what about his load?'

'Look, Jimmy, he's hurt. I doubt he can carry the load

downhill let alone up. He'll have to go. That guy, Hassan, can take him down the lower path. He can take the load and leave his here to pick up when he returns.'

Jimmy shook his head as if he could worry the problem away like a dog drying itself. Eventually he stood up and shouted to where Wart Face had gone.

'All right, you win. We'll split his load between us. Hassan can take most of the heavy cooking gear down; we can use the gas stoves instead. We'll have enough, I think.'

He was bending over Attar's sack, undoing the straps and shaking out the contents on to the ground. I went to Attar and examined his arm, twisting it gently and bending the elbow. Attar grimaced and winced a few times but it was clear that nothing was broken. A snarl from behind me made me stiffen in alarm.

'Jimmy,' I said softly. 'Get that bloody dog out of here, and tell that guy to leave it behind when he takes Attar down.'

Jimmy said something to Wart Face who scowled and replied venomously. Jimmy shrugged.

'No can do, I'm afraid,' he said. 'He needs the dog for hunting, and protection apparently.'

'He doesn't need protecting.'

'Well, yes, but there it is. I'll try and make him keep it away from us. Okay?' He smiled his most disarming smile.

'Good.' He had already decided that I agreed. 'Right then, Hassan will take Attar down to Gaumukh and then catch us up. If we split the loads between us it shouldn't be too bad and we can have a break in a bit. I don't like it here,' he said looking up at the looming granite cliff above us.

The lammergeiers had gone but the beetling crest of the wall still appeared to be on the verge of collapse.

'Hassan says there is a good place to stop further up the valley. There is water about an hour away.'

'How on earth does he know that?' I asked. 'You said he'd never been here before.'

'I know. Odd isn't it? But I bet he's right. He seems to know these things. Knows the land I suppose.'

I grunted. Jimmy's carefree attitude to Attar had left a bad taste in my mouth. Attar had recovered some of his good humour until I told him that Wart Face would accompany him down and then the smile vanished. Wart Face picked up Attar's sack and strode off without a word. The dog loped ahead of him.

I paid Attar the money we owed for his two weeks' work and added almost as much again as recompense for his troubles. I didn't tell Jimmy. He would have complained about baksheesh for someone who was so patently useless and taken it back. Attar trudged reluctantly away after much hand-shaking and profuse thanks. I waved him off and turned to find Jimmy gone. He was already a distant figure in a shroud of dust, head down and walking hard. I wondered whether he felt as guilty about Attar as I did. Probably not. I shouldered my sack and realised that Jimmy had put the entire extra load into his rucksack.

A hot acrid hour passed. An hour of sweating gritty discomfort. Once past the granite cliffs an ibex path crept close to the rim of the steep tottering moraine slopes dropping into the glacier. The slopes were near-vertical walls of con-glomerated mud, scree and rocks. Some boulders the size of houses hung out over the glacier awaiting the next rainfall to topple them thunderously on to the ice four hundred feet below. On the left massive and chaotic boulder fields ran up into the lower flanks of Sudershan Parbat. Occasionally the path disappeared under the debris of fresh landslides and the way ahead was blocked by huge granite blocks perched one upon the other in uneasy balance.

The sparse vegetation had vanished. Here the land was too fluid for life such as that. Lizards sometimes darted into the shelter of dark cracks on my approach, frightened from their sun-baked lethargy. They were small creatures, no more than six inches long, and I wondered how they had reached this high remote valley and what the first bleak winds of winter would do to these heat-loving, dappled-skinned, soft reptiles. I kept an eye out for them, hoping to photograph one sunbathing, motionless, head pointed to the sky, with glittery black obsidian eyes and flicking tongue, and an incongruous snow mountain looming as a backdrop, but they were too quick for me.

The struggle to survive up in that high valley must have been brutal indeed. A place where death was random, meaningless and violent. There were lammergeiers, griffon vultures, eagles, crows, white-beaked ravens, and choughs circling the currents of heated air, ready to wheel and swoop in a swift-taloned black-shadowed rush on the solitary lizard. There were marmots and hares and other unwary rodents, also stalked from the sky, hiding amid the scattered rocks and boulders from where they scratched a meagre existence on this narrow shoulder of thinly scattered soil between mountain wall and glacier. There would be sheep and mountain goats at the head of the valley, if the hunter was to be believed. Wolves even though I doubted him. Foxes, marmots, voles, mice, fluffy grey hamster-like rodents, scuttling furtively from the safety of crevices and undercut boulders. To know they were there and yet rarely seen was testament to the shadow of fear under which they lived; hunting and hunted, and menaced with the sudden overwhelming destruction of their hostile sanctuary.

At the end of the tortuous boulder field I rested against a razor-edged granite slab cleaved by winter frosts from the crags above. It lay tilted from the edge of the debris at an inviting angle. I lay sideways across the smooth surface of the rock and closed my eyes, cheek pressed to the shadow-cooled surface. Sweat cooled and salt dried in my hair.

A desert wind had risen, blowing the aroma of sand and bitter dusts up from the receding valley where we had once been. I listened to the wind, intent on hearing what message the distant deserts had. There was nothing; only soft flurries on my clothing, and the tak-tak-tak of a rucksack strap whipping the grey gold flecks of my broken sarcophagus. A low-pitched, almost inaudible vibration of the rocks hummed softly as the wind curled between them, squeezing through defiles, trickling sounds of dusty pebbles shifting around the foot of monolithic rocks. High above me the air made rushing, hustling sounds as it flailed the mountain ridges, but low down where I lay the air was resonant with secret sounds, with the breath of the earth that smelt of bleached bones and desiccated soil.

Opening my eyes, I stared at the crystals in the granite. A pin-cushion lichen, red like a garnet, thumb-nail size, grew like a spatter of blood from the grey gold surface. In the cool shadow the rock seemed polished with oil, slick against my skin with a hard unfriendly smell of sulphur, a stink of ozone and cordite still clinging to it from the crashing explosion of its birth from the mountain.

The wind died. For a moment utter silence reigned until my confused ears readjusted and the cracks and pistol-shot reports from the glacier mingled to form the background sounds of the day.

It is never truly silent in the mountains. They move constantly in huge plundering collapses and minuscule creeping movements, obeying the laws of gravity. In apparent silence the air shivers with the echoes of the hills. The deep noises of the earth pressured inexorably upwards mix with tremulous vibrations as the flesh of the mountains is ground away by the slide of a thousand glaciers. Even sand, sliding in gossamer-thin avalanches down the flanks of small dunes, can be heard singing shrilly. Some say it is the Sandmen singing for your soul, coming for you in the silence of the desert to fill up your eyes and smother your sleeping breath. You can hear symphonies drawn out in the sibilant fall of powder snow on a silent face; hear water music in the gentle sluicing of ice water, trickling first tentative steps over fresh crushed gravels at the start of its voyage to the sea. It is never silent. The word is meaningless in the mountains.

As the wind faded I sat up and searched the valley for signs of Jimmy. Ahead I could see that the narrow shoulder I had trailed spread out in a semi-circle formed between two ridges on the mountain side. There was a hint of greenery, and blue-grey shadows suggested a less harsh region. A small figure, silhouetted against stark white slopes, stood on a rock pinnacle waving a twiggy arm slowly above his head.

I broke from the reverie and stood waving a reply. Coming from shadows into the full midday heat felt as if the air parted around me, flowing like water bending around egg-shaped river rocks, cascading shockingly between my shoulder blades as the sweat sprang from my pores in salty pin-pricks. It sucked my breath away, momentarily draining me of strength, and I swayed as if drugged.

I heard the busy hiss of the gas stove before I rounded the pinnacle upon which Jimmy squatted grinning at me like a gargoyle.

'You look knackered,' he said.

'Bushed, mate.' I collapsed by the stove. 'It's too bloody hot for this lark.'

Jimmy jumped down from his perch and sat in the shade of the pinnacle. He stared fixedly up the valley to the jumble of ice cliffs and the snow slopes leading to a broad saddle. On either side of the col ridges soared in graceful concave arches. Rocky buttresses and sentinel spires of dark rock protruded intermittently from the left-hand ridge while on the right a perfect crescent of snow climbed into the sky. The blue-grey shadows of the cornices, lightly pencilled into the facing slope, smudged the sweep of ice and snow. Thin parallel fluting etched the face as if it were softly raked crystal-white sand. The two ridges framed a vista of cloudless sapphire sky.

'Can't be that far from here,' Jimmy said, shielding his eyes from the glare. 'One hour to the snow, one hour up and one down.'

I looked doubtfully at the way ahead. 'Looks a hell of a lot further to me.'

'Naw,' Jimmy said airily, 'that's just the scale fooling you. Anyway, if we take any longer than an hour going up, that ice-fall on the right will twat us.'

The ice-fall was a turbulent storm of crevasses and ice cliffs tumbling in frozen motion down the flanks of the left-hand peak. As if to confirm Jimmy's words, a dull booming echoed round the valley and a puff of ice fragment rose from the centre of the ice-fall.

'True,' I said, and Jimmy laughed delightedly.

The site where we had chosen to rest was in complete contrast to the ground we had covered. A stream of clear water came down from a shadowy dark cleft in a rock wall to the left. The pinnacle of rock had hidden the wide flat area of scrubby sagebrush and green grass nourished by the stream. The stream had broken into scores of rivulets interlacing over the level terrain like a miniature delta. Circular pools with moustaches of flowers and grass trailing into the water were dotted around, the profusion of growth giving their positions away. We sat close by one. An aluminium cooking pot bobbed on the surface. Purple poppies, daisies, louseworts and wild mint grew in tangled bunches at the edge, competing for the moisture-rich soil. The bottom of the pond was reddish brown silt so fine that, once disturbed, the motes hung in the water like dust and would not settle. Glints in the mud betrayed tiny slivers of mica washed down from where it had been crushed from the rocks far above. The pasture extended far up the valley towards where the snow line started. It was as if we had passed through a gateway to the heart of the valley.

Jimmy handed me a mug of tea and one of Attar's parathas. I accepted the tea and threw the paratha over my shoulder. I felt less guilty about Attar's absence, and relaxed in Jimmy's company. I couldn't be bothered to bring up the questions about the postcard. It had been a long hot day.

'You know something?' I said.

'What?'

'That Hassan is really getting on my tits!'

'I'd noticed.'

'No, I'm serious, Jimmy,' I retorted. 'Ever since he turned up I've hardly had a civil word out of you. All I hear is Hindi. I may as well have come on my own.'

'Got a touch of the greenies have you,' Jimmy taunted. 'Didn't know you cared so much.'

'Oh, for Christ's sake be serious,' I snapped. 'Is it going to be like this in Pakistan, then?'

'Like what?'

'Trailing round after you like a bloody lackey while you interview a world of oddballs about water!'

'Now hang on,' Jimmy said, sitting up, 'you know damn well this jaunt was going to be like this, Pakistan is climbing, here is trekking and winkling a few things out, okay. We agreed, remember?'

'Yes, we agreed, right, but I didn't agree to be ignored, and nor did I agree to the hiring of pathological nutters like what's-he-called and his devil dog. I didn't agree to be scared stupid by him, near-killed by the cook, or savaged by that bloody dog. Did I?'

'He's not mad, though his dog might be. I can agree with you there,' Jimmy said in his reasonable honest broker voice. 'But it's only for a few days, three at the most. And he knows a lot of stories – weird things, you know what I mean?'

'Well I might do if I spoke the language but I don't. And it's hardly surprising he knows weird things, is it? Most bloody nutters do. That's how you know they are mad.'

Jimmy rummaged in his rucksack, discarding Attar's load of pans, rice, sugar, tinned fish, butter and cheese, along with a litter of clothing and climbing equipment. When he had nearly emptied it he produced a tattered exercise book wrapped in a Sainsbury's shopping bag.

'Read that then,' he said as he tried to hook a pair of underpants from the pond before they sank.

'What's this?' I said, unwrapping the book.

'Well. It'll give you some idea of what I'm talking about. Why I keep talking to these oddballs, as you call them. I'm getting really close now.'

'To what?'

'To a complete story. Something that is all linked together.'

'What are you on about?'

'Just read it. Hassan won't be here for at least another hour.' He started tying his boot laces. 'I'm off to have a look at that waterfall.' He nodded in the direction of the cleft from where the stream emerged.

'I can't see a waterfall.'

'Well there must be one there,' Jimmy replied as he stood up. 'Think about it. What made that cleft, why is the wall wet so high up, and what's that rainbow doing there? Stands to reason.'

As he strode off I noticed the faint aurora of colours at the mouth of the cleft, as if sunlight were glittering off motes of dust suspended in the air.

'Hardly a rainbow,' I muttered at his retreating back. I opened the exercise book. 'DRAGONLAND!' read the title.

9

Cycle of Spirits

There are countless myths and legends associated with the mountainous regions of this planet. Fantastic tales, mysteries, archetypal stories imbued with fear and awe. I have heard many of these legends and have begun to recognise a common theme running through them all. The stories, like poorly fitting clothes, hide what lies beneath. The people from whom I have heard these stories have good reason to believe them. Fear and ignorance might account for most of the fantasy that embroiders the tales but these people are blessed with open uncluttered minds that are prepared to acknowledge the truth in them. We can believe in Christianity. Some of us can blindly accept transubstantiation – that wine becomes the blood of Christ and a sliver of bread becomes his flesh when conse-crated in Eucharist. Yet we will laugh at the myths and legends of other cultures. We laugh with the amused, conceited arrogance of fools unable to recognise that our own truths are equally as unfounded.

Well, I shall tell some of the legends that I have recorded and you can laugh, if you wish, if you believe you know everything. Remember, before you laugh, the myths you accept as truths. Think of the countless religions and the pantheons of Gods through which others live their lives. Think of something never wholly understood and yet taken for granted because otherwise you would be insane – Time, Space, Existence. Is there nothing inexplicable in your life? Can you really dismiss the notions of Chance, Fate or Luck? Perhaps you have never thought too much about it because it makes you feel uncomfortable, makes you sense that dark uncertainties would begin to erode the solid foundations of your happy existence. Ghostly shadows at the back of your mind might unsettle you with the thought that you know very little, or you know an awful lot but understand very little. Perhaps, more simply, you are scared of the dark, scared of yourself and of what you know lies in the deep dark areas of your mind. I will tell you some tales of dragons and rock serpents and if you only laugh, well, it will be some entertainment for you, a brief diversion from the boring certainty of your life.

For as far back as there are records, mountains have been a potent symbol of the bond between the heavens and the earth. The unattainable summits, often wreathed in the clouds, have risen up from our mortal world into the abode of Gods. The divine has always been associated with the highest places.

There are many Himalayan peaks banned to mountaineers simply because a deity resides on the summit. The kingdoms of Nepal and Bhutan are classic examples of this. The Sherpas who live among divine mountains call the highest mountain Chomolungma, which means 'Goddess Mother of the World', or sometimes 'Goddess Mother of the Winds'. We have named it Everest, after the great English surveyor of the last century. The sherpas live in eastern Nepal. They are the people from the east – in their language 'Sher' means east and 'Pa' means people. They are Buddhists of the Kar-Gyud-Pa sect and their religion is indistinguishable from any other facet of their lives, but their Buddhism is deeply linked with the far more ancient animistic beliefs in Bon. The two religions have blended so now they venerate a vast pantheon of Indian Buddhist Gods and Goddesses as well as the original Bon demons and spirits. Past myths and fables became irrevocably intertwined. The witchcraft, sorcery and cruel sacrifices of the old animism left their mark so that every mountaintop, forest, river and cave that previously had been inhabited by demons and horrors is now the abode of Gods.

Hindus believe that the Himalayas are the dwelling places of all immortal beings. Shiva, one of the three main Gods, is said to dwell on the awesome summit of Shivling with his wife Parvati, 'the mother of the mountains'. The terrible ice-glistening spire of Shivling's summit represents the lingam, Shiva's phallus, as a symbol of his creative side.

Nanda Devi, the highest and holiest mountain in India, is a beautiful ice-covered peak rising from an almost impregnable double ring of mountain walls; the innermost wall, known as the Sanctuary, is believed by Hindus to be riddled with caves and precipices inhabited by the demons and spirits that guarded Nanda Devi, 'the blessed Goddess of the secret snows', from desecration. Although the Sanctuary has been penetrated and the mountain climbed, those who have entered have come away with a sense of mystery, an awareness that they have left behind a special world where myths and legends and reality blend into one.

For those who have lived and climbed on the world's great mountains this is no fantasy. There are moments when the strictures of modern life are swept away and reality can become a dream; when lightning flickers across jagged serried rock spires, and cohorts of clouds, black-bellied with menace, roar against the senses and thunder explodes in deafening blasts, and the smell of sulphur fills the air, mingled with the smell of the earth sucked up couloirs in saturated wind-driven mists. When raging with thirst and without water, you can smell it in the snow, and in the constant slide of powder snow in a storm there is an uncanny sense of life upon the mountain. All sense of scale can collapse until the summit, two thousand feet above, seems reachable with an outstretched hand, and the ground half-hidden by drifting clouds seems lost in infinite depth. There are times when the clouds seem solid and the temptation to step out on to them is almost irresistible. An incandescent dawn rising above a sea of cloud-footed peaks after the interminable dark fury of a night storm stuns the mind. It is possible to lose oneself on the flanks of a mountain; lose all sense of time and depth, even the sense of being. There is mystery to be found there; an incomprehensible sense of other beings that sometimes ambushes you at unguarded moments.

The Gods of Greek mythology dwelt on Mount Olympus and played their games with the fate of mere mortals. The Old Testament records the meetings of God and the prophets on mountaintops. Mount Sinai and Mount Nebo are where Moses takes instructions from the Lord. It is the Mount of Olives in the New Testament.

It is no coincidence that we forever strive upwards. We see success in terms of ascent, never descent. Heaven is above, Hell below. We build upwards more often than outwards or down. We know next to nothing about exactly what lies within our planet, yet we have travelled out to the stars. The builders of the Tower of Babel tried to reach the heavens and meet their God. Who did the builders of the Empire State aspire to meet?

The mountain people living a harsh and precarious existence dominated by the vagaries of the mountains have a more colourful and imaginative concept of what we vaguely refer to as a sense of mystery. They have clothed that sense in stories, given shape and form to something we may say is fanciful, but that they know from long experience is real.

Not so long ago, a few centuries perhaps, the mountains of the European Alps were widely regarded as evil-bringers, destroyers, to be feared and avoided. They meted out punishment in the form of landslides and avalanches, floods that swept away crops and houses, storms that made people cower fearfully as the lightning danced flames across the high peaks and rocks crashed into the valleys. Glaciers were the domain of dragons and monsters, riven with crevasses and echoing to the thunderous roaring of ice walls collapsing. They were labyrinths of ice, greenish-blue maws of nightmare dimensions that swallowed the unwary and spat their chewed remains from their snouts decades later. Mountains were fearful places; dangerous regions that were uninhabitable and barren. The Mont Blanc range was formerly named Les Montagnes Maudites, 'the accursed mountains'. The Church encouraged the belief that mountains were the refuge of dragons and demons; the inaccessible fortress kingdoms of Satan. In 1690 the Bishop of Geneva, Jean d'Arenthan, had even travelled to Chamonix, the village at the foot of Mont Blanc, to exorcise the glaciers of their demons.

The greatest range of mountains on the planet, the Himalayas, are a complex grouping of separate mountain ranges lying roughly east to west across the top of the Indian continent. From the Hindu Kush – literally 'the Killer of Hindus' – in the west, through the Pamirs north of them, eastward across the stupendous peaks of the Karakoram, with the Kunlun Shan range running north-east into China, and further east the Himalaya range dominates the magical kingdoms of Nepal and Bhutan in a seemingly limitless horizon of summits.

A fearful region indeed. One of the last great 'blanks' on the map. A land of terrifying contrasts. The highest mountains and deepest river gorges, the largest non-polar glaciers, the most destructive rivers. It truly is the land of Giants, both real and mythical. It is a land of cataclysmic violence still erupting from the earth in the massive throes of its creation. Even as it grows steadily each year it is being destroyed at almost the same speed. The huge rivers were not spawned by the high snows of the mountains. They were there before the mountains rose and today they slice down through the great ranges, cutting them into inaccessible valleys, tearing the new-born rocks in savage violence down into the plains of India and Pakistan. Peoples of infinite variety have settled in these mountains, some blessed with fertile hillsides canopied in vast forests of birch, pine, larch and rhododendron, others scratching a living from a lunar landscape that is swept away almost as soon as it has been settled. There are lands of lush and moist hillsides, home to countless species of plant and animal, and land such as the bleak high desert plains of Tibet, near lifeless, and perhaps one of the most inhospitable places in the world.

It is natural to see the ranges as one and call it all the Himalaya. Yet each range is distinct in the character of its inhabitants and the nature of its terrain. Indeed their names seem to reflect this.

The Hindu Kush, the killer country, is a land of borders, of violence and passion, whose people are defiantly independent.

The remote and bleak Pamirs form a land of death and desolation, mysterious and alien, with mountains turning to bleak rounded deserts. Its people, the nomadic Kirghiz, reflect this in the savage brutality of their lives, the weather-worn contorted faces and blank flint-eyed stares mirror the desert landscape in which they reside. Their womenfolk suffer the highest rate of miscarriages in the world.

'The Mountains of the Spirits', the Tien Shan range that borders the remote Kunlun Shan, was the last great mountain region to be discovered. Surrounded by deserts, it was feared more than any other place. This was the true home of all spirits and demons, residing in an untouched expanse of silences and whispering winds, where travellers cowered and hurried past, haunted by mirages and desolate cold winds of life-destroying aridity. Unvisited and unlived in, the summits loomed over vast empty distances silent but for the moan of the wind, the whispering of demons.

The Kunlun Shan range south of the 'Mountains of Spirits' is said to be the coldest on the planet – a region of frozen beauty where men go only to rob the land of its treasures and flee like hunched-over tomb-robbers laden with their spoils of lapis lazuli, silver and jade.

The Karakoram, the land of rock, is a wasteland of precipices, bleak rock walls and spectacular mountains. It is one of the most violently active volcanic regions, where landslides and avalanches, earthquakes, rivers and vast glaciers combine in an orgy of destruction. A land of warriors, thin-faced, dark-bearded Pathans living by harsh codes of honour and vengeance; embroiled almost continuously in vendetta and strife as they reflect the elements around them.

The eastern Himalaya is where Chomolungma, 'Goddess Mother of the World', stands serene above the beauty of Nepal and the almost lifeless high Tibetan desert plains. In ancient Sanskrit 'Himalaya' means 'the home of the snows'. The most beautiful of the ranges, the most abundantly verdant and fertile, here man has chosen to stay in large numbers, unlike the lonely nomadic lives of the people in the other ranges. It is a land where religion and mystery are inextricably woven into the fabric of everyday life, where religion is believed to have flown in with saints riding the skies on the backs of tigers, and Goddesses dwell on lofty summits. Here the constant aura of mystery seeps through the region like pungent aromas escaping the cooking pot. Prayer wheels spin, cymbals resonate, prayer flags flutter juniper smoke-laden prayers up to the thirty-three heavens of eternal bliss, where the Mahayana Buddhist Gods reside. Here indeed is a land of beauty and charm, where religions, rather than standing apart in violent schism and iconoclastic discord, are cheerfully mingled together. Here animism, Hinduism, Buddhism, sorcery and witchcraft mix into a bewildering confusion of gods and beliefs, superstition and enchantment. Enchanted is the best description of this beautiful area.

If you stand on a high col or upon a crystalline white summit and look at a vista of mountains stretching away from you in all directions you could so easily be ambushed by a sense of movement as you watch the peaks begin to flow away from you. In the early morning the cloud will fill the valley as the sky, fresh cleaned by starlit night, is flushed with the first incandescent glow of dawn and the mountains appear to rise and fall with the heavy swell of a slow deep ocean. Plumes of snow streaming from summit ridges curl over the ice cornices, hanging like tidal waves over the abyss. Gradually the movement becomes apparent. If you look suddenly away, or close your eyes and stare at blood cells drifting across sun-reddened lids, you will find the flow has stopped. Remain still, utterly motionless, braced against sudden winds and stare fixed at one unfocused spot in the far distance and wait for the sluggish start of the waves. There is, you will notice, a peculiar fluidity in mountain ranges. Massive, elemental and uncompromising they may be, deep-rooted in the bowels of the earth, there for ever it would seem, yet they are moving. The earth's greatest mountains are young and growing, pushing inexorably higher. At the same time they are being carved down, pared away by water in its various forms. Hence their shape, hence the fluidity. The Himalayas have risen from the death of the once-great Sea of Tethys. It is not difficult to see the storm-torn waves of that ancient sea frozen in the snow summits surrounding you. It is when they begin to move again before you, when imperceptible shifts in focus occur and you realise that they have moved away, that you encounter the mystery of the mountains. Then all things become believable, all things past shimmy out of focus and fear rises darkly in a flood.

The fossils of ancient crustaceans lie upon the summit rocks of these huge mountains trapped for ever in the limestone of the ancient sea bed of Tethys. In a high remote valley, with steep-flanked slopes sprouting sagebrush and gnarled wind-withered trees where ibex feed and lammergeiers spiral the thermals above, I found a starfish locked in a dank waterworn rock wall. I lay on a stone bed of primaeval ammonites and listened to the roar of meltwater in the glacier below. In the maelstrom of a savage storm I saw a mountain come alive. The snows flowed around my legs and the crashing sounds of wind beating the ridge above me numbed my mind. I tried to hold on, digging arms and legs into the white wave-tops, closing my mind to a rising panic. For a moment I was lost, washed down and over, drowning on powder snow melting in my lungs, thrashing my arms in desperate swimming motions until I surfaced on to a suddenly still shore. When the storm passed and weak sunlight filtered down through ragged wind-torn clouds, I saw the glacier beneath me, a sinuous river of ice flowing southwards to a dark forested valley. Small avalanches boiled down from the sides of the mountains flanking the glacier, filling the air with a deep rumbling sound that rose and fell on the wind. It was the noise of surf on steep-shelved beaches.

These ranges are a battlefield. Water is the ruler here. It is everywhere. Here it is visible in the sea of peaks, the white horses of the corniced ridges, the serpentine flow of the glaciers, and the heavy laden monsoon clouds banking in from the bay of Bengal which carpets the land with fresh supplies. Giant avalanches, collapsing ice cliffs, rock-studded green ice walls of deep crevasses, snow fields glinting in the midday sun, frozen waterfalls, and icicles fringing a blue-cold cave mouth are testament to its presence. In all forms it moves down from the mountain sides, destroying at a rate of erosion unequalled anywhere else. It heads for the great rivers that will carry it to the sea. Some, evaporated off, rises back to the high mountains to fall as snow, only to renew the endless cycle of its destructive and creative existence. Life giving and destroying, the true home of water is in the mountains. It starts flowing down from the highest places and moves endlessly to the sea, where pooled in unimaginable depths, it may take millennia to escape the stranglehold of deep sea currents and rise vaporously to the skies to begin again.

It comes as no surprise to hear the legends of the mountain people and see the pervasive theme of water in their stories. The mongoloid nomadic tribes dwelling in the shadow of 'The Mountains of the Spirits', the Tien Shan range, venerate water. As with all other nomads, water is the prime mover of their lives. Living in the bleak harsh deserts they see more clearly than others the spirit forces in water. Their god reveals himself to them in the elemental forms of wind, snow, ice, rock, thunder clouds, and above all water. Water is life. Every plant to them is a wonder. It is the work of their God. To stand on the shore of a great ocean that most would never see would be to stand by the divine. The paradise of Islam to which every Muslim aspires is a place of verdant greenery, cascades and streams of crystal pure water. Green is their colour, the colour of plants, the evidence of water.

I met a man in Hunza who talked to me of glaciers. He was very old and stooped with the aches of a harsh life. It seemed that he smiled too much until I noticed his dark eyes, near-black, glitter as he squinted against the stark mountain light with a hard uncompromising stare. If he smiled it was without humour. Perhaps it was simply the ravaged mouth and broken teeth and the goitre on his cheek that made him seem comical. He told me first of the daughter he had lost in the winter just passed; how she drowned in the torrent below the village. His wife sat beside him, nodding sadly. He looked up the valley with a squinty smile towards the distant white pyramid of an unnamed mountain and spoke slowly of the glacier he had offended when he was a young man. The torrent below the village sprang from the snout of this glacier. He said that glaciers were living beings. I could not fully understand whether he meant that it was alive or whether something living was trapped within its creaking frozen body.

He said it feasted on the snows of winter, gorging itself through its massive jaws. Its jaws – crevasses, I presumed – filled steadily with the heavy winter snowfalls and gradually closed. With the coming of the high summer sun they would creak hungrily apart and the belching gurgling sounds of its empty stomach would echo up from deep within. The clamorous babel of surplus water being excreted through the labyrinth of icy tunnels that formed its monstrous gut could be heard from high above the valley. It fed on snow gulped in greedily from regular storms, compressed and crushed into ice, ground up and chewed with awesome power as it gnawed its way through the very rock of the valley walls. It vomited torrents of filthy water from its snout and churned its wastes, the crushed rock of the valley, into sinuous chaotic lines of moraine.

He described a brutish being possessed of unimaginable power nurtured by an all-consuming hatred, an abhorrence of itself, of its captivity, that led to a blind destruction of all those who strayed too close. He spoke of a single entity with a mind racked with malevolent impotent thoughts. He said that some of these ogres managed to reproduce themselves, breaking free down an adjoining valley to reach new sources of snow and growing into a separate distinct offspring flooded with its parents' malignity. With the coming of spring, and winter's grip unclenched by the sun, it stirs into life with furious bellowing crashes as it shakes towering ice cliffs free from where it humps over buried islands of rock. Immense explosions boom within the pluming clouds of pulverised ice fragments sweeping down the valley towards the old man's village. At night the monster sleeps in the frozen high mountain air.

Each year the seasons hold it back. The summer heat melting its progress so that only water pours down towards the village, irrigating the fields of barley and spinach and infuriating the impotent glacier. Deep in the ancient echoes of its memory it remembers a time when it reached far past the village, when there was nothing there to antagonise it, no warm-blooded puny creatures to infuriate it with their ignorance.

Aided by small earth tremors, it can sometimes break out of its lair and roar wildly down the valley, though never enough tore free to threaten the small community of farmers. A few houses perched high up the valley had been destroyed, a few acres of hard-won pastures were buried beneath the landslide of mud and boulders, but no lives were lost.

They were lucky, the old man said, to have such a weak glacier. He knew of two villages that suffered the scourge of great and violent glaciers. His cousin among many others had been killed when a creature brought the valley walls down upon their homes one hot sulphurous afternoon.

'Did you know of dragons?' I asked.

When I had described the dragons I knew from legends he looked stern and said it must be the same creature.

'But they fly,' I replied. 'These cannot fly?'

'They are slow, and lazy,' he said, 'but very, very strong.' His wife nodded. 'You must see where my cousin lived, and you will see the power.'

He never told me what had been done to offend the beast. He said his daughter was dead now, and the debt had been paid. He smiled at the dark valley where the glacier crouched, hidden from view, and his wife nodded and swayed back on her heel as she squatted in the grey glacier dust of the Hunza valley. I wrote his story in a small notebook after they left, and as I finished, a distant booming came from the head of the valley as some ice cliffs collapsed and the knee-high field of green barley before me seemed to shiver and sway in a wind that I hadn't felt.

The story the old man told was not new to me. The idea that mountains were living beings, or that things lived within them, was commonplace. I once heard a guide telling an attractive female client, as he pointed to a huge snow field stained red from top to bottom, that the mountain was bleeding with grief. It did look at first sight as if a wound was seeping blood through a white gauze bandage, despite my knowing what it was. I laughed and told the guide that it was a good joke, but he frowned at my interruption.

'It is no joke,' he said sternly. I saw the woman smiling at me. 'It grieves for the deaths of two climbers who died here many years ago. Every year it bleeds for them.'

'It is only algae growing on the surface of the snow. It shows up red as it draws life from the sun. Come on, you *know* this is the reason.'

'That is what you *wish* to think,' he said angrily, looking up the red snow slope. 'I have been in these mountains before you were born. My father, and my grandfather, and my great grandfather have worked in these mountains. They know that what I say is true. There was no blood slope here before the climbers died. Come on,' he said to the woman, 'we must hurry.' He stalked away with a disdainful glance at me. I laughed at him. I wouldn't laugh now.

With the aid of modern scientific techniques we can discover forms of life that once we did not know existed. We can see the structure of things, molecules, atoms, even the neutrons within atoms. We can formulate new theories of knowledge about our world, about the universe in which we spin helplessly. Through an electron microscope we can see into a universe smaller than the wavelength of light or greater than anything we could previously imagine, depending on how we view it. We can peer myopically at the world of viruses and microbes and slowly comprehend what lives within us, within the massive complicated world of cells from which we are formed. We can witness the simplest forms of life, the viruses that infest us. Their ancestry reaches back to the origins of life itself, back to the primaeval soup from which life emerged millions of years ago. Viruses are not separate living cells, as are bacteria; they are chemicals capable of replicating themselves. They are not separate things living within us like parasites; they become part of ourselves. Without the electron microscope such ideas would be regarded as fantasy. It makes me wonder about the dragon glaciers and bleeding mountains. If there are worlds within worlds as tiny and delicate as we have discovered, what else could there be?

There is a community of people that lives in the remote fastnesses of cloud-wrapped mountain forest in Colombia. They are the Kogi, and they see themselves as the protectors of the planet. The world to them is a single living being for which they are responsible. They say the planet is dying. They say that we are the killers, and that they have tried to teach us how to change our way of thinking so as to be able to save the world. We have not listened. Theirs is a highly sophisticated ancient culture and, isolated though they are in their mountain kingdom, there are remarkable parallels between their beliefs and those of other mountain people.

The Kogi hold that our world was born from the sea. They consider the sea and sky to be inextricably linked. They see the world in terms of the cycle of life and water. They understand the notion of evaporation and precipitation and accept the concept of a constant cycle of renewal. Evaporation, rain clouds, snow, glaciers, meltwater lakes and new-born rivers, sea and evaporation. To the Kogi, water is the essence of life, and they speak of it as being alive and creating life. The world began as a sea, as water, and the Kogi practise divination, which to them is an opportunity to commune with water, a chance to delve into the knowledge of the universe. As with the nomadic Kirghiz of the bleak mountain region of the Pamirs, who revere water and would travel many miles to allow a child to stand and gaze at a great river, so the Kogi regard the sea as sacred, the source of life. In their understanding of the world, the mountain summits and the sea are linked by the cycle of water. They are the opposite sides of the whole.

I met a man who understood this sense of wholeness better than most. He was resting in a smoke-filled mountain lodge perched high on the steep slopes leading to a well-used mountain pass. I had ducked into the lodge and crouched by the sweet-smelling smoke of the kitchen fire to warm the chill mists from my back and shake off the damp rain that fell on the forests of rhododendrons and maple trees. Through the open door I could see the clouds clinging tenaciously to the dripping wet trees. The sprays of red rhododendron flowers occasionally glowed through breaks in the dull grey shroud. As my eyes adjusted I noticed the man sitting quietly in the corner of the kitchen away from the heat of the fire. I nodded a greeting to him, and he inclined his head in return.

When I was warm and supplied with a glass of hot sweet tea, I approached the man who shuffled sideways to allow me space on the rug-covered bench. His accent was strange and difficult to follow. He did not speak Nepali, and his Hindi was halting and full of strange words that I had never heard before. He was a gentle, placid man with soft expressive gestures that seemed to employ his whole body. He was handsome, pale-skinned and tall. His hair was worn long and straight and his gaze seemed soft and distant.

He seemed mildly amused by my inquisitiveness and chided me for my impoliteness, for being too swift to ask only what I wanted to know and to have forgotten basic manners. I apologised and offered him a cigarette which he accepted with a smile, breaking off the filter with a fastidious motion of the hands. He smoked through cupped hands, careful not to allow the cigarette to touch his lips before handing it to me.

We smoked quietly and watched the rain increase in force and the foliage of the forest swaying in the downpour. After two hours the rain abated and I paid the lodge owner, a gold-toothed beaming Sherpani who rose from her three-legged stool by the hearth, steepled her hands, palms together, and with a bow of the head said, 'Namaste (*I bow to the god in you*)', the common Nepalese salutation. I noticed she looked at the quiet stranger with deep respect, as did so many others who met us during the next two days – for we walked together, stopping each afternoon as the monsoon rain poured down. He never told me his name and he paid for nothing. I couldn't understand the reverence which was accorded to him by others that we met on the way. He was not a monk or a holy man. He had left me before I discovered who he was.

As we sheltered from the rain on the second afternoon I muttered a curse at being so miserably damp all the time and he laughed at me. He said he came from Assam, where it was always raining, and his people hated it. I knew Assam to be a region of the lushest rain forests on the planet, remote, isolated by high mountains on its borders in the north-east of India, a region which grew a lot of tea, I thought, though maybe I was mistaken.

He told me that in Assam the rain destroyed crops and communities alike, washed away the soil and caused frequent landslides and floods. Assam was the home of the Naga, an ancient ancestor-worshipping people who were protected by dense impenetrable forests from the influence of invaders – one of the original inhabitants of central Asia, tracing their culture and ancestry back into the primitive darkness of the stone age. I suggested that he did not appear so primitive to me. It was many years since he had left his homeland, he replied, and he would not return. He quickly changed the subject and pointed to a rapidly building rivulet of muddy water cutting through the village.

'Can you see the snake?'

I looked across the muddy tangle of wild grasses, almost flattened by the rain. There was no sign of a snake and I glanced at my companion in confusion.

'Look carefully at the water and you may see the snake,' he said patiently with a wry smile.

I stared hard at the rivulet that twisted busily down the centre of the village. Small pebbles and fragments of soil crumbled into the flow and were swept away. The water had a spiral pattern to it as it cut through the steeply sloping muddy ground. As I stared the spirals formed the pattern of plaited hair, a continuously moving series of interlocked V-shaped, twirling dark mud down the hill. It twisted swiftly from side to side as it curled past rocks that it couldn't dislodge until it seemed to be moving.

'I can see what you mean, but there isn't a real snake,' I said apologetically.

'Perhaps it is because you do not know what to look for. In some villages near where I was born the people believed that the snake was the embodiment of the water spirits. The snake was the favourite form that the spirits chose to take when they needed to leave the water. That is why you can sometimes see the snake in such small streams as this.'

'Could you see a snake in a glacier?' I asked, remembering the old Hunza man.

'I have not done so,' my companion replied solemnly, 'but I imagine it would be possible. You see I have only looked at a glacier from a great distance.'

'But have you seen snakes in water? Have you seen these water spirits?'

'Yes. A long time ago I believed that they existed. I saw them in those days. I saw them often and in everything. But then I wanted to see them, you understand?'

'Yes, I understand. I think we would call it auto-suggestion, but does this mean you no longer believe such spirits exist?'

'Oh, maybe I do. I have seen many things, learnt many different things, and I prefer not to use the word "believe". It suggests that something must be fact, must be unchangeable, unquestionable. Do you understand? Is it not better to accept things rather than to believe them; accept that everything is possible?'

'Yes,' I said quietly, 'that is always how I have thought.'

'I know,' he replied, 'I knew that when we met. I could see it in your eyes and hear it in your questions. But you should be careful with your questions, for they can lead you into danger. If you ask too many questions, you seek too many answers, and in the end you will find something which you *want* to believe.'

'But if you ask no questions you will learn nothing,' I said feeling rather uncertain. 'You surely need to know things to be able to accept them?'

'You can know things without searching them out.' He was smiling at me with that gentle slightly paternal expression that I had come to like in the past few days. 'Come,' he stood up with a surprisingly fluid athletic motion for a man of his age, 'the rain has stopped. It is time to go.'

We walked together until the early evening, stopping occasionally to share a cigarette beneath the shade of damp steaming trees. He told me of the Water Spirits of his past which dwelt in the high cold rivers, moved in hollows, were not the water but were part of it. Like viruses, I thought, neither good nor evil for they had been here long before such concepts could exist. They created the shape of the mountains, directing the work of water in the rivers to form valleys and lakes, and eventually seas. They took the form of serpents for this was the closest shape to the movement of water. If careless they could be caught in the form of fish, and when the fish were eaten the spirits took the form of the water in the eater and returned eventually to the outside where they were washed back into the rivers; or rose in the vapour of cooking pots and escaped as rain. It was easy to see snakes in the steam rising from cooking pots if the sun was shining at the right angle.

The spirits had different characters according to their environment. In rivers they were happiest. Busy with their work. In the deep seas it is said they slept in slow-moving currents to recover from their labours. Drifting in clouds in the sky, they were lazy in the heat of the sun. They would be swept towards the high mountains to be frozen and trapped. Sometimes high-flying choughs would come to their rescue by swallowing them and flying back down to swoop over the rivers and release them. If not rescued, they could become extremely dangerous as they tried to escape the ice and snow in which they found themselves imprisoned. They could not move fluently through the water hollows because all movement had frozen. Desperate to return to the rivers, they fought their way down from the mountains breaking everything that stood in their way, until they returned to the limitless world of streams and rivers and seas. They could not be killed. It was said that sometimes a whole serpent became trapped in the glacier ice when carried up by greedy unthinking vultures. These were the most violent ones. The angry ones that crashed and roared and scared people.

I asked whether his people knew of dragons, and he said that sometimes the water spirits were represented in the form of dragons. It seemed strange, he said, for dragons had always been connected with fire and not water. I told him that today in the West dragons were associated with fire but in the distant past they had long been associated with water. The myths of some desert races hold that dragons dwell at the bottom of wells. To peer into a well was seen as staring into the dragon's eye. They were water-dwelling, all-seeing, omniscient beings, fearsomely dangerous and powerful. Did he know, I asked, that the word dragon comes from the ancient Greek word meaning 'to see'?

'Questions, questions, questions,' he said. 'You have asked too many.' He shrugged in his eloquent way and smiled. 'Tell me of the Water Spirits in the West?'

'No-one believes in them now, but there are many stories of them in fairy tales and past legends.'

I told him of the Kelpies. They were water spirits of Scottish folklore. Mischievous and malignant spirits that tried to entice travellers into the water where they would be devoured. It was said that if anyone saw a Kelpie he or she would die by drowning. My friend liked this tale.

We reached a fork in the path. I wanted to go left on the path that switch-backed steeply through dense lichen-covered trees to a village on the crest of a ridge. I could see the pear shape of a stupa and a prayer flag fluttering where the path wound out of the trees far above on the ridge line. He said that it was time for us to part and he thanked me for my company. He warned me again about questions, then left with a soft wave of the hand. I felt strangely bereaved when he had gone and only much later did it occur to me that I had never asked his name, nor what he did. It seemed then that he had learnt far more about me without once asking a simple question . . .

I read the last page in the book with difficulty. Jimmy's spidery handwriting had become smudged by moisture and the book creased through being stuffed carelessly into the depths of his rucksack. I looked up towards the rock wall where Jimmy had gone in search of a waterfall. There was no sign of him. A thunderous boom echoed from the ice-fall at the head of the valley. Another soft puffy cloud of ice particles rose above the jumble of cliffs and crevasses. It was past noon, and the full heat of the sun was beginning to eat into the fragile icy glue that held the ice-fall together. I wrapped the exercise book in the Sainsbury's shopping bag and put it away in Jimmy's rucksack.

The stream meandered down into the meadow of sagebrush and flower-rimmed pools from a gravel ravine that cut into the hillside. The walls of the ravine grew above me as I walked carefully up the left bank, mud and screes leading me up to stepped tiers of rocky buttresses. It felt oppressive and danger-ous. I didn't like being hemmed in and kept glancing fearfully at the top of the walls on either side, half-expecting a sudden volley of rocks to appear as black dots in the open sky above. Eventually, as the rock walls crammed close together, I was forced to squeeze between jammed boulders at the edge of the stream which now rushed with greater fury. The water, under pressure from the constriction of what had become a granite gorge hardly wider than my shoulders, roared angrily in its furious descent. When forced to stand in it, I felt my legs being dragged away, as though gripped by two huge fists. Above the sound of the stream I heard a deeper sound, thrumming above me.

A huge chockstone jammed between the walls blocked my progress. At first I could find no way past and began to wonder what had happened to Jimmy. The stream leapt over the obstruction in a carefree shower of spray bursting out over the gorge below. I was soaked in seconds and began to shiver. The water was icy.

Feeling on either side, I realised there was no way up the edges. I was pressed against the chockstone, arms out-stretched, groping for gaps as the deafening deluge of melt-water blinded me. Something hit me painfully on my right shoulder. I glimpsed a black fist-sized rock spinning out into the torrent as I sat heavily on the bed of the stream still clutching at the water-smoothed rock. From my sitting position I was astonished to see the glitter of sunshine sparkling on a drizzle of mist at the back of the chockstone. Crouching in the stream, I grasped the base of the chockstone and ducked my head under the pounding cascade. There was a hollow space beneath the chockstone and rays of sunshine formed a golden shaft of light at the back of the recess. There was a way under and up the other side.

After tortuous wriggling, and some panicky coughs as I inhaled mouthfuls of icy water, I emerged from behind the chockstone blinking in the harsh sunlight. Standing slowly upright, I popped my head and shoulders into the sun and took in an unexpected sight.

10

Waterfall of Bones

Jimmy squatted on a large boulder examining a huge ibex horn. He was surrounded by towering rock walls, a full circle of rock sixty feet across, open only where I stood. I turned to look back down the gorge and saw the mountains on the other side of the glacier framed between vertical black walls only five feet apart.

'God Almighty!' I yelled at Jimmy, who looked up in surprise.

'Pretty good, eh?' He waved the horn in an expansive gesture, as if showing me round his recently inherited castle.

I clambered out from behind the rock and stood unsteadily atop the rock gazing at an eighty-foot column of water that descended like an icicle from the centre of the circle. A rainbow spray of mist could be seen where the stream plunged down from space in an unbroken column of seeming solid white. It fell free of the rock walls into the dead centre of a foaming pool which debouched into and over the top of the chockstone on which I stood.

'Bloody hell, I can't believe this.'

'Come over here,' Jimmy yelled above the roaring water, waving the ibex horn imperiously at me.

I scrambled cautiously round the pool on banks of grey

shingle. Jimmy sat on a boulder deeply embedded in gravel. I looked nervously above me. The boulder was a different colour from the surrounding walls. It seemed to be a completely different rock.

'Do you think that's a good idea?' I shouted.

'What?'

'Sitting there,' I yelled above the roar. 'That thing came from up there.'

Jimmy looked curiously at the boulder, then at the rock walls, and then nervously at the top of the cascade.

'Ah, so it did.' He hopped down from the rock and walked to where the walls bulged and formed a protective overhang. I squatted beside him, shivering.

'Amazing, isn't it?' Jimmy said, still holding the horn. 'You would never know it was there from outside. It's so deep in the cliff it is hidden. Bloody wild, eh?'

He was grinning manically, and his eyes glittered with excitement.

'Where did you find that?' I pointed to the horn.

'Oh yeah, I forgot.' He looked at the horn again as if he hadn't seen it before. 'There's loads of them. Come on, over here.' He set off in a crouching run, as if going into combat from a helicopter. I laughed and followed him slowly, wary of falling missiles. There would be none of the normal whistling, thrumming sounds of rockfall in here, I thought, not above the water – just thwack and you're dead. I began to hunch my shoulders and crouch over as the sense of danger lurked ominously above me.

'Look!' Jimmy pointed in a circle around him. He was standing in a graveyard of bleached bones. Shattered skulls and splintered rib and leg bones were strewn in a wide circle. Some skulls sported huge sets of distinct knobbly ibex horns. Smaller skulls showing bared canines were those of fox and possibly wolf. Mostly they were goat and sheep bones.

'Wow!' I kept looking from side to side. 'How did these get here?' And as I said it a chilling thought popped unpleasantly into my head. 'Oh shit! Jimmy,' I said, 'you don't think this is a bear's lair do you?'

His grin disappeared and for a moment he looked wildly round the beach area of the pool.

'No, can't be,' he muttered without conviction.

'Why not?'

'Well . . . um . . . tracks! There are no tracks.'

'They wouldn't show on this ground.' We had instinctively drawn closer, watching each other's back.

'How would it get in here?'

'Same way as we did.'

'Naw! It would be scared of the water.'

'Still doesn't explain these, though, does it?' I pointed to the bones.

'Well, I suppose not, but a bear couldn't drag these up behind that chockstone, and anyway they don't eat goats, do they?'

'I don't know,' I said dubiously, 'grizzlies are carnivorous. I reckon they would eat anything they could get hold of.'

'Still couldn't get them up here.'

'Avalanches,' I said, 'that's it – avalanches. They came from up there.' I pointed at the circle of blue sky above us. 'Look at the bones. Most of them are broken. They've come from above. Must have.'

The tension evaporated as the solution became clear and we laughed at each other's fearful expressions. Looking at the drift of bones and skulls I imagined the fearful rushing slide of an avalanche with the flock trapped in its grip. Looking up, I imagined the air full of tumbling, kicking goats swooping down in a spray of winter snow. The black specks of lammergeiers above the carnage would have coveted the twisted carcasses as the summer sun melted the banked snow. Circling high above the pool, the great birds would be uncertain of descending into the cramped grotto – peering red beady eyes down at the unattainable feast.

'Yes,' Jimmy was kneeling, sifting through the larger bones. 'Look at this one.' He held up a beautifully spiralled horn.

'What is it?'

'Dunno.' He turned it in his hand. It was spiralled like a double helix, gradually narrowing to a slender tip. 'Markhor, perhaps, though I'm not sure they live in these parts.'

'Like ibex, you mean?' I laughed and kicked a double-horned ibex skull to make my point.

'Well, I'm no expert.'

'You and Attar were yesterday morning,' I said with a grin.

'All right. I get the point, but . . .'

There was a sharp cracking sound, swiftly followed by a volley of reports. Jimmy held the horn protectively over his head as I dived painfully into the suspect goat-smelling shelter of the largest group of bones, both hands across the back of my head. I heard a high-pitched yelp and glanced over to see Jimmy crouched on his knees clutching the horn to his head. The impact sounds stopped exploding around us. Jimmy leapt to his feet, threw the markhor horn into the pool and lurched towards the chockstone.

'Come on,' he yelled, 'let's get the hell out of here. Quick!'

He jumped feet first into the gap and jammed. His head and shoulders protruded from the flow of water over the chockstone and wriggled furiously from side to side. I could see he was swearing. I began to giggle, and by the time I reached him I could barely control myself. The fear of another rockfall added a manic nervousness to my laughter. By the time Jimmy's head finally dropped beneath the water, mouthing inaudible obscenities, I was kneeling helplessly in the icy water feeling the hot rush of urine on my thigh.

We stumbled from the mouth of the gorge into the blistering heat of the sun. Our clothes steamed. I was still racked with giggling fits as we reached our lunch site. Wart Face and the beast were waiting for us. The beast snarled at me and cured me of the giggles. Wart Face scowled unpleasantly.

Both our rucksacks had been neatly re-packed and placed

against the rock pedestal. I glanced suspiciously at Wart Face who was talking urgently to Jimmy and wondered whether he had seen anything he liked when he had packed them. The stove hissed sharply as the water boiled over the pan and extinguished the flames. Tea leaves swirled amid the bubbling dark brown tea. Three cups were filled by Wart Face, and Jimmy and I poured some reviving warmth back into our steaming bodies.

'He says we'd better get a move on if we want to cross into Guligad Bamak tonight,' Jimmy said through a cloud of sweet-smelling tea vapours.

'I would have thought it best to wait until tomorrow,' I replied. 'Wait until early morning when it will be nice and frozen and safe.'

'He says there is a way to avoid any danger from the ice-fall.'

'Yes, well, his idea of what is or is not dangerous is pretty bloody suspect.'

'We can at least have a closer look,' Jimmy said. 'If we don't like it we can camp there and do it straight off in the morning.'

'I suppose it makes sense,' I said reluctantly, though I knew that it wouldn't matter what it looked like, Jimmy and Wart Face would go up and I would have to follow.

Jimmy stood up and spat tea leaves into the pond. I noticed that Wart Face and the beast hadn't bothered to wait for our decision and had set off towards the ice-fall walking in long heavy-booted strides. His hound loped like a wolf beside him, head down and forward, haunches low to the ground.

As I shouldered my pack I noticed it felt lighter. Jimmy was placing the exercise book in the zipped top pocket of his sack.

'That's nice of him,' he said, 'he's taken all of Attar's load out of my sack.'

'Yeah, he's taken mine as well,' I said. 'Probably doesn't think we are capable of carrying them.'

'Who cares,' Jimmy replied, hefting his sack into a comfortable position on his shoulders. 'By the way did you read that thing?'

'Yeah. I read it.'

'Well?'

'Oh, I liked it – most of it anyway. I liked the idea of the mountains as oceans, as moving. I've always thought that as well. But I wasn't too sure about the stories. You don't believe in them do you?'

'Why not? We believe in ideas that are just as strange.'

'Speak for yourself!' I said tartly. 'You won't find any skeletons in my cupboards.'

'Oh no? You were pretty religious a few years ago.'

'Ten years ago, in fact, and I'm not any more.'

'Yes, but you were once, and I'll bet it still lurks somewhere inside you. No-one truly stops believing.' He set off walking and I followed.

'Yes they do.'

'So, when one of those ice cliffs comes thundering down on top of you, are you saying you won't pray?'

'Yes. Well I hope not. I mean, you can't tell until it happens, can you?'

'Exactly. That's just my point.'

Hassan Ghyias was not a patient man. Nor was he violent. It was a strange thing that his ugliness made others think of him as dangerous and yet his silent manner was often mistaken for the sign of an untiringly patient man. Glancing at his dog, he allowed himself a rare smile and the thought, *but they are right to fear you dog. You are both ugly and violent. Even I do not trust your fear of me.*

The dog sensed his thoughts and looked inquiringly at his master. Its belly was hollow and aching with hunger, its mind beginning to boil with hatred. Only fear held it in check, but the hunger was eating away the fear.

'We will hunt soon,' the Hunter murmured as he stood and

shaded his eyes from the low evening sun, searching the hillside from which he had come. The dog snarled.

There was no sign of the two men. He had seen them reach the pass. *They would be safe coming down this side. There were no crevasses or ice cliffs to threaten them, only the darkness.* He sat down again and tended the stove. The dog snarled, baring its yellowed fangs. With blinding speed the Hunter cracked the dog across the nose and forehead with the shaft of an ice axe that he had ready for just such a moment.

The dog had known why he held the axe and had bided its time, waiting while the hot hungry hate built inside. The Hunter had been too fast; he was always too fast, though one day the dog would get him.

It sprang up and backwards at the blow, its jaws making a sharp clacking noise as they snapped shut on empty space where the Hunter's wrist had been. A sharp stone thudded into the side of its head between the ear and the eye. It ran from the man with a piercing yowl, its hate and hunger abruptly quenched by fear.

The Hunter poured tea and stared up the darkening valley. It was not that he was a silent man. True he spoke little and only when needed. That was the way of things. He was patient when he needed to be. Even the dog, on long stalking hunts, could be patient, stifling the slavering excited whines of hungry anticipation. If it was needed. Most talk, he had discovered, was unnecessary. Like fear, talk had a purpose, but everyone had too much of both.

The younger man, he thought, *he is interesting but he asks too many questions. He can control his fear, he did so on first meeting, and that was good. The other one is angry and full of fear.*

'I will leave tomorrow,' he said aloud. He had to kill something soon or he would be forced to kill the dog. The dog was useful, strong and fast in the hunt. Without the dog too many wounded beasts would have been lost. The food that the boys provided was no good for the dog. Hassan would hunt and leave the boys. Strange that he thought of them as children. They were old enough to be married, with many children of their own, but to him they seemed like empty children. They knew nothing. They needed him and others. *Like that fool of a cook who was interested only in his looks and his clothes*, he thought without malice. He knew what the younger boy, who was so full of questions and half-heard stories, wanted to know but he couldn't tell him. *He must find out for himself*, Hassan thought sadly, *and with luck he will know when to stop asking questions and step back from his search*.

There was a clattering of stones but even with his trained eyes he could not make them out in the gloom. He heard a murmur of voices, and then a loud shout of protest followed by the sound of an avalanche of stones. More shouts, and then he saw the pin-prick of yellow light bloom out from the dark shadow of the moraine bank ahead of him. Hassan re-lit the stove and placed the cooling pan of tea back on the ring of hissing blue flames.

They stumbled into the light of a small fire that the Hunter was feeding carefully with his dwindling stock of firewood. Shadows flickering across his face softened his features and, but for his brooding inescapable stare, he looked for a moment almost human, even kind.

Jimmy slumped on to his rucksack and hung his head wearily between his legs.

'What was it I said?' he asked in a low voice, 'Three hours, four at most. Jesus! We've been on the go for seven and a half hours since the waterfall.'

I collapsed beside him, too tired to laugh.

'Yeah, and you said I was fooled by the scale.'

'Can't be right all the time,' Jimmy admitted grudgingly.

'How big of you to admit it at last.'

It was hard to know which had been the worst part of the crossing. I thought that the lung-bursting race under the ice-fall was a good contender. It had felt as if I was running the hundred metres, except that it went uphill for so long that I had been unable to move faster than a stunned tortoise. The knee-deep waterlogged snow had reduced us to a staggering, mushy crawl.

I had tried to get angry, to work myself into an infuriated charge up the slope with the thought that, if they had listened to me just once and gone in the morning when it would have been frozen hard, there need not have been any of this agony. But I had been too exhausted to raise more than a flicker of indignation. Only when the slope on which I had been slumped, gasping for breath, shook with a terrifying rumble did I galvanise my legs into a last desperate rush. I had stared with horror at the plume of the ice-avalanche sweeping across my tracks fifty metres behind me. Then glanced for an instant at the leaning green wall of ice above me before the adrenalin hit, and I charged off after Jimmy, clawing and scrambling in the wet white mush, and uttering small high-pitched squeaks of pain and fear.

Jimmy had glanced down on hearing the avalanche. He must have seen me thrashing across the slope, a ludicrously puny stick-like silhouetted figure. By the time I caught him up at the col, Jimmy had the map out and was naming the peaks he could see rearing up in the late afternoon sunshine.

'Very phallic isn't it?' I said looking at the ice-sheathed wedge of Shivling's classic mountain shape.

'Yeah. It's Shiva's linga, that's what the name means.'

'Oh!'

I looked at the other side of the Gangotri glacier where three stupendous mountains stood with immense shields of golden granite dropping four thousand feet on the west side of their summits. Jimmy wittered on about Krishna's weapon and Shiva the destroyer while I lay back exhausted and stared at the sky waiting for him to shut up.

'. . . but this Indra bloke, he was the main man years ago in the ancient Aryan religions. He was a warrior god, you know – dead violent and he drank a lot.'

'Don't you think . . .'

'This Indra chappie . . .' Jimmy carried on regardless. '. . . what I liked about him was he used to specialise in slaughtering dragons. You see? God of weather, of rain, and dragon killer to boot. There are connections everywhere if you look for them.'

'Look,' I said firmly, 'don't you think we had better get on? I mean it's already taken us twice as long to get here as we thought it would.'

'We'll be okay. It's all downhill from now on.' He rummaged in his rucksack and pulled out a gas stove and pan. 'Let's have a brew and then go.' He handed the stove to me.

'And I suppose I have to make it, do I?'

'Yup, I made the last one.'

Jimmy turned to scan the vista of peaks ahead of him.

'All right then, if we have to talk about it,' I said as I dug a wind shelter in the snow for the stove. 'How come Shiva created the Ganges and yet Shivling isn't the source of the Ganges? The Bhagarathi river is as far as that map shows.'

'Well, that's true, but water from Shivling and all those hills feeds that river, don't they? And anyhow, there are other tributaries said to be the source. The Alaknanda, or the Yamuna, or whatever, it's not important. It's the myth that counts.'

'What myth?'

'It's not so much a myth as something the Hindus believe, especially the ones who worship Shiva,' Jimmy said. 'They reckon that Bhagarathi, the king I was telling you about, made some sacrifices and asked the Gods to let the Ganges come down from the heavens and they obliged. But Shiva, realising the river would be angry and would destroy the earth when it fell from the sky, stood on a mountain and caught the water in his hair and let it down slowly. Ganga, the river God, tried to destroy Shiva, but his hair was too dense and matted and she became tangled. So then he could let the river flow smoothly on to the earth . . .'

'That's it, is it?' I looked incredulously at Jimmy and then at the towering spire of Shivling. 'You believe that, do you?'

'No, no. I don't, but the Hindus do. You've got to admit it's a good story.'

'Yeah, well that's all it ever will be,' I said derisively.

'Maybe, maybe. You never know. There's nowt as queer as folk, as my pissed-up grandma used to say before she were beaten to death with a bottle of stout . . .'

'Oh shut up, you babbling idiot. Here, grab this tea and shut up.'

'See that peak straight ahead of us? Vasuki Parbat, it's called.'

I shaded my eyes. 'Which one?'

'The one poking out above that ridge, to the left and further back from the Bhagarathi's.'

'Oh, yeah. What about it?'

'It's named after the great water serpent god of the underworld . . .'

'SHUT UP!' I yelled. 'I don't want to know any more. Bloody hell, I think this water lark is going to your head.'

'Don't joke about it. There's more to it than you know.' Jimmy sank into a sullen silence.

It was certainly downhill, as Jimmy had said, but over horrendously broken ground and through a chaotic jumble of rock debris and boulders into a valley seemingly hotter and more arid then the one from which we had escaped. Jimmy had set off after me and dawdled on the way. It was only after darkness had descended that he caught me up.

'Is that you, Jimmy?'

'Who the hell else would it be?'

'Ah. Thank God for that.' I stepped from the shelter of a dark boulder to see Jimmy turning on his headtorch. 'I thought someone was following me. It's been with me for ages. Really creepy.'

'What do you mean?' Jimmy asked.

'It was a feeling, you know, a sense of someone in the

shadows when you can't see or hear them. It felt sort of threatening.'

'When did you first notice it, then?'

'A while back. When we got off the glacier proper and on to the top of that moraine bank. It was still quite light at the time, which seemed odd.'

'I know what you mean,' Jimmy said, looking around him. 'I've felt the same. I kept looking back, thinking someone was following. I thought perhaps you'd got lost and somehow ended up behind me.'

'No. I've been here nearly an hour waiting for you. Funny thing is that when I stopped, the feeling went away. You don't think this place is haunted?'

'Thought you didn't believe in ghosts?'

'Well, I don't really. But it's unnerving to . . .'

'You don't seem to believe in anything, but it is odd we should have the same feelings at the same place.'

'Hhmmm. Over-active imagination I expect. Comes from reading all that tripe of yours about spirits and gods and ghosts. Let's get on. I hope your ugly friend has got a torch or we'll never find him.'

I turned on my heel and stepped cautiously into the pool of light from my headtorch.

Suddenly Jimmy leapt on to my back with a blood curdling shriek.

'YARRRRRRRGGHH . . .' It echoed off the surrounding rock walls, mixed with the echoes of my horrified scream.

'God! You bastard!' I eventually blurted out, still clutching both palms to my chest. 'You vicious little twat!'

'I thought you didn't believe in ghosts?' Jimmy said through his laughter.

'Bugger off.' I turned and stalked away into the darkness, tripping over a rock almost immediately, which only increased Jimmy's glee. 'Come on,' I yelled, 'and don't do that again.'

'Boo!' Jimmy replied, snorting with laughter.

*

We sat silently drinking the Hunter's tea. Peering over the steaming rims of our mugs at shadows moving outside the circle of flickering firelight. Once we both jerked our heads up in alarm as one shadow took solid form and a gleam of reddish yellow shone briefly in the darkness. The Hunter's arm whipped out and there was a meaty thwacking sound, stones scrabbling and a mournful howl.

The dog retreated and lay in the shadows nearby, flat on its belly, forepaws stretched out and chin resting on its paws. Its nose wrinkled at faint odours drifting down from the yellow glow of firelight. The smell of food made its belly ache and saliva drooled in slimy strings from its jowls. It fixed its gaze on the dark silhouetted figure of the Hunter, waiting for its chance. Occasionally a deep rumbling growl shuddered through its clenched teeth.

The Hunter had cooked rice and dahl, and a thick stew of green and brown lentils, with beans that he added from his own supplies. He spiced it strongly with chili powder and dried tomatoes, and a handful of garlic cloves crudely crushed between his thumb and the blade of his knife so that there was a pungent bite to the bland mush. The rice was gluey and clumped into salty balls that the Hunter scooped up from the pan with his thumb and two fingers and dunked into the dahl. He squatted on his haunches with his baggy shalwar trousers tucked back between his calves and his knees and leant over the two pans to eat. He spilt nothing.

We sat opposite him on our sacks eating from plates with spoons, gulping tea to quench the burn of the chili, and gasping when we bit into whole cloves of barely crushed garlic. Though hungry, we ate slowly out of tiredness. All thoughts of ghosts were forgotten in the secure glow of the fire. Jimmy, for once, was quiet.

When the meal was finished we struggled clumsily with the tent. In the light of one weak torch the three carbon fibre poles appeared to be the same length until we had threaded them into the wrong sleeves and swore and fought to bow them into positions they would not fit. After a weary argument Jimmy left the task to me and went to talk to the Hunter in low murmurs. I began again, this time with systematic care.

'Hassan is leaving,' Jimmy said when he returned with two mugs of sweet tea.

'Why?'

'I'm not sure. He said he doesn't like this place, and something about the dog that I didn't understand.'

'What do you mean, he doesn't like it here?' I asked from inside my sleeping bag. 'Seems a bit vague, doesn't it?'

'Yeah. It does a bit. He had a queer look in his eye though, as if something was disturbing him. I asked him about dragons in the glaciers but he wouldn't let me finish; just snapped something at me and left.'

'Well, that I can understand.' I popped my head out of my bag and reached for the tea. 'You're taking this business a bit far you know. And as for a queer look to his eye, it's not bloody surprising. Most pathological maniacs do, you know.'

'How the hell are we going to carry all the extra gear over the Chirbas pass tomorrow without him?' Jimmy ignored the jibe.

'I was rather hoping for a rest day tomorrow, a little exploration, a wander around, you know.'

'Not a bad idea. We have far too much food and gas now, with both Attar and him gone.'

'Good, that settles it. We stay here until we have eaten so much that we can manage the loads.'

'No we won't. We haven't got that much time if we want to get back to Delhi and then head for Varanasi. We'll cross over the day after tomorrow and throw away what we don't need.'

'Did you pay Wart Face?'

'Hassan, you mean?' said Jimmy. 'Yes. He didn't want it at first. I think he thought he had let us down.'

'He has, but no doubt he got over his guilty feelings and accepted in the end.'

'Listen, Chris, give the guy a chance, will you,' Jimmy

snapped. 'You make no effort with these people. You just jump to conclusions without any good reason. At least I speak the language. You're damn near racist, for God's sake.'

'Oh, come off it!'

'No, you are,' Jimmy insisted vehemently. 'What has Hassan done against you, eh? Or any of the other people I talk to? Absolutely nothing, and yet you dismiss them out of hand, and everything they say.'

'Well, you listen to me, Jimmy. That bloke is bad news. I don't have to speak the language to know that. As you once said, it's all in the eyes, and that bloke's eyes terrify me. You're too mixed up in your stories to notice, but it is there, mate. Take my word for it, that guy spells trouble.'

'No, he just seems that way. I'll admit he's not good looking, and his dog sure doesn't help things' – I snorted contemptuously – 'but . . .' Jimmy continued, 'you haven't heard him talk. He knows things; stacks more than he'll tell me, but he has that aura about him. He's no native idiot, as you seem to think. He might be a hunter but he's also far more than that. I'm not sure what because he clams up for some reason, but of all the people I've talked to he is the only one who seems to know what I'm after. You though, you know nothing about him, you dislike him and distrust him and he knows it.'

'Okay, okay, spare me the lecture.' I held my hand up defensively. 'But I can't say I'm sorry to see him go, even if it does mean we have huge loads when we cross into Chirbas.'

'Fair enough, but I reckon you should lighten up your attitude. You can learn things here, good things. Things that can change your view on life, certainly on people.'

'I came here to climb, Jimmy,' I pointed out, 'and we've done precious little of that.'

'Not here you didn't. We came here to trek, remember, and visit Haridwar, and Varanasi. We're going to climb in Pakistan, not here. Anyway, it's far too late to climb now. The monsoon will be here any day.'

'We've had over two weeks of perfect weather, for God's sake, and we've done nothing.'

'Well, we couldn't have climbed anyway. We haven't got permission.'

'We could have sneaked one in on the sly.'

'And get caught? There are more liaison officers per square mile here than anywhere in the world! And if that happened there would be no coming back, would there?'

'Sod it!' I burrowed into my bag. 'Who said I wanted to come back. I could have done without this in the first place,' I muttered through the down bag, then reached out and fumbled with the headtorch hanging from the ceiling until the fading light flicked out.

11

The Tenant of
Guligad Bamak

The clouds filled the valley below our camp. It lapped at the
bank of moraines above the glacier and rolled back like the
chaos of a leaking washing machine. Occasional glimpses of
rubble appeared through rents in the cloud carpet as the weak
morning sun began to burn it away. I zipped up my polar
jacket against the frosty burn of the air. My breath left a
vapour trail and the wet ground between my legs steamed.
The sun hadn't reached us. A thin skim of hoar frost coated
the tent and Jimmy's snores rumbled from within. I burped a
cloud of vapour and the garlic of the night before repeated on
me.

There was no sign of the Hunter or his dog. The fire was a
small pile of damp ashes. I noticed he had left behind his
greasy rough blanket and the canvas bag that he carried
everywhere. By the time I had produced a pan of tea the sun
had struck the tent and the hoar frost was sliding off the
rounded dome of nylon in scratchy slivers of water crystals.

'Brew's on, Jimmy,' I yelled. There was no reply.

The temperature inversion was retreating into the darker
depths of the lower valley, revealing the glacier. A spine of
dirty grey ice, striped with the shadows of crevasses, formed a
pattern like scales on the back of an albino crocodile lying

half-submerged in a steep-sided wallow of mud. The valley walls rose steeply, dark where the morning sun hadn't reached and browny green where the soft light touched. It was very different from the previous valley. It reminded me of a remote Alpine valley I had walked up in Austria, but there were no pastures or stacked domes of dried summer hay. As far as I could see beyond the snout of the small glacier, the valley was entirely forested. The sides marched away from me in a series of overlapping ridges that stepped down from the mountain flanks where silky tendrils of morning cloud still clung in places to the upper branches of high pine trees. Some trees grew singly from rocky outcrops and stood out starkly, black and spiky.

The soft morning light gave great depth to the valley and I looked at ridges, in gradated shades of bluish grey, plunging into the shadows of the dark and forbidding valley floor. Above a huge open wedge of lightening blue sky lay an ominous opaque layer of silvery cloud. It was an innocent-looking nebulous streak across the sky but beneath it, in familiar snaking spirals, I recognised the signs of a weather front moving in. It appeared to be coming from the west.

'Hey Jimmy,' I shouted, 'the monsoon has arrived.'

There was a muttered curse before his dishevelled squinting head popped out of the tent door. He peered sleepily at the sky and shook his head. 'That's coming from the wrong direction, you idiot!'

'I know,' I grinned at him. 'I just wanted to wake you up since that's what you've done to me with your bloody snoring all night.'

'Thanks.'

'There's tea in the pan.'

He crawled out on his hands and knees in a tattered pair of black underpants. He possessed only one pair, he had claimed proudly. Black, he said, didn't show the dirt. One pair for two months. Judging by the way the rubber waistband showed through sweat-rotted gaps in the cotton, I couldn't see them lasting the distance.

He stood up stiffly, mug in one hand and the other in his underpants scratching furiously.

'Christ, I seem to have a colony of ants living in here.'

'I doubt any self-respecting ant would dare live there,' I said.

He put down his mug, pulled open the waistband and examined himself curiously. 'Well, there must be something,' he muttered. 'Feels like a herd of lobsters.'

'Maybe a wash might help,' I suggested. He gave me a shocked look.

'No way.' He thrust his hand back into the fray and scratched furiously. 'That would be cheating.'

'Your friend seems to have gone walkabout. His blanket and stuff are still here. I thought he'd gone once you paid him off?'

'Not in the dark,' he replied as he examined a specimen from his underpants. 'He's probably trying to beat his dog to death. Did you hear it last night? Sounded like the Hound of the Baskervilles.'

'I think it had a go at Hassan.'

'Maybe it's dragged him off and eaten him.' Jimmy laughed.

At that moment Hassan appeared. So suddenly did he appear it was as if he had materialised from the air. One moment we were talking, the next Hassan was standing quietly with his hell hound submissively at his feet. He nodded curtly at us and said something to Jimmy. It was then that I noticed the blood. He held his right forearm protectively across his chest. Blood dripped on to the faded grey of his baggy trousers. The dog sniffed the fresh blood smells appreciatively, its eyes rolling up in their sockets to glance furtively at its master as its nose twitched.

A fearful laceration extended from elbow to just short of the wrist. It seemed as if the whole soft underside of his forearm had been laid open. A purple sausage of exposed muscle bulged out along the line of the gaping wound. I noticed that a thin length of twine had been tied tightly around the dog's muzzle. Blood matted the fur behind one ear but I couldn't see a wound.

The man held a bone in his other hand and was pointing it in the direction from which he had come. He spoke rapidly to Jimmy, gesticulating with the bone. It was a large bone and curiously familiar. I felt a shiver tingle up my back as I realised what it reminded me of. Jimmy said something urgently and pointed to the man's arm, stepping forward as he did so. The dog rose from its belly into a crouch and a menacing growl reverberated from its chest. The man barked at the dog which immediately laid its ears back, ducking its head low to the ground but staying in the crouch, ready to spring. Even with its jaws tied I took an involuntary step back.

'Get the first aid kit,' Jimmy said curtly. 'I'm going to treat him whether he likes it or not.'

I rummaged in the tent until I found the plastic shopping bag full of bandages and medicines. I could hear a heated argument between Jimmy and Hassan. When I emerged I found that the dog had crept away to a discreet distance while Jimmy and the Hunter sat beside the stove. Vapour steamed from the pan as Jimmy re-heated the tea.

'I suppose it was the dog?' I handed Jimmy the bag.

'Yeah,' Jimmy replied. 'Last night, when we heard all that barking. He says he found a man, a dead man, up the hillside from the camp.'

'You *what*?'

'He's found a skeleton.' Jimmy looked at Hassan. 'And that's its thigh bone, I think!'

I looked at Hassan holding his injured arm with the femur resting in his lap. The dog was also staring at the bone.

'Apparently he followed the dog, thinking it had detected some game, and found it chewing away on that thing.' Jimmy upended the bag and scrabbled among the contents until he found what he needed. 'Obviously the dog didn't like having it taken off him.'

'No, I can see that,' I said queasily inspecting the wound. Hassan showed no sign of pain or discomfort. He held the arm out towards me as I squatted by his side. 'It needs stitches.'

'I know,' Jimmy answered. 'The problem is I've got these adhesive stitches, and I've got thread and stitching needles, but no anaesthetic.'

'Well, use the plaster things then.'

'I don't think they will be good enough and if we don't close that wound he's going to be in deep trouble.'

'He might be anyway if that thing is rabid.' I eyed the dog suspiciously. 'Why doesn't he shoot the beast? I would.'

Jimmy spoke to Hassan, who nodded curtly.

'Right, Chris, get some water on the boil and we'll try to sort this out. He says I can stitch it though he doesn't seem too keen.'

'Don't blame him.'

'Oh, I don't think it's the pain he's bothered about. He says it will mend by itself. He reckons he has some potions or powder or something that would do it.'

'Look, even if we clean and stitch it I reckon he'll be lucky not to get it infected.' I rattled a few pill boxes lying on the grass. 'He'll need antibiotics.'

'No, he won't take pills. He thinks they are bad for some reason.'

Hassan watched the two men curiously. *I will go*, he thought, *when they have finished with me*. He looked down the forested valley, and then at the dog. It cowered under his gaze. He knew there would be good hunting in the forests. It had the look of land that was unvisited. The hunting would be easy if he could shoot with his bad arm, and the dog could be controlled.

The fearful one flinched as the hot salted water was poured

on to his wound. Hassan remained motionless, almost unaware of what they were doing. He gazed into the dark valley, looking for the secret places where the animals would be. There would be tracks near the river leading back into the wooded hills. The dog would follow well. It would be keen, even with its jaws tied shut. He had often tied the dog on the trail, to keep it silent.

He watched impassively as Jimmy clumsily sewed the first stitch with the fine curved needle and thin dissolving thread. He glanced at Hassan's face, expecting pain, but was met with a blank indifference. For a moment he locked eyes with the Hunter, suddenly frozen by the dark unnerving stare, then looked away. The detached giddy feeling washed over him again as it had on first meeting at Gaumukh. It seemed as if momentarily he had been overwhelmed with a bout of vertigo, as if he were perched on the edge of an endless fall, fighting the lightheaded urge to let go into a vertiginous swoop of space with the lurching stomach of acceleration and a mind empty of fear, utterly relaxed, uncaring . . .

He shook his head and the Hunter smiled to himself. *The boy was not scared*, he thought, *he sees it and is not scared because he doesn't know what he is seeing*.

Jimmy inserted the needle again.

'Are you okay?' I asked.

'Yes,' Jimmy said, shaking his head again. 'Yes, I'm fine. Just felt a bit dizzy, that's all.'

I gazed at the half-closed wound. 'It's making me feel pretty ill, just looking at it.'

When Jimmy had finished, the Hunter stood up and called the dog. It skulked over reluctantly and crouched shivering at his feet. The Hunter looked curiously at the stitches in his arm, as if he were unsure how they got there. When Jimmy approached with a bandage, he shook his head. He bent down and picked up the thigh bone. The dog lifted its head, following the bone with hungry eyes. Pointing behind him, he said something to Jimmy and then handed him the bone. Jimmy accepted it gingerly, holding the stem fastidiously between finger and thumb. And with that the Hunter left, pausing only to sling the rifle in its greased cloth across his shoulder and pick up the long-strapped canvas bag and rolled blanket. The dog followed at a respectful distance until the two had dwindled into specks amid the moraines.

'Weird,' Jimmy said, watching them disappear from view. 'Strange bloke.' I noticed the pallor that had come over his face as he stitched was fading, but he kept shaking his head as if an insect was bothering him.

'You don't look too good to me,' I said.

'He was weird, wasn't he?' Jimmy ignored my concern for him. 'Did you notice a strange aura about him ... not charisma, something more than that, as if he had his own atmosphere, a sort of power around him. Did you notice?'

'I didn't trust him nor did Attar.'

'Oh, Attar noticed,' Jimmy said. 'He knew it straight away. You could see it in his eyes. He would never meet eyes with Hassan, always kept them averted.'

'That's fear, nothing else.'

'No, it was more than that. I don't know what but there was definitely something there. You could almost feel it.'

'Well, whatever.' I was glad the man had gone and wasn't for elevating him to some god-like status. 'What do we do about this?' I pointed to the bone.

'Let's go and have a look.'

Jimmy stood up and reached into the tent for his trousers and a shirt.

He lay in the shadow of three huge boulders on a flat table of knee-high granite. The boulders formed a crude shelter. Two on either side of the shelf were capped with the third that sat atop them, forming a bulging roof. Water dripped from the lip of the roof on to the shelf below. Smears of ice glinted in the tight joins between the boulders. A small patch of dirty old winter snow was banked behind the skeleton. The rock seemed unnaturally dark for granite. Lichens spread in patches mingling with the flecks of dark crystals in the granite.

He was on his back, the remains of a rotting blanket draped around one shoulder and along the length of his body nearest the back wall of the rocky recess. There was a damp musty smell in the air. The folds of the blanket had a liquefied appearance as if soaked with the slime of his decomposing flesh. Yet the bones were picked clean. There was no smell of putrefaction.

The skull was thrown back and sideways from the neck so that, as he lay there, he appeared to view the scene outside his chosen resting place with a lonely imploring gaze. The blank eye sockets and the ragged triangular hole of his nose gave him a disturbingly poignant expression. His jaw hung open, slackly askew, so the rictus grin of his shattered teeth seemed peculiarly comic, as if he were laughing when he died. I half-expected him to utter some compelling shriek of laughter.

His right arm emerged from the edge of the blanket in sticks of white bone, lumpy-knuckled at the elbow where they had fallen apart with the loss of the skin and muscle. The forearm lay separated from the upper arm and at the wrist it fragmented into a mess of bony nodules, dislocated knuckles and thin twiggy finger bones that seemed to grasp the hem of the blanket. The dog had torn the thigh bone free from the last grip of the skeletal hand, scattering the joints and finger ends. Where the shelf ended his left leg hung over the edge covered by the blanket. His lower right leg lay in a mess of tibia, fibia and broken-up foot bones below the shelf. It had been wrenched from under the protective shroud of the blanket when the dog had savaged the thigh bone free. A curved scoop of pelvis jutted out and there was a gaping hole in the collapsed midriff showing the stacked vertebral blocks of the spine; an exposed column of bone flecked with brown tendrils of corrupted flesh.

Jimmy leant forward and carefully replaced the thigh bone

retrieved by the Hunter. He bent down on one knee and gently collected the scattered remains of the foot and lower leg, placing each piece by the thigh bone. When he was satisfied he had found all the bones he picked a wet fold of blanket from the shelf and draped it over the exposed bones, covering the obscene hole of the midriff. He stood up, wiping his hands on the front of his shorts. We had said nothing since leaving the camp. Silently following the Hunter's directions, we had picked our way cautiously up an old stream bed, surrounded by oppressive walls of tottering boulders paralysed into unstable balance when the waters had disappeared. Where the skeleton lay the shelter of boulders abutted a steep overhanging wall of dank granite. There was a bleak aura of dungeons in the dark, oppressively shadowed niche.

Jimmy's face had a frozen expression as he scrambled over the boulders leading out of the stream bed and up to the niche, but his eyes had an odd glittery excited look when he turned to watch my progress.

I felt guilty, standing there in the shadows, like a voyeur with a two-way mirror staring at the secret nakedness of unsuspecting lovers. The skull seemed to stare accusingly at me as if demanding what right I had to gaze at its pathetic exposed bones. I looked away, down into the sunlit forested valley. I shivered. It was cold in the shadows and the sight of the sunshine below invited me to leave. A familiar tingle bubbled up my spine. I remembered Harry kicking my hands away and refusing to let me out of the grave, and the hollow knock as I fell back on to the exposed coffin lid.

'What on earth was he doing up here?' Jimmy asked.

'What?'

'Well, look at him. Barefoot, dressed in a blanket, and that's it.' Jimmy was searching around the skeleton. 'That's all he had.'

'So?' I wanted to leave. 'He was probably a holy man. Come on, let's leave him in peace.'

'At sixteen and a half thousand feet?' Jimmy looked vexed.

'Why did he come here to die? I mean, who would wander around up here dressed in a blanket and nothing else? Doesn't make sense.'

'He probably got caught out,' I said looking reluctantly at the laughing skull. 'He was probably a hermit or something like that and just got caught out. You know how it is, the weather changes, he gets lost and dies of exposure.'

'I don't know.' Jimmy kept staring at the skeleton. 'I mean, this is way off the track. Even if he crossed the pass he wouldn't be up here, would he?'

'He would if he was looking for shelter, for a cave, or something similar.' I turned away to leave. 'Anyway, if he had been caught in a full bore white-out he wouldn't have known where he was going.'

Jimmy shook his head vehemently. 'No way would he have been able to cross the pass in bare feet. He must have come up here deliberately.'

'What if he did? It doesn't really matter now, does it?' I said with annoyance. 'These guys are well weird. You don't know what he might have done. He's dead now, so why not leave him be.'

To my horror, Jimmy settled himself down cross-legged on the shelf and pulled out the tattered exercise book from his jacket pocket. He faced the valley with the bony remains laid out behind him.

'What are you doing?' I asked incredulously.

'Oh, nothing.' He was looking at me with a strangely distant gaze. 'I'm going to stay here a while.'

'It's a bit out of order, isn't it?'

'Why?'

'Come off it, Jimmy! If you can't see it I'm not going to tell you.' I turned and began to scramble back to the stream. I heard him laugh, a familiar and irritating snigger that he let out when he knew he had wound me up. I clamped my lips tight shut, determined not to respond with a shouted angry swear word that would make him chortle with delight. The warm touch of the sun as I emerged from the stream bed chased the lurking shivers from my back and I ran down the scree-slope in long sliding strides to where the tent bathed in sun above the glacier.

The Hunter reached the edge of the moraines. Below him he could see the dirty snout of the glacier and the spurting torrent of meltwater boiling out into a wide pan of fine gravel and grey mud. Sunlight sparkled on the dancing wavelets rushing down the valley floor and motes of silver seemed to glint on the surface of the pan as the sun mirrored off glittering scales of mica in the grey mud.

There was an easy way down the moraine bank to the edge of the glacier stream. The dog had bounded down from boulder to boulder, stopping occasionally to worry at the twine tied round its muzzle. The Hunter followed carefully. He walked with effortless casual strides yet already his body had tensed and his senses become fully alert. The hunt had started, and the dog, recognising the change, could barely restrain its excitement. It stood on the mud bank on stiff legs with its coat bristling up and its eyes fixed on the Hunter's slow descent. It nodded its muzzle in a futile attempt to bark and then swung round and began quartering the area of mud and gravel for some scent of quarry.

The tree line came almost to the water's edge. A thin open strip of grass, wild flowers and sagebrush ran between trees and water. The Hunter walked on this border as the dog searched the water's edge. He kept his eyes on the tree line, alert for signs of an animal passing from tree to water. Half a mile from the snout the mud flats ran out to be replaced by water-rounded boulders and a steep overhung earth bank.

At a bend in the river a large tree had fallen across the grassy border. Its topmost branches hung out over the churning waters and a tangle of broken branches along the trunk barred further progress downstream. The Hunter turned and headed into the shadows of the trees, flicking his hand at the dog which reluctantly came to heel and followed in a low wolfish prowl; its flanks quivered with excitement. As the Hunter ducked under the first low branches he unslung the rifle and with a smooth one-armed motion slid off the greasy cloth and stuffed it into the bag draped across his shoulder.

The goat was an old animal. It limped heavily, holding its right foreleg clear of the ground. It knew the Hunter was coming. It had smelt the odour of him on wafts of icy cold air billowing up the valley walls from the river. It had also smelt the rank canine stink of the dog. As it hobbled into a clearing the sharp stench of them reached it again, but it was too exhausted to flee. Its rib bones protruded in pathetic racks from its flanks where the hair had fallen away. It turned rheumy eyes in the direction of the scent and lowered its massive horns in a weak gesture of defiance. It was barely able to lift its heavy head back up to scan the land in which it had struggled so long to survive.

A tall pine rose straight up from the two large boulders in the centre of the clearing which was perched on a rocky shoulder jutting from the spine of a wooded ridge that dropped into the valley. The goat had struggled up through stands of fir and spruce, its hooves scratching on the stony forest floor where stunted pale-leafed plants stretched for the sunlight above the canopy.

There was a clear view of frosty sunlit peaks at the head of the valley and the sinuous track of the striped grey glacier carving down from the snows. The air was redolent with the scent of sun-heated pine needles and the distant hints of lavender and burnt-out sagebrush and sand dust wafted from distant alpine meadow lands. The goat raised its head to the gentle wind coming down the valley. Its nostrils dilated, sucking in a last flood of harsh cold mountain memories.

The shot crashed round the high valley walls and the goat was jerked back on to its hind legs. For a moment it tried feebly to push itself up before a sudden snort of blood gushed from its quivering nostrils and it folded gently forward and laid its heavy head on to its forelegs.

The Hunter laid his rifle alongside the goat's body. The dog edged towards the blood-spattered snout until a harsh command urged it back.

A poor kill, he thought, *but enough*. He pulled the hind legs apart by standing on one hoof and pushing the other away with his hand to keep the skin of the groin tight. Reaching down with his other hand, he pressed hard down on the lower belly and a jet of yellow urine spurted from the goat's bearded penis. The carcass made a groaning sound and blood gurgled through the tight-clenched teeth. With a deft stroke of the blade he cut from anus to ribcage and pulled the intestines from the steaming cavity in a neat sac of unbroken membrane. He tossed the grey-blue veined mass to the dog which pawed frantically at the twine round its nose, driven almost to distraction by the stench of bloody offal.

When the carcass had been skinned and jointed, carefully wrapped in hessian sacking and stored in the canvas bag, he cut the twine, pressing a heavy foot on to the dog's head to prevent another bite.

The Hunter sat by the pine tree watching the dog gulp the mess of pine needle-coated guts from the bloodied earth. He gazed up the valley at the distant moraine bank. A minute dot of colour amid the grey rocks showed where the camp was located. He thought of the young man and the skeleton man under the shadow of the boulders. For a moment he wondered whether the boy would recognise himself in the blanketed bones and then he dismissed all thought of them from his mind. He would never recall them again.

12

Naming the Moon

It was a bare room. A large curtainless sash window let in the stark flat light of a misty wet morning. I was staring across the diagonal of the room at damp grey serried rooftops, a landscape of red bricks, sooted black, and a forest of cracked chimney pots. A thin gauze of mist hung over the rooftops and rain ran in trickles down the window pane. In the foreground a white-sheeted double bed dominated the room. A figure stood beyond the bed staring out of the window. There was no colour. I seemed to be in a photograph. I wanted to get out.

Alice lay on the bed. At least I thought it was Alice, but I couldn't talk to her and she didn't seem to notice me. She was naked and very lovely. She lay on the bed with her back propped against a soiled grey pillow. A tangle of sheet like a discarded shroud was draped across her belly. Her legs were crossed, feet tucked under her thighs and there was a hint of wispy black peeping from beneath the edge of the sheet where it crossed her loins.

She seemed overcome with sadness. Perhaps it was the black and white, the shadows and contrast of the grim room with its flat light and rain-streaked window pane. It was the sort of window that would always stick, jammed shut by the glue of too much paint and wooden frames warped by

173

continual damp. The paint was flecked with sooty dust in the corners of the joints and dribbles of hardened gloss ran like white syrup on to the sill.

I tried to wave to her but I couldn't feel my arm, and anyhow she wasn't looking. She ran her fingers through her hair, using them as a comb as she pushed back the long straight dark locks into a pile above her forehead. She wore a bracelet on her ankle that I had never seen before and there was a white band on her finger where a ring had been. Her eyes were wide dark pools and something long and spiralled seemed to uncoil in my stomach as she looked at me. She did not see me. I didn't think it possible that her eyes could be sadder.

A bare light bulb hung on an old worn three-ply flex from a jagged hole in the plaster of the ceiling. On the wall by the window light rectangular shadows mirrored the wood lines that separated the panes of glass. A crack ran waist-high across the wall. I expected to see cockroaches skittering across the bare concrete floor with busy antennae waving for a scent of food.

When I looked at her again, Alice had dropped her arm but was still staring through me. Her breasts were heavy languid curves, stark white on top and black shadowed beneath each swell. Her nipples stood erect from wide dark aureola. I wanted to reach out and cup a breast in my hand and felt myself harden. I wondered if she would feel it. I couldn't reach her and softened.

I looked at her face and saw a change. She wore eye-liner drawn thick and dark in a rising thinning line from the outside edge of each upper eyelid. It accentuated her cheek bones and gave her an alien appearance. It looked as if she had oiled her long black hair.

Alice never wore mascara, or an ankle bracelet. Her nipples never stood proud like that; we had laughed that no amount of kissing would suck them out of their concave shape. And her breasts were small and upturned not hung heavily down like these. Where had her friz of golden auburn hair gone? The sheen of colour through which I had looked at the rain coming in from the moors above Derwentwater was now oiled black slickness. *But that is Alice, I know it is. I would know her anywhere. Why has she changed everything? What's going on?*

She rolled on to her side and the sheet slid off her hip. There were stains on the sheet. I saw a pair of leather shoes beneath the window. Men's brogues with pin-hole patterns on the toes. There was a tie on the end of the bed and a black sock. They hadn't been there before.

Alice moved again, and I glanced at her, then back at the shoes. They were gone. A man stood by the window looking out at the rain. He wore black shoes and pair of black jeans. His naked torso was muscular, like that of a dancer. There was a white scar running diagonally from shoulder blade to belted waist. His hair was matted into tangled dreadlocks. *He would smell foul*, I thought, *if I could smell*. It would be an unwashed acrid stench of sweat and there would be the faint odour of fear in the room.

He held the brogues in his hand and turned to look at Alice whose back was to him. He took in the curve of her buttocks and thigh, her feet and calves drawn up under her, her spine arched over in foetal curl and her face buried in the sheet, a swathe of dark hair spreading out from her head like matted blood. I knew the room would have the fetid fishy bouquet of sex, of mixed juices spilled. I saw tiny beads of perspiration dappled across Alice's brow and the glint of moisture on the downy hair of her upper lip. I strained to get into the picture but a smothering soft wall held me back.

The man smiled as he stared at her and I tried to cry out. I recognised his face – the scar and the wart and the sneering contemptuous expression, and I looked at where he was staring. At the junction of her upper thighs where a dark shadow nestled. I heard a deep canine growl and saw Alice flinch, and a spasm of shivers rippled across her haunches . . .

*

'Are you all right?' I heard Jimmy's voice muted in the darkness. I felt his hand pushing against my shoulder and struggled to reach the surface. It was dark and I was held back, my heart was pounding as I felt panic building. I wrestled with the soft clinging walls that sheathed my head and shoulders and I heard Jimmy laugh. A gush of icy air stung my face as he pulled open my sleeping bag.

'Hey! Calm down,' he said. 'You've been dreaming.'

'What?'

'You were dreaming and talking in your sleep.'

'Oh. Right.' I sat up, bare-chested in the icy wind, and rubbed my eyes. We were bathed in a silvery light that made everything appear to have a leathery texture. I looked around. Jimmy lay beside me in his bag. Beyond him a silver sweep of snow curved into the distance to be swallowed by an arch of black night studded with stars. Our nest was a hole in the snow six feet long by four deep and just enough to squeeze us in side by side.

'Good God. I'd forgotten where we were.'

'I know,' Jimmy said. 'You've kept me awake with all your chatter.'

'Sorry.'

'It's okay. I couldn't sleep anyway. I should have taken those pills you had. I've been awake for ages, watching the stars.'

'Oh,' I replied until a frightening thought occurred. 'Was I really sleep-talking?'

'Yup.'

'What did I say.'

'Nothing I could understand but it sounded interesting. In fact it sounded suspiciously like a wet dream to me.' He said it with a mischievous grin. I looked at him carefully. *Had I said her name*, I wondered. *Does he know?* If he did he gave nothing away except a trace of a smirk from the cowl of the bag.

Chris, you're a fool mate, he thought, *as if I didn't already know!* Jimmy had listened to the increasingly frantic fight with the down bag and the occasional muffled shout. He heard 'Alice' only once in a sort of strangled cry. When it seemed that Chris might tear the bag he had called his name and broken the dream.

This place where they had chosen to sleep was serene and aloof from the world they came from. It would have been easy to talk so far removed from home, so isolated, but Chris had kept silent. *Why? Alice had told him long ago!*

Jimmy shuffled up into a sitting position with his back against his rucksack, insulating him from the icy touch of their snow-walled lidless coffin. He heard Chris fumble with the cooking pot and stove. There was a whoomph of ignition behind him and then a faint blue light and the hiss of gas.

He looked across the curve of the col on which they had bivouacked. They were facing the way they would descend in the morning. The snow gleamed in the moonlight a bright silver hanging in the black horizon of the sky. He had lain for hours watching the night sky bloom. He loved these still moments when the mountains revealed themselves in silent understatement.

The intense calm and striking beauty conflicted with his knowledge of their meaningless savagery. It was strange the way he anthropomorphised mountains and never animals. They of all things seemed to have souls, to have an infinitely deep slow pulse of life in them. He thought of the stars and the planets in this way and sometimes fancied he could feel the mountain lifting inexorably into the sky.

He had counted four shooting stars firing across the night. *What is it they say about them? A great man has died when they appear, or has been born . . . What did it matter?* The atmosphere was so clear that the stars shone with an astonishing vividness and he felt he could reach out and touch them.

How many stars could he see at one glance? A hundred thousand million? There must be life out there. It is a mathematical certainty.

He thought of Titan, the largest moon of the ringed planet, Saturn. The rings consisted of orbiting boulders, snowballs and dust circling in layered rings around the immense planet. Snowballs drifting in the icy blackness of space. He liked the notion of ice in space, water, the element of the water people.

Of the many moons of Saturn only Titan has the potential for life. The other moons are too small to maintain a stable atmosphere, including a small moon called Tethys. Seven hundred miles across of solid ice. He smiled at the name. Tethys was the ancient sea from which the mountains had been born. Tethys hangs near Titan, on which life would one day briefly flower. He searched the night sky for Saturn but knew he wouldn't find it. He had never managed to remember the positions of stars and planets. To know they were there seemed to be enough.

'Here,' Chris said, passing him a steaming mug. 'Careful! It's very full and very hot.'

'Thanks.'

They drank in silence, shoulder to shoulder, blowing across the hot vapour of their mugs.

'Do you know where Saturn is?' Jimmy asked after a while.

'Haven't the foggiest. Why?'

Jimmy told him about the rings and the moons, and Tethys and Titan.

'So why do they reckon Titan will eventually have life, then? Or is this another of your barmy water theories?' Chris said when he'd finished.

'No. It's got nothing to do with water. Well not that much,' Jimmy replied. 'You see, they've discovered Titan has an atmosphere.'

'Who's they? And so what – lots of planets have atmospheres.'

'They don't actually, and "they" are the space lot, the NASA scientists. When the two Voyager space crafts went past Saturn they took samples and pictures and stuff. Anyway, Titan has an atmosphere, right. It's mostly made of methane but it also has other things in it. I can't remember their names, but some of them are the essential building blocks for life. They reckon that some of the molecules are the same as those that form compounds in DNA. And DNA is the number one honcho for getting us where we are today.'

'How do you mean?'

'Well, DNA is the basis of life. Ergo, Titan has not only an atmosphere but also the potential to produce life, see?'

'Yeah, well, so do you, but that doesn't mean you will, and anyway, if that's the case, why didn't they find life forms?'

'Ah! Now that's the interesting bit. You see they reckon Titan is in the same chemical stage as we were before life formed. The problem is that, firstly, Titan is too cold, and secondly there isn't any water.'

'Right,' Chris said resignedly, 'I was wondering when water was going to come into it.'

'No listen,' Jimmy said, 'this molecule, what's it called . . . hydrogen con . . . hydrogen something. Hydrogen cyanide, yes that's it, hydrogen cyanide.'

'Yes . . .'

'Yes, right, this is the stuff that can form something else and then form DNA. Amino acids come from it, and they were in the primaeval soup from which we came. But you can only make these acids from hydrogen cyanide if you have WATER!' He said it with a grin and a triumphal sweep of his arm, as if the stars were about to applaud him.

'Brilliant!' Chris said sarcastically. 'Yup, bravo. Super! You seem to have forgotten that you said there is no water on Titan so that seems to rather stuff the old extraterrestrial life a . . .'

'No, no. Hang on.' He had an irritating expression on his face. 'If you remembered that Water People bit I wrote, and if you had bothered to take any notice and not been so cynical you would remember the little lesson in cosmology I put in it. You know, the bit about the sun cooling down, running out of fuel, exploding into a huge red giant and so on. Well, in doing that it will annihilate the inner planets, us included, but it will warm up Titan. Water will be released and, Hey Presto! So there will be life. Good, heh?'

Chris was intrigued. 'I wonder whether we'll be capable of colonising Titan by the time that happens.'

'I doubt it somehow,' Jimmy laughed. 'It won't happen for another six billion years and I doubt humanity will be around by then. And anyway, it wouldn't be much use because the sun will collapse again into a white dwarf and Titan will refreeze and that will be the end of that.'

'Oh, how sad. You just get all the million-to-one ingredients together and thrash away producing life and then poof someone turns the lights out.'

'I know,' Jimmy laughed, 'life's a bitch.'

We were silent for a while, looking out at the measureless sweep of the sky. A chill wind began to sweep the col and we huddled down into our bags, lying flat on our backs with just nose and eyes exposed.

'What time is it?' I asked.

Jimmy peered at his watch. 'Just after three.'

'Is that luminous?'

'No. I can read it by the moon. It looks stunning tonight doesn't it?'

'Sure does,' I said. 'And the weather looks as if it's settled down again.'

'We should be down in Gangotri tomorrow if all goes well,' Jimmy muttered. 'It was a good crack, going into Guligad, wasn't it.'

'It was certainly an experience to remember,' I said, thinking of Attar, and the skeleton, and the wounded Hunter. 'It's good to get away from Hassan anyway. That bloody skeleton gave me the creeps last night.'

'I thought it was the best bit, actually,' Jimmy said sleepily. 'Still can't figure that one out.'

It was one of those endless timeless nights when sleep didn't come and we seemed to drift through the night sky above as it wheeled its dazzling jewels across the infinite black silence of the universe. Our breath hung in frosty clouds until zephyrs of dawn wind blew it apart.

I remembered all the other mountain nights we had spent together and felt that this one was the finest. All those hours spent huddled without sleeping bags shivering through the coldest hours of a blue black dawn, or flinching from the thunderous explosions of Alpine storms, the rock ridges aflame with lightning and the sulphurous cordite stench drifting in the shattered air. There had been standing bivouacs on cramped ledges with the soft powder building between us and the rock walls threatening to push us off, and comfortable organised bivouacs with food and sleeping bags and a quiet cold night with the same stars wheeling in a different hemisphere.

It was the serenity of this night that seduced me, and the wonder in Jimmy's words that almost had me believing him as he told me his stories while stretched out on his back, staring into the future strewn across the sky, speaking in a hushed voice as if apprehensive of retribution, pausing occasionally to catch his train of thought, and letting the awesome silence of the night fill the vacuum.

'It's never really silent you know,' he said.

'I know,' I said after a long pause. 'Never still either.'

'No. I meant space.' He waited, as if trying to catch the sound of it. 'They have radio telescopes or dishes, or whatever they are, that hear a constant faint sound of radio waves coming from all areas of the universe. They seem to think it is the sound of the Big Bang still echoing back to us from that initial explosion. Weird, isn't it.'

I said nothing. Looking at the stars, it was impossible to imagine that first stupendous fireball of creation, or believe that it could still be heard. A faint hiss, a whisper from the universe, a ten-thousand-million-year-old aside still reverberating through the vaulted stars. And later, as the moon waned in brilliance, I asked Jimmy if he knew the names of the seas on the moon but there was no reply. Sleep had snared him, and I gazed alone at the shadowed seas on the face of the moon that water had never filled.

The names told of the mesmeric power of our lifeless moon, touched the nerve of wonder we have when we see it in full glory hanging precariously, as if about to fall, above our tiny world. The Sea of Rains, and the Sea of Clouds, the seas of Moisture, Vapours and of Nectar on a land without atmosphere. There was the Bay of Rainbows where the spectrum never glowed and '*Lacus Somniorum*', the Lake of Dreams which was for ever dry. The seas of Tranquillity, Serenity, Fertility and Ingenuity where such things would never be sensed. There was a place called Hell and the Lake of Death. As it rolled heavily down from its zenith I wondered who had named those shadows on the surface with such gentle grace. They struck a chord of hope in me every time I looked upon the face of the moon, and, as if the moon were drawing me to it, the faint quivering unease that Jimmy might be right crept into my mind.

Atmospheric tides, currents of air and waves of wind; it was striking to realise how we perceive so many things in terms of fluidity. Even the moon with its empty arid seas and windless surface has the consolation of dragging our seas back and forth in eternal tides that lap nearly 80 per cent of our world.

I shivered again, despite being warm, and remembered the sounds of footsteps circling the tent on our last night in Guligad, and Jimmy asleep while I stared wide-eyed into the darkness of the tent and thought of the skeleton lying broken on the granite slab above the camp. Or the sense of being followed as we toiled up the frozen neve in the early morning. I had turned repeatedly to stare down the slope and once had been convinced I had seen a figure on a ribbon of a snow ridge moving slowly upwards. Despite what Jimmy said, the presence was there, like an icy wind on my spine, and still I turned and turned to catch the figure out, but it knew I knew and was careful not to let me have a second glance.

*

By midday we had trekked the last weary miles down a forested path and emerged to see the vivid yellow walls of the Gangotri temple, the spiritual source of the holiest of rivers. We rested in the shade of cedar trees and I checked to see that the major's brass pot hadn't leaked any precious water. Jimmy had laughed at me because I had been too tired to trudge to the source and had filled it three miles downstream where a solitary baba stood on one leg in the freezing shallows and chanted. He wore a g-string and had daubed religious symbols in rice paste on his forehead and shoulders. He took no notice of us and kept up a steady chant with his free leg bent up so the heel pressed against his groin. His hands were steepled in prayer.

Now I felt guilty, and wondered whether I could lie to the major. Somehow I knew that he would sense my shame but he would be too polite to say anything. He would merely be disappointed in me.

'Do you think I should go back?' I asked as we watched a crowd of naked holymen bathing and chanting on the river bank.

'We'd miss the night bus, and he'll never know if you lie.'

'Oh, he'll know all right. I'm a terrible liar.'

'Well, it's not that important anyway.' Jimmy pointed to the bathers. 'Look at that lot. They're even further away but it's obviously still a damn holy place.'

'I suppose so.' But inside I felt I had betrayed the major's trust.

'That temple', Jimmy continued, 'has a stone in it that they all pay homage to. They believe it is the one that King Bhagarathi did his penance on and where he persuaded the Goddess Ganga to come down from the heavens. I think the major will still be pleased, you know.'

The bus roared noisily out of the village in the dark of late evening with a billowing cloud of diesel fumes and fifty-seven passengers on board. We had managed to grab two of the twenty-five seats and were crumpled under the weight of our rucksacks in the centre of the bus. Jimmy glowered moodily out of the window, clutching the small and smelly infant thrust upon him by an old woman in a black sari.

We left as the evening ceremony of *aarti* came to an end and the pilgrims, waving lights and throwing garlands of flowers on to the roaring waters of the river, tramped back to the road to board the waiting bus. The driver arrived last. His hair and shirt were soaking wet from his last washing away of sins.

Fountain of Wisdom

'So, Mister Banks, you have returned safely.' The major sat back in the wicker chair and scrutinised me with a wry smile. 'Safe, but thinner. Would you agree, sir?'

'Christopher,' I said. 'Please call me Christopher, and yes I probably have lost a bit of weight. Nothing drastic though. I didn't get sick.'

'Yes, that is good.' The major nodded. He turned to talk quietly to a young boy standing barefoot on the burnt grass of the garden. The boy nodded, smiling broadly, and stepped forward to clear the table of our plates and cutlery.

'That was superb,' I said as the boy left. 'I've been dreaming of a meal like that for what seems like a lifetime now.'

'Yes, it was of good quality.' The major smiled. 'I was sorry your friend could not be with us.'

'Yes, well, Jimmy's pretty ill at the moment,' I said, tearing off a piece of chappati that I had rescued from one of the vanishing plates. 'He may have Giardia.' I chewed happily on the burnt and salty dough thinking of Jimmy throwing up across the cockroaches in the hotel lavatory.

Serves him right, I thought. He had probably caught it at Haridwar. He had insisted on stopping there on the journey down from Gangotri to witness the evening *aarti* ceremony on the banks of the Ganges. During the evening he had wandered off to talk to groups of Sadhus squatting near the river. I had found him hours later eating voraciously in a lean-to kerbside food stall. He seemed unperturbed by the frightful appearance of what he was stuffing in handfuls into his mouth.

It turned out that he had become engrossed in conversation with three ash-streaked Sadhus with tangled dreadlocked hair, stainless steel bowls and saffron orange blankets. Their paste-daubed faces and red-rimmed eyes showed they were deep into an intoxicating ganja-smoking session that had lasted all day. As darkness fell they stood up, threw off their blankets and ran naked towards the river, brandishing tridents, the weapon of their adored Shiva, and curved swords, to join a massed throng of chanting enraptured sadhus and pilgrims at the river bank. Jimmy had been left squatting amid their abandoned blankets in a state of utter inebriation, having smoked the ferocious chillums of ganja that had been handed round continuously for the previous two hours. Completely unable to talk, he had shuffled to the nearest food stall in the throes of a smoking-induced feeding frenzy. On the bus to Delhi the next morning, still with a glazed look to his eyes, the sickness had begun to take hold. To add to his misery he confessed between revolting burping retches through the open windows that he couldn't remember a thing about what the Sadhus had told him except that he was sure it was really important.

'Yeah, he's fairly miserable at the moment,' I said, nibbling the last of the chappati. 'Must have caught it in Haridwar.'

'Haridwar!' The major's eyes lit up with pleasure. 'So, you visited Haridwar as well. Good, that is good. Gangotri, and Haridwar, and Varanasi soon, you say?'

'Yes, and then we are off to Pakistan.'

'You are anxious to leave India?' the major inquired with a frown.

'Oh, don't get me wrong. I've enjoyed being here and seeing these places. They are fascinating, but . . .'

'But what? You don't like them, eh? Be truthful to me, Christopher. I am not easily offended.'

'I suppose I don't understand the significance of everything. I don't want to really. You see, I'm not very religious or mystically minded. I mean, Jimmy loves it. I can hardly drag him away, but I came here to climb, and we have done precious little so far.'

'Be patient. You will be back in the mountains soon. You have told me so. Why be in such a hurry?' The major poured a stream of thin green tea into a delicate china cup and passed it to me. He leant back in the chair and looked thoughtfully at me for a moment.

'I would have liked very much to meet your friend Jimmy,' he said at last. 'From what you say, he seems to be an interesting man. Very interesting for an Englishman.' He sipped his tea and fastidiously wiped droplets from his neat moustache with the tip of his forefinger.

'Oh, he's certainly interesting.' I chuckled. 'Most crazy people are.' The major suddenly looked stern and leant forward to tap the table urgently with his finger.

'Please do not speak like that,' he said with a note of anger in his voice. 'It is an insult to your friend and to me.'

'I'm sorry. I didn't mean . . .'

'I know. I know.' He held his hands up, palms out, in a familiar expressive gesture. 'Excuse my sharpness. Please, drink your tea and listen to me.'

I sat back and smiled at the major, who twisted his palm in a soft command and I picked up the tea cup and sipped.

'Your friend is right to search for these stories as you say he does. Furthermore, my friend, he is right to believe what he wishes to believe. He is not crazy. If he were then you would have to say the same of myself. You, Christopher, cannot understand the ceremonies and the symbols and the gods because you don't want to. That is your choice, and that also is right, but you cannot force your sense of right on to others.'

'But Jimmy is inventing it all. He looks for stories that fit

187

what he wants to believe and then claims that they are proof,'
I protested.

'Maybe so, but maybe also he is right. He may know things
you do not. These Water People may yet exist. You do not
know but it is possible that he does. You must allow him that
freedom as you are so gracious to allow me to believe in my
Gods. I accept that Shiva and Krishna and Rama exist, as my
late wife believed and worshipped Radha and Sita and Parvati,
their consorts. For you, this seems as crazy as Jimmy's Water
People, no?'

'No, well . . .'

'Honesty please, Christopher.'

'I . . . no, you see these have always been there for you and
for all Hindus. Jimmy is inventing his gods. They are a fiction,
a fairy tale. No-one else believes them. It's special to him.'

'Christopher. It is exactly the same. Where did all the
religions of the world come from if someone hadn't discovered
them to be true. What of the Mohammeds, the Christs and
Buddhas of this world?'

'But you can't think Jimmy is one of *them*?'

'I have not met him.' The major held his open hands out in
a defensive shrug. 'It is possible. After all, everything is
possible.'

'Oh come off it, major.' I grinned at him.

'What a curious expression. I have nothing to come off. Do
you want me to leave my chair?' He began to rise.

'You know what I mean.' He was smiling his gentle amused
smile.

'Yes, I know.' He stroked his moustache with the tip of a
finger. 'You understand very little about this country. Indeed,
I suspect that there are many things that you don't understand
and so you dismiss them. Facts, you can understand. Facts,
logic, proof, evidence, and that you call reason. These are the
things you live by. Is that not so, Christopher?'

'I suppose so. What's wrong with . . .'

'Nothing, nothing at all. As I said before, it is your right.

But it is not everything. There is much more than simple proven facts. It would be a very barren life if this were not so. What about the mountains that you love so much? Why do you return so often? Because they are big, or dangerous, or exciting, or something else that maybe you cannot exactly define but you are aware that it is there. A sense of mystery perhaps, a beauty finer than that which you can see with your eyes or feel with your hands? Think about these things. Love, what is that? Can you tell me? What is beauty, or fear, or wonder? They are not facts but you accept them, just as you should accept me, and your friend Jimmy.'

'I do,' I complained. 'It's just that Jimmy goes too far; he believes it too much. It worries me sometimes, especially some of the people he meets. The Hunter, for instance – he was strange, really strange. He had a hold on Jimmy. It was weird.'

'But you should let him be the judge of that,' the major said. 'Like the woman I showed you in the bazaar, the potion seller. You take her as you find her but you cannot change her or what she believes. You may never understand this land but you must not dismiss it. You have been to holy places and seen the Godmen, and the pilgrims. They believe in a multitude of Gods yet they live happily together. They live to be re-born. They know that what they do in this life, their karma, dictates what their re-incarnation will be: one of happiness or sorrow. If you are born a Hindu then that is what you are. You cannot become one; you cannot be converted. You are born to it and it is inescapable. We do not convert others and do not force our views on others. That is why a hundred million Hindus believing in an anarchic formless religion can live happily side by side. We have no Koran, no Bible, no Gospel, or doctrines. Do you understand?'

'Yes but it isn't that perfect, is it?' I said. 'Look at the violence that sometimes explodes over India. One million dead, hacked and burnt to death, during the Partition. That's not exactly living peacefully together.'

'That is another matter entirely,' the major said with a grim expression. 'I was there. I saw the killings with my own eyes, and then collected the dead. That was Hindus fighting Muslims. That was your country's fault, splitting the nation into East and West Pakistan for Muslims and India for Hindus. England playing God and failing to realise that fifty million Muslims would not leave their homeland for new artificially created nations. That was a conflict of separatism, of recessionism, and it will happen again. It happens now in the holy city of Ayodhya where Rama and Sita are worshipped. There are militant Hindus like the Naga Sadhus who want the Muslims out of India. They claim to be Shiva's warriors. They say that we suffered six hundred years of Muslim domination after the Moguls invaded and that now is the time to repel them. But they do not fight among themselves. This is another matter.'

'Is that why our bus was attacked after we left Haridwar?' I asked.

'Not in the city?' the major said in horror.

'No,' I said. 'On the way to Delhi. I don't know where. It was dark. I only saw crowds throwing stones and shouting which woke me.'

'Ah well, I do not know. There are many problems today. You see we have an ancient culture and a modern world. It is difficult.' He paused to sip at his tea with little finger arched self-consciously out from the hand.

'Think about this when you go to Varanasi,' he said. 'It is a magical sacred city; it is the oldest continuously inhabited settlement in the world. It is *Kashi*, the city of light, one of the seven Holy cities, a wondrous ancient place; the dream place where all Hindus desire to die and be cremated. Where life is re-born and the sins of a lifetime washed away in Mother Ganges' sacred waters. You may think it is an anachronism in the heart of a nation that is a world superpower with nuclear weapons and a space programme. How can that be reconciled? Somehow it is. Perhaps because it is the heart of the matter, yet it is no wonder that there are problems.'

'That is true all over India,' I agreed. 'It makes me uncomfortable.'

'And that is because you do not know how to see as we do.'

'What do you mean?'

'The eye is fundamental to our whole culture. You use yours simply to see, to observe your many facts and reasons, to confirm how right you are because, look there, you say, look at that, there is the proof that I am right. You look at the surface.'

'I don't follow you,' I said. 'Do you mean the old adage about the blind man seeing clearly?'

'Not quite, my friend.' The major smiled, shaking his head in a see-saw rhythm. 'Take our Gods, for instance. You see only statues, some with many arms and legs, others like Ganesh with the heads of elephants, and this is strange. Of course it is, if it is all that you see. But we see in the Gods all those things which we strive to be. In a way they are a reflection, the perfect image of what we aspire to be. Everything in this land is like that. The Gods represent various aspects, human qualities you could call them, and when I look on them I am really looking at myself, at what I want to be. How close I can get to this determines the quality of my rebirth. You see, the Gods hold a mirror up to myself and to all Hindus. And I can see the Gods in other forms than sculpture. Any things associated with the Gods become a reflection for me to contemplate. That is why trees, animals, rocks, sculptures, flowers and so on are worshipped. The whole of India is like a mirror. Do you follow me?'

'Well, sort of,' I said dubiously.

'Our goal as good Hindus is to develop our awareness; to achieve through meditation and contemplation that point of perfection that the Gods embody, and seeing, using our eyes, is the most common aid to this end. If images are the embodiment of the divine then to look on them . . .'

'Is to be seen by God.' I completed the major's sentence.

'Yes. Yes, you have it, Christopher.' He slapped his thighs

191

enthusiastically with both palms. 'And do you see like this? Of course not, and by not knowing this you can never fully understand me or my culture. Never.'

'I suppose not.' I wished for a moment that I did.

'Seeing is essential. When I go to temples to pray, or make a pilgrimage to see holy places, I go to see God and to be seen in return. It is called *darshana*. In seeing I give my *darshana* to the gods and they bless me with theirs. It is both very easy and very difficult, but slowly I develop, I expand into something better.'

'Is this the same thing as the "all seeing eye" that occurs in Buddhism? You know, the eye that is painted everywhere on temples and stupas and things in Nepal.'

'No, no. Don't confuse things, Christopher. Different religions, you see.'

'Yes, but doesn't Buddhism and Hinduism get all mixed up in Nepal?'

'Probably. What does it matter?' He dismissed my protest with a wave of the hand. 'You have seen the red mark on people's foreheads? The *tilak* we call it.'

'Yes. It's a caste mark, isn't it?'

He shook his head again. 'It is an ancient mark. The third eye. Seeing is so important that we have created another eye. It is said that once, when Shiva was playing love games with his consort, Parvati, he accidentally covered her eyes with his hands. When this happened the world was covered in darkness. So Shiva created the third eye to let the light return. So now married women wear the *tilak* to acknowledge the moment when Parvati had her initiation with Shiva. Do you not think we are lucky to have such stories to tell? Do you like them?'

'Yes, they're fascinating,' I said, 'but that is all they can ever be for me. As you said yourself, even if I wanted I cannot be converted to Hinduism.'

'I suppose that is true, and it saddens me. Anyway, my friend,' he said with a roguish smile, 'I don't think you would be a very good Hindu.'

'You're right there.' I laughed. 'No doubt I'd be re-born as something awful. I'd probably come back as one of those poor male spiders that have their heads bitten off and are eaten by their mates when they first make love.'

'Not so bad,' he laughed, 'I think you are a good man if only a little blind, and you could change that.'

'I'll buy some specs.'

'Better still, you could buy a mirror.' He paused. 'You know that when the sculptors carve the image of a god they are very careful to create the eyes last. It is very important. The opening of the eyes is done with great ceremony using a fine gold brushstroke and as it is done a mirror is held in front of the god's face and the artist tries to avert his body.'

'Why?'

'So that the first thing the God sees is perfectly beautiful. He sees himself.'

'Wow. That's pretty smart,' I said with delight.

'And why do you think the eye is made last?' the major asked with a smile.

'So it can't see itself when it isn't perfect,' I answered confidently.

'No, but that is a fine answer.' The major smiled and I felt strangely blessed, almost as if I were a grateful puppy being rewarded. I wanted to please. 'The eyes are the only parts of our bodies that begin to work after we are born. Elementary, my dear Christopher.'

I laughed.

'I'm afraid I do not have the accent for your Dr Watson.' He shrugged apologetically.

'Your English is excellent,' I said. 'Far better than my Hindi.' His melodic, slightly eccentric accent was quite hypnotic when he talked at length.

'I want you to learn how to see when you go to Varanasi,' he continued, 'and when you leave, so it is possible that you can understand your memories in a better way. Maybe you could also understand your friend Jimmy.'

'How?'

'Simple, my friend, simple! Look at him with new eyes.' He stood up. 'It has been a great pleasure to meet you again, Christopher, and I am deeply honoured that you have been so kind to endure the lectures of an old man, but now I must go.' He pulled a fob watch from his trouser pocket and peered short-sightedly at the cracked glass face. 'Yes, yes, I am late already.'

I stood up and shook his extended hand. He turned to pick up his satchel and umbrella. He studied the umbrella with a smile and then held it out to me. 'Would you accept this? You will have need of it when the monsoon comes, and it is coming soon. I can feel it. Can you?'

'Er, yes,' I said. It was stiflingly humid. The air hung like a heavy wet blanket, almost unbearable after the light cool touch of the mountain winds. I had read that morning that temperatures of 135 degrees had been killing people in Pakistan, and that in southern India forerunners of the great downpour had already lashed the coast. 'But I can't take the umbrella. You see I won't be coming back to Delhi. We take the train to Varanasi and then fly to Pakistan. Oh God, I nearly forgot . . .'

The major looked surprised as I reached for the small rucksack I had brought with me and searched inside. My hand closed on the cool metal of the pot and I pulled it out with a flourish and handed it to the major.

His face lit up with delight and he reached tentatively for it with his free hand.

'Did you . . . ?'

'Yes. I filled it.' I smiled at his obvious pleasure and then braced myself. 'I didn't fill it exactly at the source. I'm sorry. I was too tired.' I explained that I had filled it three miles from the source and told him of the holyman who had been there and kept apologising until he put down the umbrella and grasped my hand.

'Thank you, Christopher,' he said fervently. 'Do not worry about a mere three miles. Just understand how important this is to me.' He held the brass pot up in front of his face and then pressed it to his heart. 'Thank you, my friend. I thought you had forgotten, but I didn't say anything for fear that it would upset and embarrass you. I put an unfair burden on you by asking you, a total stranger, to do this thing, and I had no right to rebuke you if you failed. Thank you.'

I thought he was about to burst into tears.

'I insist that you accept this as a gift,' he said, proffering the umbrella once more. 'It is quite old. I have had it for many years on many pilgrimages and many campaigns. A poor gift after what you have done for me, but please accept it as a token of my friendship.'

I could not refuse him. He waved once to me as he walked from the garden towards the hectic dusty bustle of the main road. I saw him standing at the side of the road polishing one mirror-like brown brogue shoe on the back of his calf muscle before he stepped into the mayhem of hooting taxis, scooters, bicycles, lorries and buses and was gone.

I looked at the exquisitely carved dragon-headed handle. Like the decorations on the brass pot, it was beautiful. I remembered that he had said he hailed from Rajasthan. He had talked fondly of Jaipur, his home city. Trying to describe to me the splendour of the magical wind-singing galleries of the Hawa Mahal, the Palace of Wind, set as it is in the centre of the city. He said it was a city of artists, a pink-washed wonderland of exquisite jewels, fairy tale buildings, with forts and fantastic palaces standing witness to the glory of the ancient desert-sanded state. He had exhorted me to go there claiming it to be the epitome of all that I expected of India. Only when I said we were going to Varanasi, had he stopped trying to persuade me to go. Now I had a small memory of him and his homeland in a finely carved dragon-headed umbrella. *Jimmy would love this*, I thought as I hailed a rickshaw to take me back to the hotel.

14

The Burning
Ghats

I dreamed of dragons as the train rattled and rolled south-east to Varanasi, the city of light. I sat wedged between Jimmy and a fat woman. Our feet were propped on our rucksacks and a thick tube of canvas crammed with climbing gear perched on our laps. Sharp edges jutted through the canvas. My legs and buttocks tingled with bone-deep muscle-crushed cramps from hours spent squeezed on to the hard seat. The woman smelt musky and snored incessantly with her head lolling against my shoulder.

I sat suddenly upright and awake when the train shuddered to an abrupt stop with a screech of steel against steel and a rising babble of querulous voices. I could see nothing outside. The night was inky black and starless and the thick wet air wallowed into our carriage as a door opened. It felt hotter than the smoky miasma of crowded humanity inside. Sweat poured down my face, stinging my eyes. Veritable streams seemed to gurgle over my chest and down to the waistband of my shorts where they mingled with accumulated dust to form an abrasive surface worthy of any knife sharpener. The warm salty cloth stung my raw flesh where the hip bones pressed against the elasticated waistband. My buttocks slithered on the wooden bench as if I were sitting on a water-logged mud flat.

Jimmy had not been woken. I glanced at him slumped forward across the canvas duffle bag oblivious to the steel-tipped ski-pole poking red blemishes into his forearm.

I noticed that I still grasped the major's umbrella in my right hand, where the handle poked up between my legs, and remembered the vivid hallucinatory dream from which I had been wrenched. The billowing plume of an avalanche had come thundering down a black-walled valley towards where I stood. Though wanting to run I had somehow found my feet rooted to the earth and my body unable even to twist away from the onslaught. The air had bellowed in protest and the ground shook as rocks tumbled from high black walls into the undulating spine of the snow cloud. It piled high to engulf me, and I stared up at vertiginous distended walls of frosty crystals, mushrooming into the sky, so that the valley vanished and the beast seemed to writhe in the ferocious moment of the kill.

As I trembled before this snow-borne Nemesis I saw her freeze and hang immobilised above me. Then the swollen white ramparts began to fold and settle in upon themselves and the sounds of fury faded, to be replaced by the tortured cracks of pressurised ice. The dark valley walls slowly rose above the descending snake of white.

I saw where the glacier basin lay like a forked tail above the body of a dragon that curled menacingly down the dark contours of the valley. Its crevassed back was riven into scabby deposits of broken rock that ran in stripes across its body, and snow slopes running down from flanking mountains appeared as wings sprouting from its shoulders. Its ice-taloned limbs clawed at the constricting rock buttresses of the valley. I stood at its snout staring into a cavern of icicles and a tongue of brown burnt meltwater and heard a dreadful high-pitched screech echoing from deep within the labyrinth of ice veins leading back from the throat. I awoke with a start to find that we had stopped and the fat woman was still snoring.

The train jerked into motion with arthritic creaking sounds and the slow acceleration of clunks from the tracks. The whistle sounded and white steam mixed with soot rushed past the window. I saw a pair of brown legs hanging down from the roof. One calloused heel swung back and forth through the open window. I shrugged the fat woman off my shoulder in disgust when I realised she was dribbling on me. She wobbled upright, her head lolling from side to side as if detached from the treble chins of blubber on which it sat. Then it slumped heavily on to her expansive chest. Huge rolls of fat slicked with sweat bulged at the gap between her bodice and the twisted colours of her sari. A gold embroidered veil had fallen across the duffle bag. I wiped her spittle off my arm with it and then draped it across the back of her shoulders.

The water had an oily, slick feel as it fled downstream with the current. Vaporous clouds of mist clung in small patches to the surface, seeming to run with the current. A cool breeze lifted from the river and hit the wall of humid air hanging densely a few feet above the surface. I trailed my hand in the water, letting the cool air slide up my arm. It was not yet dawn but already there was a crowding sense of menace to the sky. I glanced up, half-expecting the thunderous opening of the monsoon.

The sun silently exploded across the horizon with startling suddenness. Before long a vast semi-circle of blazing molten gold had lifted massively into the dawn sky. A fringe of spiky black trees shafted into the base of the golden pyre. The mist vapours seemed to curl and twist in agony across the surface of the river as the sun consumed them like acid splashed on ice cubes. The far bank was tree-lined and shelved into mud flats washed by the gentle flow of the Ganges, now a mature river, sliding across the great plains of India to the vast impoverished shores of the Bay of Bengal.

The memory of its turbulent icy green waters heaving under the bridge at Haridwar and the cool fresh breeze sucking down the river from the high mountains made me regret this visit to Varanasi. From that bridge I'd watched a holyman in raptures of religious delight as he clung to a cat's cradle of heavy chains in the arches below. He hung from tired arms with three-quarters of his body sucked into the powerful current until it seemed to be dragging him under. I couldn't bear to watch his ecstasy. I expected to see his tired arms loose their grip of the wet chain links and his body disappear downstream in a swirl of brown and green waters.

In the early dawn of a sultry day threatened by monsoon the river spread out like a vast brown lake from the edge of Varanasi, the eternal city of a thousand temples. Then the lifting sun had illuminated the shoreline with a dramatic wash of colour. Tiers of steps ran up from the western bank into a fantastic skyline of minarets and palaces, ornately carved façades of dark-shadowed recesses and extravagant rooftops breaking the morning sky in a profusion of curving arches, sculpted steeples, jutting steps, at all manner of angles. Wooden-hulled boats, like Arab dhows, were tied up to the stepped bathing ghats. They tilted over unsteadily on a floor of sun-gilded mud. The green crowns of huge trees peeped above the serried lines of riverbank temples. Plumes of grey smoke rose in regimented lines into the heavy air.

The city hugged a huge curve in the Ganges, facing east so that the rising sun, a vast golden sphere, struck waves of heat and light on the face of the city. Not a single building seemed to complement its neighbour yet they all clung together in an extraordinary appearance of serene composure. It was as if a menagerie of deranged architects had been let loose on the river banks in a competition to produce the most outrageous design. Some had built magnificent temples with no thought that they were slipping slowly into the river before they had been completed. Others had erected forbidding porticos, covered walks with repeated arches staring out from cool shadows; domed shrines punctured the smoke-veiled sky.

At first it was silent as we slid into the water. The opposite bank was uncluttered, fringed here and there with tall black-trunked trees silhouetted like poplars on the rim of a flat

French plain. A boy stood calf-deep in black mud, tugging at a rope attached to the nostril ring of a heavy-horned water buffalo. I heard its mournful bellow as it swung its bossed horns and stared through disturbing milky-blue eyes at the sweep of the river. A flat-bottomed boat passed close to the mudbank, poled by an emaciated man who stood with one foot crooked behind his knee as he worked.

As we neared the city shore a rising crescendo of voices murmured from the ghats and I saw throngs of bathers and pilgrims crowded on the ancient stone steps. Some were immersed to their necks. A group of young men were scrubbing up soapy lathers and splashing themselves in horse play. Old people sat in arthritic crumpled forms by the river, some laid out with their feet dipped in the gentle wash of the holy river. Either they were dead or approaching death in their last enfeebled unconscious moments. At least as they slipped from life they were assured of salvation, of sins cleansed and karma strengthened for their journey to re-incarnation. Each ghat was marked by prominent phallus-shaped pillars, the lingams, proof that this was Shiva's city.

I was content to trail my hand in the water and watch the magical city in the soft lustrous glow of morning light. Jimmy listened intently to our boatman who sat at the rear, one hand on the throttle of the tiny outboard engine, the other pointing out landmarks. Every so often Jimmy leaned out over the water and retched. Occasionally a thin stream of green bile and spittle splattered into the river and the boatman smiled and waggled his head in a classic Indian gesture. His startlingly white teeth gleamed in his dark leathery-skinned face. Jimmy would wipe the strings of saliva from his mouth and cup a handful of river water to splash across his pallid face. Despite the stomach cramps and wretched nausea, he seemed entranced by the extraordinary spectacle.

I wished that Alice could see it. The postcard sent to our hotel in Delhi had wrenched my mind back to purple-heathered memories of her on the moors above Sheffield. I ached to be back there, away from this interminable wet heat, and the crushing humanity and the loneliness of alien places. I glanced at Jimmy and wondered why he had kept it so long and said nothing. *Why couldn't I ask him? What was I scared of?* I had hoarded the card in dark restaurants, reading glimpses of what I had left behind as I ate rice and dahl and Jimmy vomited in the faecal stench of the hotel shower room. She had written with hopeful anticipation, free it seemed of the gloom of the hospital. I imagined her golden head bowed over and the familiar flick of her hand as she cleared it from her eyes. I remembered her eyes melting me and hoped they hadn't melted Andy.

Yesterday, leaving Jimmy in a foetal curl clutching his stomach, I had wandered through the bewildering maze of alleys and lanes behind the Varanasi waterfront. For a moment the oppressive atmosphere seemed to vanish as I lost myself in a mediaeval labyrinth of covered walkways, shops ablaze with silk, trestle tables groaning under the spread of enamelled, filigreed, engraved twists of silver, gold, copper and brass jewellery. Billowing sheets of embroidered silks hung in riotous profusion from the narrow walled alleys.

I ducked down shadowy dusty corridors to emerge in brilliant sunshine in beautiful walled gardens of private houses. I saw so many shrines and temples that I became confused and lost my bearings, looking back down streets I had walked up and seeing nothing that I could recognise, and then looking ahead and feeling that I had already been there. Stalls sold intricate brass work, gorgeous cloths, statuettes of every imaginable Hindu god, countless black and white lingams of Shiva, foodstuffs of every kind, wreathed in the aroma of spices and fresh fried chappatis. Each stall grouped into traditional sections according to their merchandise and the lot thronged with dogs, cows, people, bullock carts and bicycles.

Then, as I studied an image of Durga, the terrible form of Parvati, Shiva's consort, a woman stepped from a dark doorway and looked directly into my eyes and smiled. She turned with a regal sway and stepped into the crowds, lost at once, but leaving me bereft, shocked, so that I stood paralysed, unable to call out to her. I knew her at once. She was Alice in the dream, dark-haired Alice naked on the bed, with the ankle bracelet and sad spectral eyes and nipples that Alice never had.

That one smiling glance had been photographed by my mind. I could still bring back the vision of her eye-lined eyes, perfect ovals and huge black pupils, and the bright red *tilak* on her forehead and the silver nose ring. Heavy silver earrings cascaded in concentric jewel-hung circles from each lobe and a glorious blue enamelled necklace hung in a crescent round the smooth coffee cream skin of her throat. A red veil, gold-banded, draped seductively round her head like a halo, and as she turned to step into the crowds I saw her blue silk sari embellished with shimmering gold flecks rise up the fragile arch of her foot to reveal the gold ankle bracelet looped over the curve of her heel.

Hours later, when I had returned to the hotel, I re-read Alice's postcard and mixed the two images in my mind until I could no longer distinguish between the two women. I felt hot and feverish and wondered if I had caught Jimmy's illness.

'Look,' Jimmy said, pointing to the bank. 'There's a cremation starting over there, on the right.'

'Where?'

'There. See the smoke?'

I searched the endless ghats, hundreds of them crowded the length of the banks. A dark black oily smoke rose from one and the boatman angled the bows towards it. There were biers stacked high with wood and glimpses of white shrouded shapes laid on top. One bier, attended by two men wearing loin cloths and smoke-blackened towels wrapped round their heads, had just been lit. The flames caught rapidly, licking greedily up the layers of faggots as the white shroud blackened and tumbled up through waving, heat-hazed air in fragments like burnt paper. The corpse seemed to move inside the flames. The smoke lifted and a black stick arm poked out from the flames. One of the attendants, outcastes known as chandal, pushed the arm back with a flame-scorched wooden pole. His partner threw pieces of flame-released wood back on top of the pyre. They trailed sparks and grey smoke in the arc of their flight.

'Did you know that they smash the skulls before burial?'

'What?'

'They break them open,' Jimmy said as he read a tourist guide of India. 'It stops them exploding apparently.' With that he suddenly lurched forward and began retching.

'I've seen this before,' I said. 'Remember that time in Nepal.'

'Whooorrgh . . .' Jimmy answered, and I looked away from the oily smoke of one man's cremation and recalled the gloomy sight of the cremations at the Hindu temple of Pashupatinath in Kathmandu. I had visited the complex of temples and burning ghats early in the morning. Six bodies lay cloaked with saffron shrouds on individual biers that lasted no longer than these white ones. Young policemen, I was told, killed in the recent riots. I had watched their young bodies blacken and curl, and the young wives standing motionless, staring at the end of their hopes, condemned now to a life of menial domestic slavery in the families of the victims.

A steady drizzle had fallen from an overcast grey sky and the pyres had steamed as the attendants forked burnt limbs back into the smouldering coals. The Bagmati river was mud-banked, shallow enough to walk across, and I stared over the grey water at the smoke rising in front of the temples, oblivious to the rain. On isolated mud islands in mid-stream the wet ashes of poorer people's cremations formed desolate barrows. I saw bones lying in the ashes and felt nauseous. When I returned to Kathmandu in a scooter-taxi we stopped at the site of a road accident. The driver pointed to the side of an overturned lorry. A few feet from the scooter I saw an old man lying in the road. His naked upper torso protruded from under the hard steel side of the lorry. Blood pooled against the lorry and flowed along the side. The man seemed to be resting on his elbow. He looked directly into my eyes with an unflinching emotionless stare. The people who crowded round the accident seemed unaware of his plight and crowded close to the cab of the lorry shouting advice to someone inside. In a crowd of forty people the old man stared silently at me as the rain ran like tears across his face and then his eyes closed slowly and his cheek rested on the bloody road. He died utterly alone. The scooter roared into life and we drove off as if nothing had happened.

'I wasn't there,' Jimmy said, wiping bile from his mouth with the back of his hand.

'Oh Jesus, look at that,' I said, staring fixedly at the water in front of the boat.

'What?' Jimmy looked around.

'There,' I said, pointing. 'That arm there.' It floated downstream, the fingers outstretched from a wizened arm. I couldn't see what it was attached to.

'Bloody hell!' Jimmy swore. 'I've been drinking this bloody water. I read that it had proven curative powers.' He leaned over the bow and puked.

'Come on, mate,' I said. 'Let's get out of here. I'm sick of this.' I nodded to the boatman and he swung the low sided boat in a wide circle. The arm bobbed in the centre of the churned frothy white wake of the propeller. Suddenly there was a thunderous rumbling in the air and I looked around in alarm. The boatman threw his arms up and shouted something unintelligible with an ecstatic grin of delight. Looking downstream, I saw an evil black clouded sky and felt the first tremulous flurries of disturbed air as the monsoon bore down on the burning ghats of Varanasi.

'It's the rains,' I shouted to Jimmy, who mumbled a reply through slime-covered lips as he hung over the side.

By the time we reached shore the clouds had raced over the city and water teemed in needles of rain. Huge droplets bounced clear of the surface on impact and then fell back, so that looking across the broad swathe of the river it seemed as if there were a foot-high silvered spray undulating across the surface. The boatman was laughing manically, and crowds of bathers on the shore stood with their arms joyously raised to the sky, allowing their upturned open-mouthed faces to be battered by the stair-rods of warm rain.

By evening the streets outside our dilapidated hotel were rushing streams of brown garbage-laden water. Lightning forked through the early darkened afternoon sky and huge blue-bellied clouds rolled ominously in from the south.

'Time to go climbing, mate,' Jimmy said.

'Thank God for that.'

15

Trembling Slopes

At two in the morning Jimmy left. The sky was clear, a three-quarters moon glared a white light on to the cirque. Rock walls gleamed a strange silvery leather white in the moonshine. The sky was magnificent. Myriad stars spread out, glinting brightly as they do only at altitude.

'Back in four days,' he said, squeezed my shoulder, and trudged away. His headtorch glimmered a beam of yellow light ahead of him, gradually dimming as he walked up the moraines towards the glacier. I heard the familiar jingle of hardware rattling on his harness, then silence. He had gone, and I drifted into sleep.

The morning sun woke me. I was uncomfortably hot in my sleeping bag. The orange sides of the tent flickered shadows across me. From outside I heard the steady gurgle of our stream. It ran, silver-sided, through a chaotic maze of black moraine hills. Its source was the glacier, and the water spilled in pools close by the tents. Grey water, full of silt. A finely ground mix of mica, mud and water had tainted the cooking for so long now we no longer noticed. A dull booming echoed around the tents – ice cliffs falling to the glacier from Snow Peak.

I shuffled out of my bag, crawled from the bell entrance and stood up. Clear blue sky and the merciless glare of the cirque greeted me. Reaching into the tent, I pulled my sleeping bag into the sun, turned it inside out and slung it across the ridgepole to dry.

I walked barefoot across the sharp-edged gravel to a large boulder and peed a long golden rush of last evening's tea. Shielding my eyes with my hand, I squinted up at the mountain as I stood there. Jimmy had made good use of the frozen pre-dawn start. I spotted his tiny figure silhouetted against the morning sun two thousand feet above me on the ridge. There were no signs of his footsteps on the long and menacing snow slopes sweeping down to the glacier. A pang of jealousy and self pity ran through me. Already he was nearing the high point of our last attempt where we had cached a good supply of gas and food in a snow hole. He disappeared for a moment behind a distinct spire of rock jutting like a dorsal fin from the crest of snow. As he re-appeared I could see how well he was going. He was stronger now, and fitter after our two previous forays high up the ridge. The week of hot sunny days and clear freezing night skies must have consolidated the snow ridge. Last time it had been a grimly exhausting slog up deep wet snow.

I walked slowly back to the tents feeling sharp twinges in my thigh again. There was no helping it, much as I tried to convince myself otherwise – the hamstring was torn. One fall with a heavy rucksack on the black rocks near the camp had been enough. That tired slip after the long stormy descent had finished my chances on the mountain. But for that I would be up there now – dammit!

I idled away the day with little jobs that soon bored me. After restrapping my thigh with elastic bandage I tentatively began the short walk to the snowy edge of the glacier, hoping for a better view of the mountain. Soon the twinges became a continuous ache, forcing me to hobble slowly back to camp. In a black mood I fiddled morosely with my camera, changing lenses and filters, still hoping for a spectacular photograph of

Jimmy's now tiny black shape on the ridge above our snow hole, but it was no good. I threw the lot into the tent in disgust.

Cooking endless brews of sweet tea at least let me vent my frustration on the temperamental petrol stove. Eventually I retired to the shadow of the tent doorway propped up on ski sticks to shield me from the unbearably hot sunshine. I turned my back on the mountain, listened to Vivaldi on my personal stereo, and read a cheap adventure story about poachers in Africa. When the sun dipped westward behind the crest of the cirque the bitter cold of early evening drove me inside.

At nine o'clock I stepped out into the cold with my headtorch and stared up at the darkened mountain mass looming above. I could dimly make out the steep buttress seamed with ice runnels and snow patches which reared above the ridge in the final wall beneath the summit. Faint vestiges of cloud scudded across the night sky in thin streaked bands, eerily silvered by the first few glimmers of starlight. The wind moaned down from the mountain side. The weather was changing. Suddenly a flash of yellow light blinked at me. Then another. One ... two ... three. A long dark pause and I smiled to myself as the tension left me. All was well. Jimmy was safe for the night. I blinked back an acknowledgment.

Safe and high. Far higher than I had expected him to reach that day. Climbing alone he would have moved so much faster than a roped pair.

By noon of the following day I had watched Jimmy make steady progress up the summit buttress towards the easy snow slopes leading to the summit. From the speed he was moving I guessed that he had dispensed with the rope at the snow hole and gone for the summit in a quick dash. Through the 400 mm lens on my camera I could see his careful methodical movements but I couldn't make out whether he had left his rucksack at his previous bivouac site. He needed to move fast. The streamers of cloud of last night had developed into banked cumulus rapidly covering the sky. Snow plumes jetted from the summit and the ridge below the buttress. The wind had increased. At two o'clock he reached the summit and turned almost immediately back down. There was an urgency in his movements, now seeming to increase with my own growing anxiety. At three the clouds enveloped the mountain and I saw no more. At nine it was snowing at base camp and no light flickered down from above.

Next day a few inches of snow lay around the tents. The water in the pans had a skin of ice, and the mountain was hidden from me. For a brief moment in the late afternoon the clouds parted and I thought I saw a small dark movement below the buttress. By the time I had reached for my camera there was nothing more to be seen. If, as I suspected, the movement was Jimmy, then he had put the worst of the descent behind him. He could reach the snow hole tonight and it was well stocked with gas and food; enough for one person to sit out the storm for several days. My glum mood lightened at the thought, but I wondered what the descent and high bivouac in the storm had taken out of him.

Two long days passed. Days of wet snow and blanket cloud. Occasionally the wind howled from above the clouds and I shivered in my sleeping bag. At night the temperature dropped viciously. In the mornings I knocked the hoar frost from the sides of the tents and with cold fingers fumbled at the stove. My thigh was strengthening but it was too late to be of any use. There was nothing to do but wait. Empty hours spent trying to ignore the insidious worries overpowering me. Did he reach the snow hole? If he didn't, could he have dug in and survived this long without food and fuel? Was that him I had seen or a rock flickering in my vision as I'd anxiously searched the mountain?

I tried reading, but my attention kept wandering as gusts of snow rattled the tent walls, making me wonder what was happening two thousand feet higher. Only the tiresome need to feed myself and make hot drinks briefly let me forget, as I lay there, impotent and scared. *Come down, Jimmy, come down safe, youth*. The camp had become a bleak dark place of dismal black gravels, wetly snowed boulders looming through grey wraiths of mists; the loud stream was now silent as its source froze. Booming sounds muffled by the clouds echoed round the tents as avalanches broke free from the high ringed walls of the cirque. And always the sibilant wind sounds rising and fading, mourning at me from the hidden mountains.

As darkness heralded the start of his seventh night on the mountain I glanced anxiously at the sky for signs of a break in the weather. At midnight a lone star glimmered through a rent in the cloud curtain. An hour later more stars and the silver shine of moonlight broke through. The clouds were lifting. It was warmer. The wind had died.

I awoke early. The light was blue in dawn's slow start. I sat outside huddled into my down duvet with the stove hissing busily. Streamers of cloud spewed in plumes from the summit. Isolated clumps of cloud, broken remnants of the storm, drifted apart on a light southerly wind. The sun crept slowly to the horizon, announcing its arrival with the paling blue in the east, and the blue black night sky fled. There was no sign of Jimmy. I stared at the snow ridge. A small dark shape sprung a buzz of hope, then I realised it was a rock. Familiar features had changed with the dusting of fresh snow. Above the dorsal fin of rock I could see no sign of our snow hole. The tight knot in my stomach began to unwind as I prepared myself to accept the worst. A hollow emptiness replaced the tension.

I turned off the stove and slopped boiling water into my mug. More tea. Always take plenty of hot sweet tea for shock. Doesn't do much for grief, I thought. 'Come on,' I said. 'Come on, show yourself, for God's sake.'

Nothing moved. I stood up slowly. My thigh no longer hurt so badly. At the boulder I peed with my back to the mountain. When finished I turned to the tents, head down, eyes averted from the mountain. For an hour I managed to avoid looking up. I ate porridge and chocolate. As I prepared another drink I forgot myself and glanced up without thinking.

A black speck moved slowly down the ridge. Black against the now blinding sunshine.

'JIIIMMMMMEEEEEE!' I yelled exultantly, leaping to my feet and pumping my arms in the air.

The cry echoed around the tents. The small speck stopped moving. Then an arm rose wearily in acknowledgment and he moved painfully on again. I stared at him. Even at this distance I could see the exhaustion in his movements. He seemed smaller. The deep snow was hiding his lower body. He was wading down, shrugging forward in those familiar wallowing motions of tiredness.

Within minutes I had packed my sack, fastened the gaiters on my boots, grabbed the ski sticks and set off towards the glacier. I walked as fast as my thigh would allow. The sack was light, laden only with the stove, food, medicines and my camera. For a while the ridge was hidden from view as I moved through the twisted path between the high black moraine hills. I was breathing heavily as I rounded the last spur of muddy black gravel and the fresh snow of the glacier glared blindingly in the morning sun. A faint dull roaring sound echoed for a moment, then died. I climbed over the crest of the first undulation on the glacier and stopped to check Jimmy's progress. There was nothing to be seen.

It was silent within the cave. He roused himself slowly from the torpor of days lying entombed. His watch showed it to be morning. Another day. The eighth. He shuffled his body round towards the entrance and reached for his axe with wooden fingers. For the umpteenth time he poked the shaft of the axe carefully through the snow, anticipating the sudden roar of the storm and the gust of powder against his arm. Silence, and then a beam of bright sunlight streamed through the hole he had made. The storm was over.

He rolled away from the entrance and lay back. Eyes closed, he felt the weight lifting from his body. Thank God, it was over! There was no burst of excitement, no exultation. He was too tired for that. Yet there was relief. A steady calm feeling. He smiled at the roof of the cave as he opened his eyes. The roof gleamed a bluey white colour from the sunlight outside. The scallop-shaped marks of the ice axe adzes were glistening with ice. The steam from the stove and his body heat had melted the roof only for it to freeze again in the night. He dragged his eyes away from the all too familiar sight. He was going down.

When at last he was ready he stood up through the roof of the cave and blinked in the glare of sunlit snow slopes. He swayed, dizzy from days of lying still. There was a strange disembodied feeling in his head. Physically he felt fine. For sure, he was tired, and the tips of his fingers were blackened by frostbite. He had escaped lightly from the terrible descent to the cave in the storm. Often he had wondered what would have been if he'd failed to reach the cave. He'd eaten well, rationing his supply of gas carefully. Yet somehow he felt distanced from events as if he had stepped outside of himself and now watched his wallowing attempts to descend with a dispassionate curiosity. As he struggled against the snow he shook his head sharply from side to side, as if it would clear away the muzziness inside. He felt that he hadn't woken up completely. His head ached as it would with a head cold.

His memories drifted back over the past days of storm. The unnatural silence in the dark cave. A single candle fluttering a weak yellow light across the scalloped walls. The hiss of the gas stove and its faint glimmering blue light adding to the candle-flame shadows. The brushing sounds of nylon against nylon as he swept the insidious powder snow from his sleeping bag – a constant battle to remain dry and a poor remedy for the boredom and solitude.

He cursed his weakness and the deep tiring snow. The sunshine that had been so welcome now seemed a cruel extra burden to him. Soon his movements slowed, his mouth dried with his heavy gasps for air, and when he rested, slumping sideways in a careless sitting position, he faced away from the sun, seeking shade behind his rucksack.

Although he could see the two tents nestling amid the moraines, there were no signs of movement. It was early yet. He'd always known they would be there, but irrational thoughts in the cave had often frightened him into believing that for some reason they would be gone. Somewhile later, as he forged down the ridge, he heard a shout and glanced down at the tents. A tiny figure stood between them, arms up high. He smiled and waved his ice axe.

From where he stood he could see that soon he must leave the ridge and begin to descend the snow face leading to the glacier. For a moment he wandered aimlessly about, unsure. Was it safe? He kicked at the snow wearily, but there was really no choice. He knew he must get down that day. There was no gas left, and he was worried about the way he felt. His head was not right.

After another fifty yards along the ridge he turned down the slope. Immediately it was easier to move. It was much steeper than the ridge and he used the angle to make sliding steps through the deep snow. Small waves of snow hissed beyond his steps. His mood lightened and some of the tiredness went with the thought of reaching the camp. He sensed the danger on the slope but it was from a distance. He had decided to go down; he must go down despite his fears, so the danger seemed less personal. It was a gamble and he knew he would win. He had no idea how long the good weather would last but he knew that to be caught in another storm would finish him, so he stepped on down the snows. The menace put him on edge, made him tense and alert. Adrenalin strengthened him and much of the tiredness was forgotten.

As the going became steeper he was forced to turn into the slope and kick steps, using both axes for support. He could see the flurries of sugary snow falling between his legs to the glacier far below. More snow seemed to fall than he had disturbed.

From far within he felt the first trembling warnings. He was slow to react. Everything was wrong. He knew it, but he couldn't act. The sun had taken its toll, burning away his will to resist; the lethargy had overwhelmed him so that he seemed to be struggling up from deep sleep but failing to wake. He looked at his arms buried in the snow and tried squeezing his fists tight on the axe handles. As in the morning on first waking, there was no strength in the grip. He shook his head, taking a deep breath as he did so. It was far too dangerous. For a moment the warning was clear in his mind. He must return to the ridge. He must get back to the safety of the ridge, away from these trembling slopes.

He rested his head on the snow, thinking of the struggle back up to the ridge, and his fear of the slope faded. Perhaps it would be all right. The thought of retracing his steps was too much. He leant into the fifty-degree slope, almost lying against the snow, with his legs deeply buried. One hour, just one hour, and he could be safely down on the glacier. It was against all his instincts to go down and yet he didn't want to spend another long day alone on the mountain. *Never climb on slopes within twenty-four hours of heavy snowfall.* He knew it needed at least this time for the snow to consolidate. A hot melting day followed by a freezing night would settle the slope. If only he had awoken earlier when it was dark and freezing, but it was too late for that. He must go back to the ridge.

Laboriously he began to climb back up the furrow of his footsteps. Three steps up, two steps down. As soon as he had decided to go up his fears came rushing back. He had at last acknowledged his mistake, and with that he was seized by an almost convulsive panic attack. Like turning his back on a darkened doorway when he was a ghost-fearing child, he tried to run from the menace he had felt as a distant nagging doubt but which now consumed him. The slope was lethal. He must get off, quickly, quickly.

He had waited too long. The sun had done its work on the snow, and its heat had sapped his will to act with speed. Too tired to care, too thirsty, and craving the comfort of base camp, he had stepped beyond the limits. At first he thought he was sliding further down than usual after a step but a quick glance above him and to the side told him the truth. Standing upright, one arm still buried in the snow, he could see that he was moving downwards. Above, a crest of snow was curling towards him. It looked deceptively soft and harmless until it hit him. Flipped violently backwards, he slid head-down with the gathering rush of snow. Instinctively he tried to swing round and attempt an ice axe brake, but the snow pushed him under and he struggled in panic to get his head above the surface.

Four days of continual storm had deposited over four feet of snow on the mountain slopes. The hard old neve ice beneath held the massive weight of fresh powder in an uncertain bond. Now the sun had finished the inevitable process. Meltwater seeped between the surface of the neve and the new snow. Layers slumped downwards in short slides, then held tentatively in balance again. A few more slips spread out across the entire length of the slope. Hundreds, perhaps thousands, of tons of snow hung poised above the glacier. Then Jimmy began his descent. As the first huge block of snow moved, with the helpless figure trapped upright within it, a chain reaction crackled across the slope. From just below the ridgeline the whole slope began to slide down, ponderously and silently at first before it gathered momentum and surged into a deepening roar in its lunge for the glacier bay.

Within the churning mass some sections of slope swept down faster than others as imperceptible differences in the slope accelerated it away. Huge shearing forces developed at the edges of these masses of moving snow, which was no longer soft, wet and sugary – it had become a solid overpowering force. As strong as any river in spate, it rushed down with gathering speed until it began to ride on a cushion of air. At its head it pushed a mass of displaced air, creating a blast force that would kill before the following snow even touched its victim. Jimmy had triggered a monster.

It had hung poised waiting for the puny fly-like creature to disturb its quiet slumber. Time seemed stretched as he tumbled within the maelstrom. He knew at once what was happening and, though he realised it was hopeless, he tried at first to resist.

His head cleared the snow briefly and he gulped, sucking in the powder-laden air and almost immediately beginning to drown. He thrashed his arms from side to side, desperate to stay on the surface, and for a moment he succeeded. Then his twisting body crossed the sheer forces on the edge of his initial sliding mass. His hips were ripped back and up above him as the slower-moving snow gripped his lower body. The immense force flipped him head down again but not before his legs snapped above the knee. He felt nothing. His back had snapped in the violent arching twist.

He still waved his arms, or maybe the snow waved them for him, he couldn't tell. He felt numb though he didn't understand why. The powder had melted instantly in his lungs and though he fought for breath there was none to be had. It seemed hours since the start though it was only seconds. He felt no fear now that the panic and struggle were over. His chest burned with pressure pains and he sensed rather than saw which way he was moving. When he broke surface again he was blind. Snow had packed his glacier glasses. His mouth, nostrils and ears were plugged solid. He was dying, deprived of all senses, but his mind worked feverishly on. The hard packed snow leeched away the few weak tears as darkness came over him. He could hear from very far away a dull roaring sound; within the avalanche the sounds were muted. Across the glacier bay its thunderous progress echoed around the mountain walls.

Where to now, Jimmy? Dead Jimmy, long gone dead Jimmy. What now friend?

No more glory, Jimmy, long gone Jimmy. No laughing eyes, blue blue eyes; no power left to you now. Where are your dreams gone, friend?

All gone in a moment; one endless moment. A rigid body, limbs distorted, a greyish-blue pallor and your teeth bashed in. Blood trickling from your ears and snow hard packed, obscenely, in mouth and nostrils. A rictus grin – was it pain or fear? Only the merest hint of blue from your eyes as you stare at me from the snows eternally. Already glazing in the high mountain sun. A congealed, dead fish glance, turning to a cataract stare. Long gone now Jim . . . dead Jimmy.

I knelt in the wet snow and touched his face. The skin was cold to the touch and had a greyish-blue pallor, a sickly translucent appearance.

Gone, all gone in a moment. The words kept vocalising in my brain like screams in a hollow basement. I looked up at the avalanche slope. It was silent now. Innocent white slopes with shadowed edges marked the borders of the break line below the ridge. A thin line of footsteps, not more than an hour old, tracked up from the centre of the break line to the crest of the ridge. *Oh, Jimmy, what now my friend. What do I do now?*

I can't recall how long I knelt by his twisted body. It seemed like an endless star-strewn night we had passed, not so many weeks before, on a high col above the forested valley of hunters and skeletons. But there were no stars now, only the cruel white glare of snowbound mountain walls and the ferocious glare of high altitude sunlight. And we didn't talk softly in companionable solace or lie together looking at wonders moving above us. He didn't irritate me, or chuckle, or deliver the sniggering scorn that deep down I realised I loved. Instead Jimmy lay tortured and stiffening, limbs distorted, lapis-blue eyes fading to a congealed stare of dead fear, and grinned a malevolent mouthful of smashed teeth every time I looked at him.

I closed his eyes gently and was surprised at the hot splashes of tears on my hand. A tear melted a clear line down the side of his snow-glazed neck.

I thought of what he had said, as if we were having the conversation then and there. It made me keep glancing at him to check that he really had left me. But he just grinned silently back.

'Do you remember the pass in Nepal?' he had asked the night he had set off, and went on to tell me about it – how he now knew he had been close to them but hadn't known what he was seeing; how he sensed them around him like a faint aroma that he couldn't identify. Walking with silent muffled steps along the tree-lined track listening to music in his earphones, and suddenly the music stopping for no good reason and the sense overwhelming him of not being alone.

The track had been bordered on its upper slope by a dense wall of rhododendron trees, petrified in the high cold frosts of early spring. The lower slope, dropping steeply to the left, was a forest of gnarled pine trees. He had looked down the tunnel of trees that formed the path and saw red rhododendron flowers strewn on the compacted snow, flowers carried up by porters from the blooming rhododendron and maple forests far below where spring had already bloomed in coloured profusion. They had sucked the nectar and discarded the flowers so that the white path seemed dotted with blood stains.

The frostbitten leaves of the rhododendrons were like black burnt hands, each leaf curled in a tight tube, five to a stem, so that it seemed as if countless agonised hands pointed stiff fingers down at the path.

A soft snowstorm had rolled across the high pass, whitening the weather side of tree trunks. Occasionally soft thuds sounded from the forest as overburdened branches dropped their heavy white loads. The pine trees were mostly wizened fractured specimens, as if they had spent too many winters hunched against the elements to grow strong and true. There was a desolate petrified atmosphere to the ice-bound forest reminiscent of fairy tales, or of Tolkien's Mordor, a region where orcs and trolls might dwell.

Above the tangle of twisted trunks each tree fought for space, leaning sideways or down the slope towards a sunnier glade vacated by a dead and fallen colleague. The trees bore an uncanny resemblance to the classic shape of ancient traditional Japanese Bonsai forms but on a scale of thirty feet rather than two. Sometimes, where a wider clearing offered light and space, a pine would tower above the other twisted spectral forms, growing a thick trunk and rising imperiously to twice the height of its frozen colleagues before its first branches spread out.

In full summer it would have been a glorious place; a verdant tunnel of green foliage, with red, and the occasional creamy-white, of magnolia, and the smell of pine redolent on gentle summer breezes, carpeted with pine needles, the sun glinting through the canopy, drawing dappled shadows on the forest floor.

He paused when the music stopped and looked round at the shadows of softly falling snow flakes, hearing them rustle off the stiffly fragile frozen leaves. There was a sense of something dwelling in the snow between the tree trunks – a warning to the unwary that made his hair rise and a shiver tingle up his spine. He saw a bird tip-toeing apprehensively over the snow with delicate worried steps as if fearful of being taken from below.

When he had escaped the tunnel path he started the descent into the valley of dying trees. The rocky path, smeared with mud, led him down through an eerie region and he couldn't shudder away the sense of being watched. As he escaped the snow line the air filled with a misty fine drizzle. Here the dying forest seemed to have lost some age-old battle with centuries of smothering lichen growth. There was no foliage. The trees stood starkly bare like remnants of a First World War battlefield. Each groping, finger-pointing branch was hung in curtains of lichen; old man's beard, it was called, and it draped the trees so completely that they appeared clothed in crumbly tendrils of disintegrating green cloth. Water dripped everywhere. Indeed it seemed as if the trees were being slowly drowned by the water-laden mists.

Through a clearing he glimpsed a far-off hillside climbing from an apron of emerald green stone-edged terraced fields until the forest reared up in a deep blue wall of early evening light, and he hurried to escape.

But now he realised what he had sensed.

'Believe me, Chris, they were there surrounding me,' he had said with a distant dreamy look. 'It felt as if they were there daring me to see them. When I realised it afterwards I didn't go back. I don't know why . . . Scared, I suppose.'

'*No they weren't, Jimmy. They were never there,*' I answered and looked in quiet shock at his fixed and bloody grin and realised we hadn't been talking.

'I always knew about you and Alice,' he had said. 'What were you so worried about?' I stared wordlessly at him and he grinned and squeezed my shoulder.

'Back in four days,' and he trudged away.

Alice. Oh Alice, what do I tell you now? I thought. *Would you believe him, Alice? Could you believe in his Water People?*

The sun had arched down the sky in the hours I knelt wordlessly listening to his dreams in my head. Shadows crept across the glacier basin in which he lay. Roused by the icy cold of their touch I rose on snow-stiffened knees and stared down the glacier at the dark edge of the distant moraines. It would take two hours to reach camp and there was little time left before dark. I reached into my rucksack and withdrew my camera. *They would be needed as proof,* I told myself in a suddenly rational and cold frame of mind, as I bent to take the photographs of his shattered body. Injuries incompatible with life is what they wanted to see.

'And you've got all of them,' I said aloud to Jimmy's silent corpse, feeling as if I were stealing something from him each time I pressed the shutter, as if by talking to him he would be mollified.

His frozen contorted limbs wouldn't co-operate with me as I struggled to push him into the bivouac bag I had taken from his rucksack. I cursed him cheerfully for being a pig-headed bugger and cried as I zipped him into his sleeping bag.

The brightly coloured bag slid easily across the snow as I dragged it towards the crevasse. It dropped with a rustle of nylon into a long silent moment before a dull thump echoed up from the gaping slot. I fancied I could smell the greenish breath of the crevasse billow up from the blue-black depths. I carried his red rucksack, straps trailing in the snow, tied to mine on my back and headed wearily down the sinuous line of frozen footsteps that I had made in disbelieving apprehension so many hours before.

16

Meltwater

'Chai,' said the old man, proffering a chipped glass. I smiled my thanks and took the sweet milky tea. He nodded his head in an abrupt embarrassed way, then turned his attention to the fire.

I looked closely as he cooked. Other than Jimmy, he was the first person I had seen in three weeks. Of indeterminate age, near-toothless, with the mouth set hard among the leathered wrinkles of his face. Two piggy black eyes squinted mischievously from a mass of crow's feet. Whitening eyebrows and a salt and pepper close-cropped haircut added dignity to a face of incorrigible naughtiness.

He squatted back on his haunches and fed the fire small slivers of wood and helpings of straw. The flames licked the blackened cooking pot. A mixture of rice, lentils and potatoes bubbled beneath the steam. The aroma filled the small mud and stone hut. Cow dung and straw layered the floor. The fresh animal smell gradually faded to the cooking and the smoke. There was no chimney and my eyes watered. A corrugated iron door rattled in the wind and snow pattered wetly against it. Small gusts eddied round the gaps making the smoke swirl. Tears ran down. I shivered, wet and cold from the day's walk.

The old man muttered to himself as he attended to the cooking, a low murmur, like song, or prayer, whispered from his hunched-over figure. I watched his lips move. Then he sighed, a long drawn sigh that said everything, and my stomach rolled over with fear as he murmured into song again.

Was he praying, I wondered. Should I?

The meal over, not a word spoken, the old man carefully put down his plate and looked at me. His eyes were serious and sad, incongruous in his laughing face, and he said, 'Jini dead,' and sighed.

'Yes,' I said, 'Jimmy's dead,' and the door rattled to a fresh cold gust.

He had said it every night – a three-day ritual, and I was starting to welcome it; getting used to the idea.

In the past I'd imagined a time like this, I play-acted in my mind how I would react, how it would all feel. I'd almost got it right but for the loss, and the numbness. All gone, to nothing. Dust to dust, the Christians say. Fuck the Christians. He was gone as if he had never been. I thought of him as It. Glazed-over eyes and a bloodless face. It reminded me of the sheep we had slaughtered, laughing nervously with stained ice axes, unsure where to start with the knife, the huge golden eyes staring mute from the battered skull. Dead eyes that seconds ago had glowed. It was all gone away now.

The old man wrapped himself within his blanket, turned his back to me, pulled his feet in foetally, and murmured as sleep took him.

In the dark I fingered Alice's postcard, unsure if I wanted to read it again. I thought of her, and Jimmy. She, swaddled in white antiseptic sheets, with her brother's blue eyes now pale and tear-washed, a scared face framed by the glorious spread of her auburn hair on the pillows. Her pallid face shading from grey to purest white, lips a thin grey line, hardening. Smiling wanly, uncertain, and she couldn't help but give quick glances at her mother, anxious looks that asked what was happening, and more that Mother could never answer. She would smile back at Alice, lean forward and pat her hand. Then, when Alice turned again to talk to me, I would feel rather than see the sudden tightening of her shoulders, an unconscious hunching in on herself. When I glanced at her I would see the white tooth marks pressed into her lower lip.

In the morning the old man left me. He walked away from the hut with a soft wave of his hand, without turning, and the wet morning mists wrapped him from sight.

On his leaving the loneliness flooded back. With Abdul gone as well the three-day illusion evaporated.

He left laden with presents, objects I no longer needed or wanted. Cooking pots, a pressure cooker, my old rope, Jimmy's down jacket and walking shoes. They were stuffed haphazardly into an old red rucksack, torn in places, with its straps hanging loose and tattered.

I sat on my rucksack outside the hut. A damp mist gusted around the hills. From below I could hear the steady roar of the rain-swollen river. Boulders rolled heavily in the flood. Deep knocking rumbles could be heard from within the rush. We had crossed it yesterday with the help of the rope. There were no more obstacles to cross. A short morning's walk would see me safe in the village. Then the merry-go-round would begin.

I looked up the valley into the mists. There was no indication of what lay beyond. The cirque of snow peaks crescented around the spit of moraine gravels that had been our camp for so long. Some burnt and half-buried litter, blackened and soggy in the rain, cigarette butts in the gravel, a flattened area where the tents had stood. These signs would soon be washed clean.

How many days was it now? Five since Abdul had found me. Five lost days blurred into vague memory of happenings. Dazed days. Striking camp and walking out. Following Abdul's careful old man's footsteps. Abdul, solicitous to the point of irritation. Three days down. Three days of wet cloud-wrapped walking. Heavy rucksacks and the jarring downward steps. Down, down, away from the spit of moraines. Leaving the brilliant white glacier behind to be swallowed by the mists. Only a faint meandering shadow line in the snow showing where we had been. Occasionally the sun would catch the deep footprints, marking them out as a clear black line running up the glacier.

Where the mountain jutted down into the glacier bay another line, running horizontal to the bay, cut a continuous undulating wave around the cirque. The bergschrund ran a clear marker between mountain and glacier. The dark foot-steps, a continuous line rather than separated steps, weaved up over the hollows and bulges on the glacier and stopped abruptly at the bergschrund. Not far to the side a tumbled scar of fallen snow marked the path of an avalanche. Drag marks led to the open maw of the bergschrund. Above this there were no signs of movement.

A fine rain began to fall. The mists swirled low over the rushing grey waters. I stood by the cairn we had built on the way up. My footsteps, and Abdul's, still showed in scuffed dark streaks in the fine silt of the river bank. I glanced back at the hut; there was no-one to be seen. I'd half expected Abdul to have returned. He would have waited, silent and patient, until I returned to my rucksack. Then, wordlessly, he would have nodded to me, tugged my elbow and turned away expecting me to follow. But he too had gone.

I watched the mist playing down the course of the river. It seemed to steam in its rage to descend. The knocking heavy thumps of the boulders echoed up from the roaring waves. We had crossed here on the way up. In crossing it we had felt for the first time the isolation of our adventure. Filled with hopes, dreams of summit days in bright snow-blinding sunlight, we had forged on, not once looking back to this dirty Rubicon. The opposite bank was dim and blurred by the mist though the dark steps leading away to the north were still visible.

I sat down, back against a rounded boulder, and faced the

water. The cold wind sucked down by the icy waters made me shiver and my fingers shook as I re-read Alice's postcard. Childish writing of gentle thoughts that wished me well in the mountains and to hurry home. These waters came direct from the glacier. In time he would come past this boulder, sweeping past in the same violent chaos that had put an end to him. He would go on down to the village and through to the Indus until he drifted slowly in the river's wide and sluggish delta thousands of miles from here in the brackish salt waters by the sea.

He had never wanted it this way. Never thought it would come to pass, though he had accepted it was possible. At least he'd had the choice. I broke down the old cairn and re-built it taller and more secure by the boulder. I thought to bury the postcard at its base but changed my mind. The torn-up paper span for a moment in an eddy by the bank and then the current caught the pieces and they swirled from sight. I stared after them, oblivious to the cold wind, then turned and walked to my rucksack. I shouldered it and followed Abdul's tracks towards the village. That little part of her should join him, I thought, brother and sister together before it ended for good.

As I walked slowly down the valley, feeling twinges of pain in my strained thigh, a watery sun began to break through the eddies of mist. I looked back once at the tall cairn I had built by the soaring stream and beyond it at our black wet tracks zig-zagging up the moraines. The heavy knocking thumps of boulders rolling downstream echoed gloomily in from the mists.

It was a slow gentle descent. I felt no need to hurry back to people, and savoured the peace of loneliness. As the sun rose and burnt the mists away the valley revealed itself. A crumbling gorge of comglomerate mud and rocks dropped sheer into the stream. I traversed the edge of the cliff, coming upon small plateaus of green spinach and barley fed by irrigation canals, so well built that the water seemed to be flowing uphill. Small mud-walled huts with shattered timber roofs, broken down by age and winter storms, stood lonely guard at the edges of the fields. Men fought a precarious balancing act to survive in these high harsh Karakoram valleys.

A steep rocky scramble brought me back level with the stream that had broadened into a wide roaring torrent. The water was shallow as I crossed barefoot to the other bank but I felt the frenzied force with which it tried to drag me away. The shingles shifted and slinked away under the soles of my feet, and once, stepping abruptly into a knee-deep hole, I nearly fell. For a moment I was poised on the edge of balance, pressing hard against the weight of rushing water. To fall with a large rucksack would have been fatal, and when I eventually staggered on to the far bank, I shivered, weak at the thought of how I had almost beaten Jimmy on his journey to the sea.

As the valley opened out I saw where it joined the main Hunza valley. A wide grey river flowed down between broad desert sandbanks and isolated clumps of poplar trees. The river flowed down to join the Indus below Gilgit at the end of the valley. At its highest point the valley opened out on to the Kunjerab pass and the border between Pakistan and China. Kunjerab means the valley of blood, and I knew enough of the history to understand the name. Less a valley, more a steep gorge eighty miles long, slashing from north to south through precipitous mountains. The Hunza and Nagar people that live here, tough and taciturn races, had a violent history as brigands and pillagers. Settled respectively on each side of the river they commanded the gorge from the natural fortresses of their villages high on the valley walls. The silk traders coming through from China were easy prey to these fiercely independent tribes.

The gorge cut through collapsing rock walls, eroded slopes of boulders, precipices, pinnacles, and followed a tortured route up towards the border with China. Three dirty glaciers, the Ghulkin, Gulmit and Pasu, crept across the valley bringing distant memories of high deserted peaks.

As afternoon sank into early evening I stopped on a high ridge overlooking the valley. I could see the thin dark snake of the Karakoram highway twisting up the side of the river. The ancient Silk Road, linking the sub-continent with central Asia, now a smooth paved highway built at the cost of a life for every kilometre laid. It is a tenuous link with civilisation, constantly ruptured and blocked by immense landslides and washed into the turbulent rushing river. Far above the opposite valley wall towered the glistening white bulk of Rakaposhi, flushed pink in the Alpen glow of the evening sun. It seemed to block any hope of escape. I knew it would take little more than an hour to reach the small village on the valley floor but chose to go no further. I didn't want to deal with the endless inquiries, knowing that Abdul would already have told everyone he met.

The night was cold on the high ridge. As the pink and mauve shades of light died on the high summit slopes of Rakaposhi I huddled close to the small fire I had built in the lee of a cracked boulder. Thick tentacles of knotty roots protruded from the shattered rock and a gnarled pine blackened by a flash of lightning groped the darkening sky with withered spectral fingers. The moon rose and swung across the night. Later a chill wind blew down the pass and moaned and sighed across my rocky ridge top. Whispering clattering sounds came from the branches above me and a pained creaking groan from the battered trunk leaning to the force of the wind.

I awoke sweating inside my down bag as a hot morning sun baked me like a nylon chrysalis. Abdul met me an hour later on the outskirts of the dusty run-down village with a broad broken-toothed grin.

'Jini . . .'

'Yes, Jimmy's dead.' I cut him off with a smile and touched the rough cloth of his shoulder.

17

Gone Fishing

A thin drizzle sheeted in from the sea on a bitter easterly winter wind. As he rounded a crumbling mud promontory he saw the stark outline of the conveyor, an angled black line pointing seaward from the headland. Faintly, on the wind, he heard the incessant chatter of the belt, but it was the pyramid of slag growing from the sea that held his attention. The conveyor was raised up on stilt legs, four of them in a line, each higher than the other, until at its end the belt hung eighty feet above the edge of the low water mark. A wind-scattered spray of debris spilled down on to the pyramid below. Sluggish waves crept back and forth eating away at the edge of the spoil heap. The belt had been boxed in with corrugated iron sheets painted a dull industrial grey.

As Robert approached, the sound of machinery increased. The falling slag rustled in the background like the sound of waves on a shingle beach. He walked at the water's edge. The sea was a flat monotone grey against the horizon of piled rain clouds. It sucked to and fro across the stony beach, an oily black film glistening on the surface. When he looked closer he could see the grainy dark coal dust suspended in the foamy edges of the waves. Across the beach clumps of sea-smoothed coal lay scattered by the previous high tide. He had come here with Jimmy when he was only a lad. And he was gone.

Four miles back he'd first noticed the darkening sea. Ten miles of shoreline contaminated, he had heard it said. They would never have done this down south, and he smiled at the idea of Beachy Head or the perfect white cliffs of St Margaret's Bay blackened by this coal slag.

For a moment he stood beneath the rattling clamour of the belt looking up the concrete legs. A band of greenish algae, speckled black, coloured the concrete defiantly up to the high-water mark. He watched the endless spill of rock, dust and coal fragments falling to the pile. A continuous rolling of debris flowed down its conical sides. In six hours it would be gone. The incoming sea would have sucked it away remorselessly and carried it southwards. Though not far enough south, he thought. Having strewn its dirty burden on miles of beach, the ebbing tide would recede and the pyramid would rise again.

He walked on without glancing back. The trenching spade balanced easily across his shoulder, and a large bucket swung from his opposite hand. The red plastic bucket held a jumbled assortment of fishing tackle, a box of hooks, lead weights, swivels, an old spinning reel, his sandwich box, coffee flask and a telescopic fishing rod which rolled precariously as he walked.

Every now and then he stopped, put down the bucket and wandered slowly across the beach. Head down he peered closely at the few sandy patches between the stones. He looked for the tell-tale whorls of mud coiled in neat circular heaps. This was where the lugworms had buried themselves as the sea receded. There were few around now. The coal had seen to that. It blanketed the beach in a black suffocating carpet. What few whorls he began to dig on produced scrawny half-dead worms. As he pulled them out, gripping their half-exposed bodies between thumb and forefinger, a black viscous fluid oozed from them. There were no ragworms to be found.

Secretly he was relieved. He had never liked the flat-bodied worms with the fringed sides; they repulsed him. Lugworms seemed more like worms to him. Thick, black and rubbery; they stayed on the hook longer. When unearthed they moved surprisingly quickly, and he would chuckle to himself and mutter to them. Silly bugger, I've got you, come on, don't let me break you. They would wriggle convulsively back into the sand, oozing slime from their black tails as they wriggled into the side of the hole. Unless he was quick and grabbed them immediately he would have to dig again hoping not to cut them in half. Flatties preferred lugs to ragworms, he'd always reckoned. Yet these black poisoned specimens made him wonder if that still held true. In fact there may not be any Flatties left.

Two miles further on he spotted the familiar concrete wall etched against the flat and dull horizon. He never had worked out why it was there. A solid wall, twenty feet wide, pushing out into the sea. At low tide its sides glistened wetly with seaweed and algae. Sometimes he found tiny crabs scuttling in the shallow pools left by the departing sea. Long ago he remembered clusters of small mussels hanging in the seaweed. There were none to be found today. The sand was grainy black, the walls less richly clothed in green.

He scrambled up on to the wall where the sea had broken it. Rusty reinforcing spikes of iron twisted out from the shattered concrete. It was awkward to climb with the spade and the bucket. He walked to the end and sat facing out to sea, feet dangling above the water. A fine rain ghosted around him with a spraying rattle against his waterproof jacket, and the sea made slow washing sighs along the wall.

Far out where the horizon marked a darker line between sea and sky he made out the low rectangular lines of a tanker drifting south. On its way to Hull, no doubt, or maybe Rotterdam. He wondered what the coast looked like to them. A dull smudge seen through the hazy rain? A few scattered houses, and the winding wheel of the Easington colliery? Probably no less bleak than his view to seaward.

He waited patiently for the tide to fill, glancing back occasionally to see the shore receding as the oily waters swelled in towards the mud cliffs behind the beach.

Looking down into the sea he noticed it had cleared slightly. It was deep at the edge of the wall. Perhaps it had been used for loading the colliers. Certainly the water was deep; he'd measured it with a weighted line. Sixty-three feet to a sandy bottom. A mile further down the beach a small river formed an estuary of mud flats. He could just make out the sea birds standing in busy groups on isolated islands of shingle and sand. The flats glimmered reflections of gunmetal and leaded silver in the grey winter light. Gull marks criss-crossed the mud between the islands in haphazard spiky footprints. There had been cockle beds there a while back. An old sea-weathered man had pushed his sled out across the mud to collect the harvest. Now, like Jimmy, he was gone, and the shrimp boats. Only the distant specks of huddled figures picking coals from the beach near the colliery showed that the sea still provided a living – of sorts.

He flicked the dregs of his coffee to one side, replaced the plastic cup on his flask, and began to rummage in the bucket. The Flatties would be feeding in the disturbed waters of the tide.

Careful not to force the old rod he slowly extended each telescopic section, checking that the rings were clear and strongly whipped to the carbon. He fitted the small spinning reel to the handle and threaded the line up through each ring, pulling it experimentally when he was done to check the bend on the rod. With fiddly double-fisherman's knots he tied the weight, hooks and swivels into the line so it hung weight down from the tip of the rod. Above the weight two lines branched sideways from the main line on wire stiffeners. A small swivel prevented them twisting and there was a hook whipped into the end of each.

His hands were numb from the cold wind and ill-suited to the task. Stubby thick fingers failed to grip the monofilament line. Freckles spotted the backs of his hands through a tangle of reddish hairs. He frowned, as he always did, when he saw the tell-tale liver-coloured blotches on his hands. Old man's hands.

When he'd baited the two hooks, half a lugworm each, he stood up and held the rod out to his side. The tip bent back and forth with the weight of the tackle. With the reel bar open and a forefinger holding the line from running out he swept the rod back and made his cast. A smooth sweep of rod letting the weight do all the work, bending the tip back and releasing his finger from the line as the whiplash took effect. An easy fluid action, much practised. The lead flew high above the horizon in an arching climb before dropping to the sea seventy feet from where he stood. He marked the small splash between two rolling swells and let the line run swiftly out as the lead fell to the sea bed. As the line slackened he flicked the bar to close the line and wound in until it came tight and began to bend the tip. Any tighter and the lead would drag, any slacker and he would not feel the bites. He sat down again, legs over the side, and waited in the rain.

Warren lay slumped against the bow of the lifeboat. His head lolled slackly from side to side with the movement of the waves. A rhythmic slapping of water against wood seemed timed to the rolls of his head. His uniform was stained oily black, his face smeared with the viscous muck. At least it obscured the charred flesh of his left cheek. Blisters swelled here and there between the ragged strips of flesh where cheek bone, blackened by oil, showed through. It must have been a painful wound, but not fatal. He hadn't died from his wound.

Lieutenant Robert Newbold turned his head to face the wind. Wearily he peered out across the heavy swelling seas. Oil slicked across the water, deadened the waves to a slow rise and fall, as of a sick man's breathing. Hunched against the stern of the boat, he felt the wind knifing through his coat. Needles of cold seemed to melt through his muscles, and, but for the occasional attempts at warming himself, he knew he would gradually stiffen into Warren's un-waking sleep. He had craved for it during the long night hours when the wind had risen whipping oily spray into his huddled body. As a slow bleak dawn lightened the coming day he released Warren from his warming embrace. There was no heat exchange. Warren had chosen his sleep, so he moved away from the stiffening body and shuffled close up to the stern.

Occasionally in the night he had spotted flashes of light in the west – brief, violent bursts of colour, like that of a distant storm. The convoy making contacts. In the short flares of light the waves gleamed like the backs of sounding whales. Each distinct in shape and size, they undulated in lazy rolls towards him, and he fancied they bore down on his small boat in a vast army of sea demons. Then the light would die, and only the rolling motion of the boat, a low swish of water against the gunwales, and the sighing wind sounds remained. Sometimes Warren murmured to him as he glimpsed the light through gummed down lashes, and he would pull him tighter to his chest and say, 'It's the convoy, they're still with us. Don't worry, they'll find us . . .'

The whales kept at him through the night as he rocked with Warren to the swell of the sea. Black-backed, adamantine creatures from his childhood dreams come to haunt him through the night.

When the torpedoes had struck with an odd tinny clangour he had almost laughed until the stunning concussion of explosions hurled him back against the wheel-house door. Flame had flashed across his vision, strangely above him, leaving him untouched. The screams came after a moment of silence. Screams of pain and terror. It was dark in the wheel-house as he hauled himself towards the open door. He saw reflections of flame across the sea, and the sudden staccato flashes of gunfire from the escorts. Two bodies lay crumpled

against the door sill. Warren groaned in returning consciousness as Robert pulled him from under his captain. The captain
had taken the full force of the explosion. Warren, behind and
to one side, had flown back with the force of the dead man's
weight. Flash burns to the face had sealed his left eye. He
whimpered about blindness as Robert pulled him out on to
the flying bridge.

The foredeck was ablaze. Oil surged in burning waves
between the raised hatches. Three figures stood silhouetted
on the bow. The sea behind them rolled smoke at the foot of
flames standing up from the water. A dull crumping explosion
came from below and flames burst up through the forward
hatches. The three were gone. As the bow swung round
broadside to the waves Robert stared with horrified fascination
as a blackened stick-like figure swept down the ship's sides,
scrabbling vainly at the steel plates. Patches of oil burned in
vast puddles around him as he drifted away.

Robert couldn't remember how they had come to be in the
lifeboat. They hadn't launched it and he tried to recall being
in the water. He was wet through and coated in oil, so he must
have swum from the ship. Had the ship sunk? He didn't know.
And where were the others?

It seemed as if the cold had taken his memories from him.
He was numb to pain and fear had long gone. He no longer
realised what had happened except in vague disconnected
images that flashed through his mind. Somehow he couldn't
make them fit with his place in the stern of the boat.

Looking back at Warren's lifeless face, he knew only that he
had lost more than he would ever understand. Warren had
slipped away from him as the night lengthened. There had
been no attempt to fight the cold. Perhaps he had received
internal injuries in the explosion. Robert didn't think so. He
had been too tired, that was all. Too tired to care, and maybe
too young to think it all through. He had simply let go.

As a watery sun began to shine above the grey horizon he
saw the smoke. A thin line running above the sea feathered by

the wind. Debris rolled sluggishly past the boat towards the smoke – shards of unidentifiable wood and painted cork from a shattered lifebelt. A slight smudge of grey showed beneath the smoke.

It rained as they hauled him from the boat. He struggled in the netting lowered from the deck. Grey steel plate swung out and up as he looked through the net and swung with it. Glancing down, he saw the sailor with Warren. When hands reached over to pull him aboard, he looked down one last time. The body swung below him, hitting the steel with meaty thumps. A rope was bound tightly across the chest and the arms stuck out sideways so that it seemed to dance a grotesque puppetry up towards him. He rolled his legs and hips over the bulwark, barking his shins against the riveted wooden fitting.

Standing unsteadily on the deck he looked down to see the lifeboat drifting astern. It had been cast loose by the sailor who had attended to Warren. It rode high in the water and span a slow circle on the swells, as a leaf, wind-blown, swirls on muddy puddles. The sun caught the boat as it rose, and the sea momentarily glistened petrol colours of blue and purple, and mother-of-pearl shades in the weak winter light.

They buried Warren with the other bodies that they had recovered. A line of white canvas-shrouded bodies lay on the deck plates, oil seeping through in blotches on some. When lifted in turn to be slid back into the sea, nine damp body shadows marked the deck, and the chaplain's words droned in a too-fast, too-casual litany on the wind. Bareheaded, Robert watched the circle of foam flow past the ship and saw the brief white fish-belly shadow turn once in the darker water below as his brother slipped away from him.

The rod tip quivered, dipped once, and he felt the slight tug of the line on his fore-finger. He swept the rod tip back and up, and smiled as he felt the sudden extra pull of the fish. 'Gotcha!' He began to reel in. There was no struggle. The fish could never break the line, so it dragged, twisting up through the dark waters, pulling the rod tip down. They always felt bigger in the water, so he wasn't surprised to see the small six-inch fish break surface a few feet from the wall's end. It flapped convulsively on the line as he lifted it clear, still reeling in. After he had fiddled the hook free he examined his little prize. A poor specimen.

It lay white mottled belly down on the concrete. Bug eyes poked curiously up from its flat head with an expression of startled amusement. Its mouth pursed out, opening and closing, in a transparent tube, stiff-edged by thin lips. A tear in the mouth marked where the hook had caught. Its back appeared to be a dull brown until he looked closer and saw the intricate pattern of markings. Dots of darker brown and vein-like webs of bluish purple seemed to glow through from within. There was a distinct pattern to the markings that he never could understand. The fish was a bottom feeder, skimming the mud and sand for food, for ever in a swirl of silt in the ebb and flow of the tides when it fed. What would ever see such delicate markings on its back through the near invisibility of the inshore sea bed?

He flipped the fish on to its back and wiped the sand and grit from its belly. It pulsed softly with the motions of its mouth and gills. The silvery white scales were traced with regular, fine-line circles, like tiny coffee cup marks on a table. Taking the spade by the metal neck above the blade he chopped down sharply and the fish arched back, tail almost touching head, spasmed, and lay still. Some blood ran from the crush wound above its eye which seemed to fade in colour immediately. In death it still seemed amused.

As he walked slowly back along the beach the fish slid from front to back of the bucket with his stride, making wet fleshy sounds. The tide was full in, and he walked close up near the mud cliffs. The wavelets flipped at his feet, coal dust speckled the foam. Past the conveyor and the colliery and on, three miles he walked. The shore was deserted now as the sun sank low on the horizon, half-obscured by clouds and dimmed by the cold steel sea and grey-smudged sky. The sea seemed flat far out to the sun but gradually he noted the steady swell coming in to the shore in a slow heavy roll. The coal pickers had gone as the tide covered the gravels, and when he passed the conveyor the pyramid of slag had been washed away. The wheels of the belt rattled on and the slag fell direct to the water with a continuous splash.

A sudden squall rushed in on him as he reached the car, driving the rain against him. The car rocked slightly. He packed the spade, bucket and rod in the boot, put the fish in a torn carrier bag he'd found washing to and fro on the shore line, and got into the car. The rain stopped as suddenly as it had started and he watched through the spattered window as the sun seemed to raise itself for one last effort, throwing a wet silver sheen across the sea before the clouds closed it down to a watery haze.

Another tanker slid sideways on the line between sea and sky, seeming oddly vulnerable, as if it might suddenly roll over the edge of the world. Streamers of smoke drifted back from its low grey shape before it too was wrapped in cloud as another squall bustled in to the shore, the sea surface darkening as the rain swept in. He shivered as he saw its approach and hunched forward against the wheel. For a moment he thought of the boat and the night full of oil-slicked waves and flame flashes from the darkness. He had fished here as a child and fought sea weed fights through the mud-flats with his brother. He'd fished with his son before the colliery had built the conveyor. He knew that he would not return.

He drove slowly with deliberate care. It seemed that now with the past years lengthening he slowed more with each passing day. The wipers clacked from side to side as he eased the old Anglia up the sloping gravel drive. The house seemed sullen and unapproachable. Dark windows barring the light and door tight shut. He noticed the battered Mini parked by the pavement. *So*, he thought moodily, *Alice and Chris have deigned to visit. One visit in three months since the news had come in clipped Foreign Office vowels of the unfortunate accident. And Chris. What had he said to us. Nothing.*

He turned the ignition off and the wipers froze in mid-stroke. Rain drops pattered against the glass. He sat tiredly in the driver's seat staring at the house. A curtain moved aside in the front-room window. She looked out with a hopeful look of anticipation. *No darling*, he thought, *it's not him . . . never will be love.*

Her face had collapsed. A washed-out grey face grooved with sorrow lines and a prune-wrinkled mouth pursed in anxious grief. He doubted whether she would last the year. *Fools. Couldn't they have thought of us.* He felt his anger burning up his chest and wondered whether he could be civil to Chris. With a heavy sigh he stepped out into the gloomy Durham rain.

The front door opened and Alice appeared. She seemed different. She smiled a tremulous sad smile and he held his arms wide. She dropped the dragon-headed umbrella and ran to him.

Abacus now offers an exciting range of quality titles by both established and new authors. All of the books in this series are available from:
   Sphere Books,
   P.O. Box 11,
   Falmouth,
   Cornwall TR10 9EN.

Alternatively you may fax your order to the above address. Fax No. 0326 76423.

Payments can be made as follows: Cheque, postal order (payable to Macdonald & Co (Publishers) Ltd) or by credit cards, Visa/Access. Do not send cash or currency. UK customers: please send a cheque or postal order (no currency) and allow 80p for postage and packing for the first book plus 20p for each additional book up to a maximum charge of £2.00.

B.F.P.O. customers please allow 80p for the first book plus 20p for each additional book.

Overseas customers including Ireland, please allow £1.50 for postage and packing for the first book, £1.00 for the second book, and 30p for each additional book.

NAME (Block Letters) ....

ADDRESS..

....

☐ I enclose my remittance for _____

☐ I wish to pay by Access/Visa Card

Number ⊞⊞⊞⊞⊞⊞⊞⊞⊞⊞⊞⊞⊞⊞⊞⊞

Card Expiry Date ⊞⊞⊞⊞